# THE COMPLEXITY

## OF A

## A novel by Michelle Bellon

An Old Line Publishing Book

Printed in the United States of America

ISBN-13: 978-1-937004-43-9
ISBN-10: 1-937004-43-0

This book is a work of fiction. Any references to real people, events, establishments, organizations, or locales are intended solely to provide a sense of authenticity and are used fictitiously. All other characters, incidents, and dialogue are drawn from the author's imagination and are not to be construed as real.

Old Line Publishing, LLC
P.O. Box 624
Hampstead, MD 21074
Toll-Free Phone: 1-877-866-8820
Toll-Free Fax: 1-877-778-3756
Email: oldlinepublishing@comcast.net
Website: www.oldlinepublishingllc.com

# The Complexity of a Soldier

*For all the soldiers and their families: they sacrifice so much more than can ever be put into words and their integrity and ethics are continually put to the test. Thank you for your service.*

*For all the victims of abuse: It is my wish that this one simple story may give a voice to those who have yet to be heard. Until we as a whole population change our perspectives on what we will and will not allow in our society and how to handle all forms of terrorism, including child molesters, the victims will still be left without a voice, without justice. Let us make change.*

*Special thanks to Lorri Broaddus for the photography shoot: You are truly gifted.*

*Thanks to Laine Cunningham for her professional and invaluable services.*

*Thank you to my best friend of nearly thirty years, Robyn: Your love and support are forever appreciated and I am blessed to have you in my life.*

*Most importantly: thank you to my children; Mariah, Yasmine, Joaquin and Brielle. You are the shining light in my life and inspire me to be the best that I can be. I love you.*

# Contents

| | |
|---|---|
| **Prologue** | **9** |
| **Chapter One - A Change of Plans** | **11** |
| **Chapter Two - The Foundation was Built** | **27** |
| **Chapter Three - Boot Camp** | **40** |
| **Chapter Four - Family Dynamics** | **54** |
| **Chapter Five - Welcome Home** | **68** |
| **Chapter Six - Memory Lane** | **75** |
| **Chapter Seven - Match-Maker** | **90** |
| **Chapter Eight - Orders Received** | **99** |
| **Chapter Nine - Amped Up** | **108** |
| **Chapter Ten - Emily's Retreat** | **122** |
| **Chapter Eleven - A Friendship Tested** | **135** |
| **Chapter Twelve - Home Sweet Home** | **149** |
| **Chapter Thirteen - Unsettled** | **157** |
| **Chapter Fourteen - Nightmares** | **167** |
| **Chapter Fifteen - No Words** | **178** |
| **Chapter Sixteen - Second Deployment** | **184** |
| **Chapter Seventeen - Called Home** | **191** |
| **Chapter Eighteen - Retribution** | **198** |
| **Chapter Nineteen - Facing the Consequences** | **213** |
| **Chapter Twenty - Taking on the System** | **222** |
| **Chapter Twenty-One - Taking a Stand** | **234** |
| **Epilogue** | **248** |

# PROLOGUE

The sweat trickling down his back was just one of many physical irritations Rory tried to ignore as he looked down the sites of his M-16 rifle. Staring back at him an Iraqi man from one of the insurgent groups Rory's team had infiltrated on the west side of Fallujah. The infiltration had been quick, deft and successful with only two minor injuries.

With the area secured and the rebels on their knees, disarmed, Rory Nichols should have felt proud of his team. But his mind was scattered as he tried to assimilate everything. The sweat dripping down his back, the swollen, bruised feet, the parched mouth were minor distractions compared to the flux of emotion coursing through his veins.

It was difficult to feel pride when he constantly questioned which side he was really on. It was difficult to justify violence brought by his own hand when he still had yet to reconcile who was the real enemy in his own mind.

## The Complexity of a Soldier

His superior officer barked orders while the captives cursed the captors and all they represented in their native tongue. He was supposed to be a hero but the only people he wanted to think of him that way, was a wife and little girl who were thousands of miles away.

The pain of missing them and worrying about them was nothing compared to looking into the eyes of his prisoner. The pure, unadulterated hatred that poured out of the man's eyes would infect Rory's soul forever.

# CHAPTER ONE

# A Change of Plans

Rory had played his fair share of battle and shoot-'em-up games as a young boy. Blowing stuff to smithereens had always been one of his and his younger brother's favorite past times. Until that is, their father tanned their hides after catching them behind the barn testing whether a pile of cow dung would burn.

Although he'd loved to execute fatal battle strategies on his brother, it never crossed his mind that he might one day become a soldier. Joining the United States Army had never once seemed an appealing option. Midway through the summer after his high school graduation, he'd been sure of only two things. He wanted to break away from the mediocrity of the family cattle ranch, and he was irrevocably in love with Emily Nelson.

Not until he found himself in the cab of his beloved 1968 Chevy pickup staring at the dreaded pink slip with the weight of his personal responsibilities literally crushing his chest did he desperately search the recesses of his mind for any kind of solution.

## The Complexity of a Soldier

*Damn it! This cannot be happening,* he thought feeling defeated. He heaved a sigh, closed his eyes, and rested his head against the back of the bench seat. He couldn't believe they'd actually handed out those things. He'd always assumed they were a myth or a metaphor, but no, they were real and he was holding one right now.

His wandering train of thought was a useless attempt to distract himself. If he focused on the real issue, he would panic. His stomach would ache with the weight of his responsibilities and that was just no good. He wasn't the type to bitch and moan even when the going got tough. He rolled with the punches and did whatever it took to provide for his family. Just as his father had always done.

The unforgiving chill of the February evening seeped into his bones. He twisted the key in the ignition. The familiar purr of the engine came to life. As he waited for the heater to do its job, he wished he hadn't been among the fifteen men who'd received the ominous slips. That simple act had changed what would have been a typical afternoon into a dreadful mess.

Rory had settled comfortably into the routine of his mill job. His simple days began at seven a.m. each weekday. He worked hard and fast for eight hours before rushing home to see his girls and unwind in the comfort of his home.

Six months earlier, Rory and his wife Emily had experienced a radical shift in their lives. On August 1, at 5:15 a.m., they had welcomed Callista Emigene Nichols, also known as Callie, into the world. Now their schedules revolved around the cherub-faced angel with her father's sable-colored hair, and her mother's golden hazel eyes. Rory had needed to operate on less sleep, summon more patience, and learn what it meant to be the man of the house but at the end of the day, he was content.

When it had only been him and Emily, they had been excited

about their plans for the future. Then little Callie had come along. She'd been born one week before her due date in the early morning hours on a Tuesday. Exhausted and exhilarated, Rory watched in awe as Emily found a profound well of strength and pushed with all of her might.

Rory had felt unmitigated pride as the nurse placed the purple, wrinkled infant on Emily's chest. He was baffled by his complex and diverse swing of emotions. A wave of tangible strength filled him as love and happiness surged through his body and mind. At the same time, he felt a paralyzing weakness he was sure was the precursor to a full-on faint.

He pulled himself together, wanting to stay in the moment. Emily reached out. Her lip quivered as she embraced her child and the motherhood she had always longed for. Rory showered her face with kisses as his heart clenched with love.

Over the next six months, Rory was shocked to learn that not only did he love being a father he was also pretty dang good at it. He had known Emily would flourish as a parent but he would never have guessed the same for himself.

Rory had spent Emily's pregnancy dazed and amazed as his wife's body and mind had morphed. Both had evolved throughout the miraculous process of nurturing the life they had created. Eventually she had become introverted as her internal focus prepared for her new role. She finished the winter and spring quarters of her first year of college before deciding to stay home for the remainder of the pregnancy.

Both she and Rory had agreed it would be best if she stayed home to raise their child even if it meant tightening their belts a bit.

Just after they married, Rory had broken away from his dad's ranch and landed a job at the local timber mill. At twenty years old, Rory felt at least a decade older. Despite being used to hard physical labor, his body had become sore and abused from the work. Still, he didn't complain. The mill was completely different than the typical ranch work and with the job in town, he was closer to Emily.

Unfortunately, being one of the newer employees meant he was one of the first to receive his walking papers. The boss gave everyone a pep talk and said that their numbers were predicted to rise drastically around May or June. The mill would be sure to rehire them then if they still wanted the job.

What in the hell was he going to do? He couldn't go that long without income. The prospect of going back to the ranch to work under his dad's thumb had him disgruntled, to say the least. Swallowing that unfavorable option, he slammed the truck into reverse and concentrated on the short drive home.

He perked up when he walked through the front door. Little Callie was on her hands and knees on the Oriental rug in their living room. She rocked back and forth with a determined look on her face while blowing bubbles out of her pink bowed mouth.

*Dang, she's so cute,* he thought.

Scooping her up, he blew bubbles on her round belly. The familiar greeting sent her into a squealing fit. Her chubby body squirmed in his arms. Emily had been on the floor coaxing Callie to crawl. She stood and rose up on her toes to give him a quick welcome home kiss. For that moment, no worries weighed on Rory's shoulders.

"Isn't she a little young to start crawling?" he asked.

Emily answered with a smug smile of pride. "Nope. They usually start between six and eight months. She'll be seven months soon so she's right on target."

She snatched Callie from him so he could wash his hands and change out of his filthy work clothes before dinner. Fifteen minutes later, Rory was freshly showered and wearing jeans with a black t-shirt. His hair was still dripping as he stepped into the kitchen and inhaled the sweet aroma of Emily's homemade spaghetti sauce. "How's your back," she asked.

He didn't want to talk about his back. He wanted to get his troubles out in the open. His tone was flat as he spoke. "My back is doing a lot better, Em, but I had a crappy day at work. I got laid off."

Emily kept her composure. Shrugging, she reminded him that he could go back to the ranch. During that time of the year, both Rodney and Justin would welcome his help. She knew that as well as he did.

There it was again, that heavy, cramped feeling in his lungs. Rory couldn't think about that option yet and changed the subject as they sat down to dinner. Later that evening, he sprawled out on the couch while Emily gave Callie her evening bath. He was half asleep and the drone of the television murmured in the background. His eyes fluttered open when a commercial for the U.S. Army popped on the screen. He slowly sat up as his mind turned over the idea.

That could be it. That could be the answer. He just couldn't go back to the ranch with the old man. There was a recruiting office in La Grande, not far from the college. It wouldn't hurt to drive over and talk to somebody. It would be best to talk with Emily about it after he had more information, though.

The following morning at breakfast, he sipped his scorching, black coffee then casually said, "I'm driving to La Grande today. A guy at the mill gave me a lead on a job."

His stomach twisted. It was the closest he'd ever come to lying to his wife.

Emily raised her eyebrows, hesitating for only a moment before giving him an oblivious nod and spooning another bite of mushy oatmeal to Callie.

~~~~~~~~~~~

Rory walked out of the recruiter's office with a bounce in his step and a new direction. He had all the information he needed and had already made his decision. The recruiter, skilled in persuasion, had detailed how Rory could join the Army and train for the Military Police. Now he just had to convince Emily it was in their best interest.

Becoming a police officer had been his dream, but he'd put his career plans on the back burner when they had discovered that Emily was expecting their first child. On the drive home, he thought back to the day she had delivered the unexpected but joyous news. A thoughtful smile slowly spread over his strong features. It had been a Friday afternoon, the exact same day he'd been accepted to the police academy of Idaho.

Rory remembered bounding up the front stairs two at a time. He'd felt precariously close to actually floating up them. He burst through the door, eager to share his news. He had been expecting a letter the first two weeks of January and had stopped by the post office daily. When he'd spotted the dark yellow manila envelope, he'd snatched it up and bolted out to his truck. He'd considered waiting until he was with Emily to open it but he feared the possibility that it was a rejection letter.

Hastily tearing open the envelope, he'd ignored the small paper cut his impatience earned. The words on the official letter blurred together until he focused on the first word after the greeting. Congratulations, it read. He skimmed the rest to confirm that he had been accepted before rushing home. Being that it was going on four o'clock, Rory knew Emily would have been home for over an hour. She would either be in the small downstairs room they had converted into an office poring over homework or she would be rifling through the kitchen planning dinner.

Bounding through the foyer, he belted out, "I'm in. I got accepted!"

His excitement waned as he saw Emily lying on the couch with a wet cloth draped over her forehead.

*Something's not right,* he thought with a quick thud in his chest. He had never seen her sick before, other than a cold they had passed back and forth for weeks last fall. He rushed to her side and knelt down, skimming her face for clues.

"Are you sick?" He brushed his fingers over her forehead near the hairline. Her skin had an alarming gray pallor.

Emily removed the cold cloth and smiled weakly. She fluttered her lashes at him. "Um…kind of. I just got a little dizzy while I was in the kitchen. I decided to lay down for a few minutes. I feel a bit better now." She sat up slowly.

"Did you say you were accepted? Did you get your letter today?"

His lingering worry dampened his excitement but he tried to shift gears and gave her a wide grin. He sat on the coffee table and pushed the envelope into her small hand. "Yep. I was going to wait to open it together but I didn't. I'm sorry, babe."

Emily laughed as she climbed into his lap and wrapped her arms around his neck. "Don't be sorry. This is what you've been waiting for, what we've been waiting for. This calls for a celebration!"

Rory gave her a bear hug and a smacking, wet kiss then examined her pale face. "I'm not sure that's a good idea, Em. You still look white as a sheet. Maybe you're coming down with something."

## The Complexity of a Soldier

Emily averted her eyes and fiddled with the buttons on his work shirt. Rory's alarm bells went off. Emily was never one to hide anything from anyone, especially him. Tipping her chin, he looked her straight in the eye.

"What's going on with you, Emily?"

He waited but she continued to avoid eye contact.

"We're gonna sit here until you talk to me."

He held her a little tighter. Despite his hold, she squirmed off his lap and sat back on the deep cushions of the sofa. When Rory meant business there was no way of holding him off. She would only meet his expectations on his grounds.

She heaved a sigh.

"I'm pregnant." Her tone was expressionless and her eyes wary as she watched his reaction.

*What the...holy...This is awesome.* Rory stood up with his fists in the air as if he had just scored the winning touchdown.

"Yes!" He sat right next to her. "When did this happen? I mean, how do you know? I mean are you okay?" he stammered with a dazed smile.

His smile was contagious. She pressed her lips together to suppress one of her own.

"Well...I started to feel tired the week of the wedding but thought it was just stress. Then two days ago I started to feel nauseated. Once I did the math, I realized that in the chaos of the wedding preparations, I had failed to notice I was about two weeks late. I skipped class this morning and went to the doctor. He says I probably became pregnant sometime in late November. The baby is due in August."

She scanned his face before asking, "You're not mad?"

Rory chuckled at her pathetic expression, and pulled her to him. "Mad? Are you crazy? This is the best day of my life! First I get a

# The Complexity of a Soldier

letter of acceptance into the police academy of my choice then my beautiful wife tells me we're going to have a baby. Hot damn!" His brain tried to wrap itself around the fantastic events.

Emily sighed in relief and laughed as she melted into his embrace. "I'm so glad. I was worried you would be upset about the timing and all. This shouldn't change our plans. We can still move."

Rory decided not to think about the way this news would affect their future plans. Confident they would work it all out, he focused on Emily and how she was feeling. "Hey, I want to know how this doctor appointment went," he said. "I want details."

"There's not much to tell. He did an exam, took my health history, weighed me all that jazz. Oh, and he took blood work. Felt like he took enough to supply an entire blood bank but it was pretty standard. He gave me a bunch of pamphlets on vitamins and early pregnancy then told me to rest and he'd see me in a month. That's it. It kind of weirds me out to know I am fully responsible for this little person inside of me."

"Well, that's exactly why you are going to follow his instructions. You're gonna take it easy and get plenty of rest. I'm going to heat up that soup you made last night."

"You don't have to do that. I can do it."

He wouldn't hear of it. He had her lay down on the sofa while he fumbled his way through heating up leftover homemade turkey soup. He was stoked when he didn't burn or break anything. His mom had made her boys do their share of kitchen duty but it was not a place he flourished.

A week later, Rory took Emily out to their favorite Mexican restaurant when she'd insisted that she "needed" beans and rice. She was one of the lucky ones because her morning sickness had come and gone in only a matter of days. Her appetite returned with a vengeance and the color returned to her cheeks.

He'd been amused, baffled, and slightly confused as he'd watched his wife behave so out of character. She threw a barrage of questions at him ranging from how his day had been, to wondering if he liked any particular names for the baby and whether they should live in a house or an apartment when it came time to move to Boise.

She didn't allow him any time to actually answer the questions. He assumed this new, frantic side of her had something to do with her raging pregnant-woman hormones. He let her continue with her one-sided conversation, eating the chips and salsa in silence, wondering how long she would prattle with no real agenda. Emily suddenly clamped her mouth shut.

"Sorry," she said. "I'm being obnoxious aren't I?"

Rory shrugged it off and leaned back as the waiter brought their order. He waited until he had enjoyed a few bites of the delicious Chimichanga before he spoke. He wanted to bring up what he'd been mulling over ever since she'd told him of the pregnancy. Emily had assumed their plans would remain unchanged but the more he thought about it, the more he realized he wasn't comfortable with that. He'd lost many hours of sleep thinking over their options and only last night had settled on a final decision.

"I've been thinking about the baby," he said. "I'm going to put off going to the academy for a year." His serious, dry tone clearly communicated his decision was not negotiable.

Emily's voice rose an octave. "What? Why? No! I'm not going to have you postpone your dreams because of this. It would make me feel horrible."

Rory simply shrugged. "Don't feel bad. This is my decision. I've thought it over. I don't like the idea of moving across the state when you are in the middle of your pregnancy. It's too stressful.

# The Complexity of a Soldier

Plus, it makes me nervous to think of supporting the family at such a delicate time while trying to start such an intensive program. It would take a lot of my energy and focus when I should be focused on you and the newborn."

Emily pleaded with him to change his mind, assuring him she would be fine with the move but he cut her off with a stern glare. She stopped in mid-sentence and leaned back, crossing her arms in a pout. Rory rarely ever got stern with her and while she was clearly unhappy with his decision, she would not push an issue he was so adamant about. It was like ramming into a brick wall.

He reached across the table and offered his upturned palm. His eyes bored into her, silently asking her to show him that she understood and everything would be okay. She haughtily turned her head. He sighed and left his arm out, knowing her rare pouts were brief.

"Come on, Em, you know I'm right on this. I want it to happen this way. I would feel a lot better about it and I can join the Academy anytime. I love you," he added, deliberately pulling at her heartstrings.

Emily turned back to look into his handsome face. Giving in, she grasped his large, calloused hand. "I love you, too," she conceded.

As they finished their meal, Rory changed the subject, to baby names.

Rory down shifted the truck as he down shifted his mind. Focusing on his present situation, he rolled the bittersweet memory around in his head. That day he had temporarily put aside his own career aspirations to begin the fulfilling and wonderful journey of becoming a new father. Now he had a family to take care of. He had a little baby girl who needed to know she could count on her daddy. Enlisting was the perfect answer.

# The Complexity of a Soldier

*Ugh,* he thought. Emily was not going to like it one bit but he had to do it. She would understand. She had to. It made perfect sense to go this route now that Callie was older and the two of them could tolerate his absence better. The Army would pay him during his training, settling the issue of financial strain he'd worried about when he'd imagined going into the police force. This would be their opportunity to get away from small town life.

It would also be his opportunity to get back on track toward his career. Even though the circumstances were less than convenient, he couldn't contain his excitement. He was setting into motion actions which would lead him to his long-term goals. That night after he rocked Callie to sleep and laid her in her crib, he joined Emily in their bedroom. She stood over the sink in her tank top and pajama pants vigorously brushing her teeth.

"So I ended up at an Army recruiting office today," he said, "and I got a bunch of information on joining their Military Police program."

Emily spit into the sink, rinsed her mouth and put the toothbrush into its holder. She stared down his reflection in the mirror. "Excuse me?"

Rory sighed, gearing up for the argument that was sure to ensue. "Yeah, the guy was impressed that I'd already been accepted into the academy in Idaho. Once I take the entrance exam, they'll go over my scores and do a psyche evaluation. He's sure he'll be able to guarantee me a spot in the MP school at Fort Leonard Wood in Missouri."

Panic flashed over Emily's face. He continued before she could interrupt.

"They combine basic training and advanced individual training so it's a nineteen-week program but after that I can start working. I'll be an MP."

## The Complexity of a Soldier

Emily turned to face him and leaned against the sink. She brushed her hair with a vicious ferocity that made Rory nervous. "Nineteen weeks?" she said. "That's nearly five months!"

Rory could feel her anxiety. He walked toward her to soothe away her worries, yet remained staunch in his decision. "I know but I really don't want to go back to the ranch, Em. This would be a step in the right direction for my career. The pay is decent and I would be able to support this family a lot better than I have been. Of course, I will miss my girls during training but it will go by fast. Then we can move together as a family to wherever they transfer me."

His eyes swept her face imploring her to see how much this meant to him. She was trying to keep her chin up but her hesitation and the sadness that had crept into her hazel eyes revealed her struggle. They had never been apart before. The idea of being separated for a full five months was daunting for both of them. Still, Emily would support him in this endeavor because she would never be able to live with herself if she refused him this opportunity.

"I suppose Callie and I could be strong for five months." Her face turned into a pout. "It's a little scary to think of moving wherever they tell us, though. It's like we don't have any say over our own lives."

Rory stroked her silky hair. "I know but it will only be like that for the four years of my contract. After that, I will be able to get a job at any federal, state or county law enforcement agency anywhere we want to live. This will change everything for us, Em."

She might have resolved to accept this new twist but she was battling a surge of emotions. Her lip quivered and her voice trembled. "When would you have to leave?"

Rory stroked her brow and placed soft kisses down her cheek to her lips. His heart squeezed as she fought back tears. "I'm not sure exactly. I have to take the entrance exam, do their psyche evaluation then go from there. I think basic training will start in April."

Rory followed her train of thought, knowing she was doing a quick calculation. He wouldn't be back in time for Callie's first birthday. "I promise to send baby girl a gift," he said, anticipating her train of thought. "We can throw her another party when I get back, if you want."

Emily gave him a sad smile. "How is it that we have always been able to read each other's thoughts so well?"

He pulled her to him and felt the warmth of their bodies melt into one solid flame. "Because we just fit like that, babe."

~~~~~~~~~~~~

Emily braced for the upcoming transition, trying her best to embrace and support everything Rory did to prepare for his departure. Over the next five weeks, she held her breath and her tongue while he aced his entrance exam, apparently said all the right things during his psyche evaluation, and began the paperwork to launch his military career.

They set up Emily as his power of attorney so nearly all of his pay, other than just enough to cover his own essentials, would be deposited into their account at home. He was determined to make everything run as smoothly as possible while he was away.

He was also determined to be in prime physical condition. He ran and lifted weights in their garage every morning to prepare for the physical strain that would be placed upon him during basic training. Things were changing before her eyes and it was all happening too fast to catch her breath. A week before Rory flew out to Missouri he came home with a high and tight military style haircut.

# The Complexity of a Soldier

"I know their just gonna chop it all off again when I get there but I thought I would beat them to it to try to get used to it." He ran his hands over his nearly bare skull.

Emily felt a lump rise in her throat. The simple yet drastic change had taken him instantly from a youthful twenty-something, to a strong man. She couldn't believe he could still make her heart stop with his muscular frame standing at six three.

She had always marveled at how he seemed to occupy so much space. It wasn't just his physical size. It was something Rory just carried around with him. It was a bigness she couldn't quite put her finger on but which she was always aware of. It was as if when he stepped into a room the environment had to expand just so his large presence could be accommodated.

His nearly black hair had always been slightly on the long side with a hint of a wave. The persistently rumpled, boyish look had offset his strong features. He was still incredibly handsome with the shorter style but somehow different enough to trigger something unrecognizable in her subconscious. It sent a shiver up her spine.

He was still her husband, she reminded herself. She shook off the odd sensation, pasted a smile on her face, and resisted the urge to wrap herself around him and beg him not to go. *Get yourself together,* she thought. *It's only going to be five months out of many years of a long marriage. Look at the big picture, think of the long term goals.*

Before she could respond with more than a pathetic, half-hearted smile, Rory dashed up the stairs. He returned moments later with a baseball cap on his freshly shaven head. She saw that he regretted the haircut because it was yet another reminder of his upcoming departure. He had meant for it to be a preparation of sorts, not a rubbing of salt into the wound. He was hoping to recover any insult or injury he might have unknowingly caused her.

## The Complexity of a Soldier

He was taking her feelings into consideration and that settled her nerves. She gave him a winning smile and rushed into his arms, nearly knocking him off his feet. She yanked the ball cap off and tossed it to the ground. "I like it! You're sexy!"

Rory flirtatiously raised his eyebrows. "Sexy, huh? Sexy enough to take me upstairs and roll around under the covers?"

She buried her face in his neck and nibbled his tender spots. "Maybe later, Soldier, once Callie lays down for her nap."

Their teasing and flirtation helped ease the tightness in her stomach but still she wondered how they were actually going to do this. They were taking on a new venture, a new chapter, seizing it as an opportunity for bigger and better things. Everything would work out just fine, like Rory claimed. It would change everything, he'd said. But she couldn't help worrying about how it would change.

# CHAPTER TWO

# The Foundation was Built

On the morning Rory flew out, he woke around four in the morning and lay with Emily curved in his arms. He listened to the slow in and out of her breath, marveling at how happy they were. He couldn't believe he had been blessed with her as his wife and beautiful angel-baby Callie.

Rory had never been one to take girls or dating too seriously. His innate aversion to the small town had extended pretty much to everyone who lived there. It wasn't that he hated the people in his hometown; in fact, he liked them very much. They were what his dad referred to as "good people." He just knew they were all limiting themselves. He was adamant that he would not do the same.

*Until Emily came along,* he thought as a small grin tugged at the corner of his mouth.

The memory of their courtship filtered into his sleepy thoughts. Her family had moved to Baker City, Oregon when her father had been transferred. The branch his company had recently built there added to the bank's chain. Emily's family was obviously wealthy, so Rory had steered clear of her assuming she was as pretentious as she looked.

After only a few weeks, Emily made many friends with her outgoing nature. She charmed everyone with her American-beauty good looks, her honey blonde hair and her warm hazel eyes. Rory's guess that she would join the cheerleading team had been accurate but he'd been surprised when she had also joined the debate team, the social justice association, and seemed purposely to avoid settling into any specific clique.

Despite instincts that warned him to keep a safe distance, Rory had been drawn to her. That had only irritated him. He reasoned she was the first student in years to come from the city so he couldn't help but be intrigued.

Although he had experienced his fair share of being led around by raging hormones, he wasn't interested in a long-term relationship with any of the local girls. His disdain and repulsion for the small town that operated in its own little dimension separate from the rest of the world blanketed how he viewed its inhabitants.

In his opinion, they all shared the same limited perspectives and small-minded beliefs. He wouldn't have been surprised if they all shared the same brain. No matter how hard they fought it, most if not all of his peers would replicate their parents' lives. They would remain in the backwoods town for the rest of their lives. Even their children would follow in those footsteps. The never-ending cycle was nearly impossible to break.

Not Rory. He refused to stay anywhere near Eastern Oregon and absolutely would not be caught dead running a ranch like his father. He loved his father, respected his ability to run the ranch and maintain his formidable physical prowess, but he had no intention to fill his shoes. He didn't necessarily want big city life but he definitely wanted to meet different people with radically different backgrounds and perspectives. Then his own children would see life with a broader vision and would have a greater understanding of the world.

Since Emily had moved from Boise, Idaho, a comparably larger city, he figured she must be just as repulsed by the scaled-down surroundings. He had been living in it his entire life and although he had many friends, he was ready to move on without looking back. And that's exactly what he intended to do.

Rory avoided interacting with Emily their entire senior year. Days before graduation, that changed. Their class piled onto the school bus for a forty-five minute drive to a job fair at Eastern Oregon University.

He had mixed emotions when he found himself paired up with Emily for the day. He was awkward and nervous as they slowly made their way around the booths gathering flyers, business cards and notes. She opened something new inside him that day, something he wasn't even sure he wanted to acknowledge. He talked more than usual and shared his plans for bailing out of town and joining the police academy.

She shared with him her desire to have a family.

At one point he was uncomfortably distracted as he watched the way she spoke. Her mouth moved in a delicate and intoxicating pattern, and her perspective was enlightened. She relayed how small towns really weren't all that different from big cities. He was shocked to realize that he really didn't know exactly why he was so set on leaving or what he was running toward or away from. For the first time, he questioned the motivations that had pressed him to leave his hometown in search of something…more.

Emily stirred in his arms and brought him back to the present.

# The Complexity of a Soldier

Their precious child was asleep in the room just down the hall. He was weak with the prospect of not seeing them for nearly half a year. He felt a sudden and intense urge to somehow back out of his contract with the Army. He came dangerously close to succumbing.

Unfortunately, that was not how he was constituted. Shoving aside doubt, he stroked Emily's soft skin from her shoulder down to her wrist. Soon she began to stir and stretch in his arms. He nuzzled the back of her neck, taking in her scent and warming her senses with soft, gentle kisses that whispered of his hunger.

Emily responded as she always did, with earnest. Her touch always lit fires in him, even when he was at his lowest. Their love-making started out slow, almost painfully so, but toward the end Emily's mood became desperate. Her anxiety crept in around them. They both knew this would be the last time for many months. She was reluctant to let him go. He wanted to hold onto the moment forever, never sharing their secret world with anyone or anything.

Her intensity ignited something that took over rational thought and had them ferociously grasping for each other.

Rory had never craved anyone the way he consistently craved Emily. His muscles went taught with anticipation as her body hummed in response to his. They pushed each other over the edge with a passion that was near violence. Each frantic to stake their claim, to burn the memory of the moment into the other's mind so while they were apart, they would remember who they belonged to.

~~~~~~~~~~~~~

After their bodies settled into the serenity of the night, Emily listened to Rory share his earlier reflections. As usual, she found herself wide awake. Her body buzzed in the afterglow of their passion while he drifted off to a pleasant oblivion. She found herself reminiscing as well.

She had been acutely aware of Rory's discomfort that day at the job fair. She smiled shyly when she'd realized that he was likely reacting to her presence. Rory was a popular guy and although he was adored by many girls, he had kept his distance from most of them. He struck her as the strong, silent type. Not introverted, just reserved. She was flattered that he was acting radically different with her, and quietly hoped it was because he might like her.

She had always sensed he was rebelling or distancing himself from something, she just didn't know what. Curious, she secretly hoped they would have a chance to talk as they went through the day together. Maybe she could break through that tough barrier.

Emily had always been known as incredibly sweet and sensible. She forever strove to keep her grades at four-point-oh and joined clubs she believed in so she could go to college. No one knew that the only thing she ever desired and dreamed of was to marry and have a family of her own.

She never shared her aspirations with anyone, especially her family. They all came from wealthy lineages with a firm belief in education and an intense work ethic. They weren't tyrants and she knew they would love her no matter what she chose. Still, it would be a hard pill for them to swallow if she immediately settled down and played the stay-at-home mom role rather than followed her father into banking and management.

Besides, Mr. Right had yet to come along. She was still young, and it was best to plan for college as her 'until then' plan. Eventually she would end up in the role of a soccer mom chasing toddlers but for now she carried on with her families' wishes. That kept things smooth and moving along as expected.

In her opinion, the job fair was superfluous for most of her classmates. Many wouldn't bother with anything other than their parents' farms, ranches, or other local businesses. As sad as it seemed, many had no plans, other than where the next party would be held and whether they could score beer and dope.

When Emily had first started school in the new town, she'd dated a few of the guys on the football team. Once they'd discovered she wasn't one to put out in the back seat of a car, they adopted her as their sisterly, smart friend. She became the one they went to when they needed a tutor for geometry or pre-calculus.

That suited her just fine. She definitely didn't intend to become a mommy while still in school and end up married to the football captain, who was sure to wind up working in his daddy's brake and muffler shop with a full-on beer gut by the time he was twenty-two.

Emily prided herself on being practical and moved in a logical, linear fashion. Her feathers were rarely ruffled. Even when she did lose her patience or allow her anger to seep through, she recovered so quickly that others were often unaware that she had slipped out of her mild manner at all.

But as she and Rory had worked through the crowd, she had been distracted. Her stomach was fluttery as she felt his strong male presence to her right side. At times the large gym wasn't very crowded at all. Then a flux of people would filter in and the pair would find themselves squeezed together as a speaker gave a demo or power point presentation about their company.

Rory automatically took a protective role. He guided her through the crowd with one large, warm palm at the small of her back. A buzz of electricity went up her spine. If they began to feel too squeezed he would step in front of her and block the crowd from pushing in too close. Emily enjoyed the feeling of being watched after. She reached for his hand as they shuffled out of the stifling hot gym to enjoy their lunch on the campus lawn.

The cool spring breeze caressed their faces but a profound

sense of disappointment filled her when he casually let go of her hand. Emily rubbed her clammy palms against her jeans and looked around awkwardly. Did he want her to give him space? Maybe she had taken too much of a liberty grabbing his hand like that. Part of her wanted to give in to the blush that was threatening, but another, more daring part of her wanted to reach out and somehow bring him closer. She decided to test her bravery.

"If you want to go find your buddies you can," she said, "but I am going to go sit under that big maple tree if you want to join me?"

It was more of a question than a statement. Rory looked into her questioning eyes. He seemed almost surprised. "Sure. I'll go grab our backpacks from the commons while you go stake it out for us."

He set off toward the student union building. She let a small sigh escape as she watched his tall, stocky form move efficiently and purposefully across the lawn. He took every step as if determined not to waste any movement.

She strolled to the large tree wondering about Rory and how she suddenly wanted to get to understand him on a deeper level. He had barely paid attention at most of the booths but had perked up enough to ask questions at the law enforcement table. Police work was obviously of interest to him so she would get him talking about that.

Once they were both under the umbrella of the ancient maple tree, they dug through their lunches in an uncomfortable silence. Finally Emily took a drink from her bottled water and took the plunge.

"So," she said. "You snagged some of the brochures on that police academy in Colorado. Are you thinking about joining?"

Rory had just finished his sub and leaned against the trunk of the tree. Stretching out his long legs, he palmed a soda can in his hand and nodded.

"Yeah, I have been looking into a few different criminal justice programs on the west coast. There are some good ones in California but I like the sound of this one."

Emily noted that he watched her when he thought she wasn't looking. She knew something was bubbling underneath the surface for the both of them. Though the thought was tantalizing, his restless unease meant that he wasn't sure what to make of it yet.

"What about your family?" she asked. "What do they think of your plans to move a couple of states away to pursue a dangerous career?"

Rory shrugged and stared at the luscious green leaves fluttering in the breeze. "They're fine. They have been expecting as much since I was about ten years old. I can't say they love the idea but it is what it is, and they just accept it."

"Why have they been expecting it? Have you always wanted to be a police officer?"

"No, that interest developed in only the past few years, but I've always made it clear that I wouldn't be taking over the ranch when I grew up. I was determined to get out of this twilight zone town."

Emily tuned into his tone of disgust when he spoke of the town. So that's what Rory was rebelling against…his family's expectations and the idea of following in footsteps rather than treading his own self-made path.

"Yeah, I can understand that perfectly," she said. "The entire side of my father's family comes from a long line of bankers. It is pretty much assumed since I am the only child, I will naturally follow suit and fill in daddy's shadow."

Rory glanced at her. His expression revealed his sudden realization that they were more similar than he ever imagined. She saw him relax as the idea settled.

"But you don't want that for yourself?" he asked.

Emily shrugged and looked away, focusing on nothing in particular. "Not exactly. I am going to go to school and get a business management degree but if I have anything to say about it, I don't plan on ever doing anything productive with it."

That statement baffled him.

"Why would you go to school and get a degree in something you aren't even interested in? Why not just go for whatever it is you're really passionate about?"

Emily couldn't believe she was about to reveal her true intentions and dreams to a guy she barely knew, but somehow she felt he would understand and wouldn't judge her.

"Because what I really want to do, doesn't require a degree. It pretty much has to just kind of evolve on its own, so I might as well go to school in the meantime."

"What do you want to do that doesn't require school?" His gaze narrowed. Curiosity was written over his face.

Emily flushed and she cringed inside as she prepared to bare her soul. "I want to be a wife and a mommy."

The moment the words were out of her mouth, she realized how stupid they sounded out loud. She immediately wished she could take them back. She worried that she had shared too much and had thoroughly annihilated her chances with him. She bit the inside of her cheek and silently chided herself for having rambled on and managing to sound like a brainless idiot. She tried to recover but found herself stammering and making it worse.

"I mean, not like right now, or anything, but, umm…you know? Someday. Oh, never mind. It sounds stupid." She waved her hand as if trying to wave away her last few comments.

Rory was obviously taken back. She could imagine him

picturing her, the pretty cheerleader who came from such an achieved family, turning in a future executive status for nursing babies and cleaning up baby spit. It was probably a far cry from what he had envisioned for her. He cocked his head.

"It's not stupid at all," he said. "My mom is just like that. She lives for us boys and running the household while dad works the ranch. It took me a minute to shift gears but yeah, I can picture you being the ultimate mother, still pretty and organized rather than frumpy and disgruntled. You'll figure out how to make it seem easy. Yep, I can picture you running a tight ship and keeping some lucky bastard in line." And with that he took a deep slug of his coke.

Emily's eyelashes fluttered as she processed what he'd said. Was it a good thing that he had compared her to his mother? She was relieved he hadn't made fun of or chastised her. She glanced down at her hands hoping to hide the nervous smile she was unsuccessfully trying to suppress.

They both relaxed into the conversation as she changed the subject to their upcoming graduation. Eventually they rejoined the others for the last few demonstrations of the afternoon. As students filed onto the bus for the lengthy ride back over the mountain, Emily sat toward the back and scanned the crowd for her best friend Abby. They had much to share. However, Derrick plopped down next to her and tried his best to flirt and make her laugh.

Emily didn't really mind and lost herself in Derrick's ridiculous antics. He was famous for being the class clown and was effortlessly hilarious. He had made it clear that he was interested in dating her but she just couldn't see him as boyfriend material and relentlessly turned him down. She listened to him ramble along, surmising he must be a glutton for punishment as she broke into fits of laughter.

# The Complexity of a Soldier

Rory was one of the last students to make his way onto the bus. As he filed toward the back, Emily caught his eye just as he spotted Derrick, who was immersed in one of his exaggerated stories about mudding on the mountain in his new truck. The two of them were friends but seemed to bond by constantly flicking each other crap and testing each other's boundaries.

"Hey, man, you better get out of my seat before I have to remove you myself," Rory warned in a mock-serious tone.

Derrick leaned back with a grin smeared across his face. "Eat dirt, Nichols. Emily needs a real man."

Rory snorted. "Exactly. So run along, little boy, and let daddy have a seat now."

Emily held her fist to her mouth to hide her smile. She was tickled that Rory was asserting himself and appeared to be staking a claim. She knew it was ridiculous to think that way but her eighteen -year old ego was eating up the attention.

Derrick stood up and puffed out his chest with a challenging stance. He still had to look up because Rory was a good six inches taller. Rory seemed to fill up too much space within the small confines of the smelly bus, and she was quietly relieved that he and Derrick were only messing with each other rather than seriously squaring off.

Rory moved so fast neither Emily nor Derrick were prepared. Within seconds, Derrick was bent over with his head firmly squeezed in Rory's thick biceps. As the head-lock tightened, Derrick's face became redder. Derrick was laughing hysterically, much to Emily's relief. The last thing she wanted was to witness a fight between friends, especially if it was over her.

Rory released his hold, hauled Derrick upright and gave him the half hand shake, half hug thing guys did. Both of them smiled ridiculously. Derrick slapped Rory as hard as he could on the back.

## The Complexity of a Soldier

"That was smooth, Nichols. Smooth."

He rubbed his cherry red neck. He spun on his heel and sat two seats back with Jackie Sorrel, carrying on as if nothing had happened. Rory eased his lengthy frame into the green fake leather seat next to Emily. He flashed a bright and devilish grin that made her stomach do somersaults.

"So tell me about where you lived before moving to this pit," he said.

Emily thought about his desire to move away from the stifling regimen of his hometown. "You know, Rory, I don't think I can tell you anything earth-shattering about living in the city. I mean, in all reality, there are pretty much the same kinds of people living the same kinds of lives with the same hopes and fears there as here. They just come in larger quantities and live closer to each other."

She looked out the window. While she saw miles of untouched, unspoiled land spread out the way it had been for thousand of years in a beautiful, peaceful existence, he saw isolation and emptiness. Her vision stayed slightly unfocused as she looked past the images flying passed them. The bus rattled along the highway as she pictured the smoggy, traffic-infested drive to school she had endured in Boise.

"I was looking forward to moving to a smaller town," she said, "probably just as much as you are looking forward to getting out of one."

She watched him mull over her statement and wondered what he could be thinking. They continued to talk. They got to know each other and discovered that they were both eager to learn more. As the bus pulled into the school parking lot nearly an hour later, Rory sat straight in his seat. He craned his neck to get a full-on look at her.

"Do you want to go out to a movie or something this

weekend?" he asked.

Emily bit her bottom lip to suppress a huge grin. "Sure that sounds fun."

Rory's gaze slipped from her eyes down to her dainty mouth. Then he scooped his backpack off the grimy floor and slung it over his shoulder. "Great! Graduation is Friday afternoon but I can pick you up Saturday evening around six-thirty, if you want. We can catch the seven o'clock showing. I don't even know what's playing but you can pick, it doesn't matter to me."

*Sounds like a first date,* she thought. Movies were a perfect first-date venue. There wasn't exactly a lot to choose from, though. The theatre was a rinky-dink setup with only one screen, so they typically only played two movies every couple of weeks.

"Six-thirty is great." She said. "Do you know where I live?"

Rory shifted his backpack as they filed off the bus. "Yeah. Your family bought that huge two-story on Second with the four large columns on the front entrance."

Emily still wasn't used to how everyone in town seemed to know everyone else's business, and just nodded. So they parted ways, each of them distracted and even baffled at how their entire dynamics had shifted radically between the time they had stepped on the bus that morning and barely seven hours later.

It was all still alive and clear in her mind as she lay in his arms, comforted by his presence and devotion to her and their child. But he would be gone tomorrow. She would feel his absence like a hole in her chest, like a festering wound.

She could do it. She would do it. Both she and Callie would get through the next five months together. It was all they could do.

# CHAPTER THREE

# Boot Camp

Boot camp was just as Rory had imagined it would be. The only exception was that they were fed aptly to ensure they ate enough to keep up with the physical exertion. His drill sergeant was thorough. The men learned to meet all of his expectations for keeping the barracks clean, their appearance flawless, and to respond with an enthusiasm close to psychosis when he barked out an order. Rory attacked the military way of life with the attitude that he was just doing another job. He wanted to do his best and keep his nose clean while doing it.

He categorized everyone in his unit by the reasons they had joined. There were three groups. There were the guys who were there because military life ran in their family for generations so there was no other choice or expectation. Others didn't really have any other plans so they were using the military as a stepping stone into college or another career. Then there were the guys who were a little bit on the edge of society and who joined as a last-ditch effort to keep themselves from ending up in jail or dead on the streets. Rory figured he fit into the second category.

During his first week, he was assigned KP duty with a guy who fit the first category. John Thomas came from four generations of military men. He was extremely stocky and on the short side at only five-six. He preferred to be called J.T. His quiet, blue eyes shone out of a stern, hard-looking face. Though the two men were radically different, they struck an immediate friendship that resembled brotherhood.

"Hey, who'd you vote for in the last election?" J.T. asked one evening. "Wait, wait. Let me guess. You're a small town country bumpkin like myself and your dad's a rancher. I'll bet you voted for Bush. I've yet to figure out why but the populations who would benefit from a democratic policy most, tend to vote Republican. It's a perplexing phenomenon."

"I didn't vote," Rory said.

Disgust flashed over J.T.'s face. "Why in the hell not? I bet your dad voted. And do you know why? I'll tell you why. He's got a business to run and knows if he doesn't use his vote, his voice, policies will pass that threaten his investments, his life-blood. It's important stuff."

So they were gonna talk politics.

Rory kicked in his own opinion. "Listen, man, I get what you're saying but I've never really bought into the whole majority rules thing. I mean, the concept itself is good but if anyone thinks it's being implemented properly after the last election debacle then they're only fooling themselves.

"I mean, it was completely unconstitutional for the Supreme Court to make the final decision. Even after the recount and another recount, the candidate with the majority of votes still lost the election. Tell me how that's democracy. I don't vote."

## The Complexity of a Soldier

He ended with finality, hoping they would drop the discussion. No such luck.

"So you do have an opinion," J.T. taunted. "That's good to know. Not that it makes a bit of difference if you don't vote. Apathy is not the answer, my friend."

"It's not apathy. It's simply understanding how things really work. I am not going to kid myself into believing that big government is my friend."

"Look around, buddy," J.T. snorted. "You're surrounded by big government at its finest. You're serving the leader and his army. What the heck are you doing here?"

"Just doing a job. It's a means to an end."

Their animated conversation was attracting an audience of fellow soldiers, so Rory shifted the topic. But that was only the first of many heated discussions. They made a habit of filling their down time with controversial debates on topics ranging from politics to religion to sports to drinking exploits. While they saw eye to eye on numerous issues, their approach was vastly different. Rory's emotions ran deep but he kept them close to the vest except with only a select few who had earned his trust.

J.T. was more of a philosopher. He made his feelings and opinions about pretty much anything that came up in life known. He contemplated the deeper meaning of his existence and of those around him. He was constantly curious about the motives of human nature and why people did the things they did.

Rory gave J.T. a hard time and said he was making things more complicated than they actually were. But in reality, many of J.T.'s insights and opinions struck him deeply. He respected his friend's ability to see the bigger picture. He enjoyed the elaborate and enthusiastic manner J.T. adopted when he got worked up about a subject he felt passionately about. His nostrils flared and his voice bellowed during his many emphatic discourses.

It occurred to Rory early on that although J.T. was doing what he was expected to do and probably what he even believed he wanted to do, the callous, rule-abiding military life wasn't really a good fit. John Thomas looked hard on the outside but seemed to have a soft inside, a trait incongruent to their choice of career.

Night after night, J.T. retreated to his top bunk to scribble in a tattered, pocket-sized notebook until lights out. Initially Rory assumed he was writing to a girlfriend or his family. One night, curious and feeling obstinate, he snatched the notebook from J.T. and read the first few lines.

The quiet desert sun beat down its brilliant rays, echoing a thousand years of praise....

J.T. leaped off the bunk and snatched the notebook out of Rory's grip. Preparing for the inevitable onslaught of insults, his blue eyes fired under his thick brown lashes and dared Rory to push him to his limit. Rory stood with a gaping grin on his face.

"What the hell is that, J.T.? Are you a poet and I didn't know it?"

The ridiculous rhyme was harmless. Rory ignored J.T.'s obvious anger and enjoyed the banter that reminded him of his younger brother Rodney back home.

J.T. turned his back and shoved the notebook under his bunk. "Go to hell, Nichols," he said gruffly.

But Rory couldn't let it go. It was much too entertaining.

"Come on J.T., lets hear a sonnet or something. Pretend I'm a pretty damsel you're wooing and lay it on me."

J.T. turned on a dime and rammed his shoulder into Rory's gut. The blow knocked the wind out of him and put him flat on his back. Rory was shocked by his short friend's strength and gasped as he tried to pull air into his lungs. He remembered how his brother had taunted him and how he would be on the other end of the beating. A pathetic laugh croaked out of his straining chest.

All of that took only seconds to flash through his mind. The force of the body hit had J.T. down with Rory, so Rory wrapped him in a head-lock. They rolled around the floor throwing punches whenever they could. Rory howled with laughter.

"Jesus, J.T.," he hollered. "I was just kidding. Chill the hell out!"

Rory's laughter only fueled J.T.'s anger. Just as Rory decided to stop messing around and immobilize his opponent, their sergeant walked in. The men scrambled up off the floor and into a stiff salute posture.

"Well, gentlemen," the sergeant yelled inches from their faces. "It looks like the two of you like to roll around on the floor, so I suggest you get out the cleaning supplies and clean every inch of this floor first thing tomorrow morning directly after P.T. and formation. That way the next time you decide to make out, it will at least be clean!"

Rory still couldn't understand the Army's desire to make everyone deaf by the end of basic training but he knew it was all part of the game. In unison, he and J.T. barked, "Yes, Drill Sergeant!"

The large bald sergeant stared them down for another five seconds. His eyes bored into them, daring them to eyeball him. When they maintained their composed forward stare, he turned his back and stomped off.

"Lights out in ten minutes ladies." His voice echoed throughout the barracks. Rory and J.T. waited until he had exited the building before they relaxed. J.T. walked back toward their bunk.

"Dude, I'm sorry," Rory said. "I was just kidding around. I won't tease you about your writing again. I actually like that kind of stuff. My mom has it all over the house."

J.T. gave him a sideways look, "Yeah, right. I doubt you can read at all, like the rest of these monkeys."

Rory put his hand to his chest in mock pain. "That really hurts, J.T."

He flashed a huge grin. John Thomas finally cracked a smile of his own and they shook hands. Neither one of them looked forward to the next day, especially once J.T. mentioned they would be cleaning the floors with toothbrushes.

"What? No way. That's just how they do it in the movies." Rory's voice didn't sound convincing.

J.T. just shook his head. "Dude, where do you think they got it from? My dad and granddad have all had their fair share of scrubbing floors with toothbrushes. We won't be able to stand up straight by the time we're done. It's gonna suck."

Rory stared, realizing he was serious. "Yeah, that's gonna suck."

The next day they woke at four-thirty for P.T. Their masochistic drill sergeant apparently thought the two of them needed extra physical exertion to remind them of their rightful place among the ranks. He had them run the obstacle course two more times than usual, counted out twenty extra push ups then counted out ten extra pull ups, all before joining formation. Then a fat, cold rain began to pelt them.

Rory stood in the icy downpour. Steam rose from his sweating torso. His chest heaved as his body tried to take in more oxygen. *J.T. was right,* he thought. *This frigging sucks!* He clenched his jaw and forced himself to concentrate on getting through the rest of his training without causing any more trouble.

He and J.T. joined everyone in the mess hall to shovel food into their faces during a ten-minute breakfast before marching off to their barracks. By the time they hit the four hour mark, Rory's knees were bruised down to the bone, his knuckles were raw and near bleeding, and his back was screaming to be stretched. He leaned back to rest on his heels. His nose crinkled as the smell of Lysol and sweat permeated his nostrils.

The twenty minute break for lunch was like heaven. They ate in silence, dreading the rest of the afternoon. Just after four, they wrapped up the last section of the back right corner. As they were putting the cleaning supplies away, the sergeant appeared to survey their work. Both Rory and J.T. stood at attention and waited for the litany. The sergeant looked up and down both rows of bunks then faced them.

"Well, gentlemen, I hope the next time you want to stick your tongues in each others ears for a little make-out session you'll think twice before you do it in my barracks." He was silent for five counts before adding, "Now drop down and hold push up position!"

They dropped as quickly as their sore bodies would allow and held themselves in the push up position. Five excruciating minutes passed. By the end, both men's arms were shaking and sweat dripped down their faces and backs. They prayed they would make it. Normally they could have handled the five minutes just fine but after their grueling day, their shoulders were on fire and hot needles ran through their veins.

*If I could just land one solid punch in that guy's face,* Rory thought. He risked a sideways glance at J.T. He was pretty sure they were both thinking the same violent thoughts.

"Attention!"

They stood on trembling legs. Their arms felt like Jello as they saluted.

"At ease." The sergeant turned on his booted heel and walked out.

# The Complexity of a Soldier

Rory's absence weighed heavily on his conscience so he called Emily at every opportunity. Unfortunately their conversations were short. There was always a line of impatient soldiers waiting for their turn on the phone. If anyone went over ten minutes, they harangued the speaker until he couldn't hear the person on the other end.

Emily talked quickly to fill him in on Callie's rapid growth, as well as how his parents were doing. Apparently Rodney, being a senior in high school, was giving them a hard time. He spent a lot of time out drinking with his buddies and several times had been hours late for the morning milking. Their father had gone stinking mad one night and kicked his butt out of the house but their mom eventually talked sense into the both of them. Lately things around the ranch had settled down to a more normal routine.

After every call, Rory reluctantly got off the phone. He felt a longing he hadn't known was possible and spent the next hour or two in an irritable mood. Without fail, J.T. would flick him crap about "moping around like a little girl" until his temper sparked. They would come close to sparring before remembering their penalty from the last time and would settle for a few quick jabs when no one was looking. The remainder of their evening was spent playing cards on Rory's bottom bunk until lights out.

For Rory, it was like having his brother around except somehow he felt an even tighter camaraderie with J.T. He felt in his gut that J.T. was the type of guy he could count on to cover his back if he ever got into a sticky situation. He was someone who would stand up for what was right.

One evening when they were heading back from the showers, a

shrill scream echoed from the woods. The trees stood directly behind one of the training facilities not far from the only women's barrack. Instinct took over. Both men dropped their things and raced into the dense foliage. The woods were silent so they weren't sure exactly where to go. They were fairly deep into the trees before they spotted two men wrestling with one very frantic young woman.

One had her from behind. His thick arms threaded through hers and his hands were clamped behind her head. Although she was writhing with all of her might, she was unable to escape. The second man had one large palm over her mouth. His other hand fondled her breasts through her olive green t-shirt. Her eyes were wild.

Both of the perpetrators noticed Rory and J.T.'s approach at the same time. Hearing their boots crashing through the brush, they let go of the girl and fled in opposite directions. The woman fell to her knees and scrambled into the bushes whimpering like a wounded animal. Rory and J.T. bounded past her, each of them targeting a different man.

Rory's long stride caught up to one before he'd taken five steps of his own. They hit the forest floor with a force hard enough to crack the man's chin against a jagged rock.

J.T. had to chase the other culprit slightly further before he took him out with a tackle to the knees. Both landed a few angry, solid punches before a sharp whistle trilled through the evening air. A group of angry drill sergeants hauled everyone to their feet. All four men were told to keep their mouths shut and were drug into separate interrogation rooms at main headquarters.

While J.T. seemed unaffected and completely ambivalent about their predicament, Rory was more than a little stressed out. There could be dire consequences if their superior officers found their fight in the woods to be a major offense. He gave his statement in a small solitary room with only two chairs. The officer held a small recorder in his right hand. Rory knew J.T. was probably doing the exact same thing in a similar room down the hall. His mind raced as he imagined how he might redeem himself if he were kicked out of the program.

The interrogating officer was not unpleasant but remained passive and stoic. Rory knew that was meant to be intimidating. He kept his story minimal, relaying the sequence of events without adding any conjecture or supposition. Hopefully that would avoid conflicting with J.T.'s story.

Four hours later, both Rory and J.T. were released. The woman they had rescued had relayed every detail of her encounter to the doctors at the military hospital and again to the military police. Apparently she was very shaken up but grateful to her saviors. She was equally determined to finish her training. She refused to let those jerks scare her off.

Rory and J.T. were both shocked when they realized that not only were they not in trouble, they would be recognized for their heroic behavior toward a fellow soldier. Neither one of them wanted to be patted on the back for doing what anyone in their position should have done. Their main concern was for the girl, although they were curious about what would happen with the perpetrators. No matter how many people they asked, though, they never did find out what happened to the other men. They only knew they had been swiftly and quietly removed from the premises.

Plenty of suspicions and rumors about what actions the Army would take against the men circulated. Many soldiers were confident that the pair would be kicked out on attempted rape charges. Plenty of others firmly believed they would only receive a slap on the wrist, undergo "rehabilitation" then finish their training in an undisclosed location. After all, the Army was reluctant to lose soldiers.

This idea bothered Rory deeply. He couldn't stop imagining that woman as Emily, his mother, or God forbid, his young daughter. What if no one had been around to help her, to bring her to safety? Who would ensure that the woman's trauma and violation received justice? Would it all be swept under the rug so the Army could keep up its numbers?

It was the first time but not the last, that Rory would question the system and exactly who benefited from it.

~~~~~~~~~~

Once basic training was officially over, their daily routine changed significantly. They shifted into their advanced individual training courses. They still had four-thirty P.T. and formation every morning. Their classroom studies covered Miranda rights, military law, evidence collection, search and apprehension, reports, vehicle inspection, interrogation and interviews. They also learned response techniques to special incidents such as rape, attempted suicide and domestic abuse.

After lunch they would return to the training facilities where the classroom shifted from books and academics to physical combat maneuvers. Their days were filled with intensive self-defense, hand -to-hand combat, and the skills required to take down a perpetrator in difficult situations. Both Rory and J.T. flourished in this part of their training. When they weren't actively participating in the classroom, they were hitting the books in the study hall.

Keeping busy was the only thing pushing Rory toward the last of his training. His homesickness for Emily and Callie was causing him physical strain. His appetite began to go down the toilet. His stomach clenched with an anxiety he'd never felt before. Every night he prayed for his girls' safety.

J.T. was acutely tuned into his drastic mood shifts. Rory appreciated his increased efforts to distract him. One evening Rory was particularly agitated after a phone call with Emily. She was typically good-natured and loving but she and Callie had both been fighting the flu for three days. Callie had been up countless times throughout the evenings fussing and miserable. Emily was frazzled, exhausted and still feeling under the weather so she had been curt and bad-tempered. When Rory had tried to sooth and encourage her, she responded with a guilt trip.

"Don't patronize me, Rory," she snapped. "You're not here. You have no idea what it's like to basically be a single mother."

He knew she was just as shocked by her harsh and bitter remarks because she apologized immediately. She claimed she was just tired and felt terrible for her stinging words. But it was too late to take them back. When she suggested they wrap up the conversation to avoid any further argument, he begrudgingly agreed.

Rory felt the burn of her comment and wallowed in guilt. She was without him all the way across the country, raising their little girl by herself, just as she'd said.

Late that evening, he and J.T. drank a few beers with a bunch of guys from their barracks at a pub located near the base. They were on a twenty-four hour pass and were supposed to be having a good time. Rory stared off into the distance ignoring the chatter while his buddies hatched a plan.

They had spotted their drill sergeant walking into a small Chinese restaurant just down the block. He and his cohorts had parked their government issued sedan at the corner. J.T. nudged Rory.

## The Complexity of a Soldier

"Come on, man, let's do this!" he prodded with a wicked grin.

Rory shrugged him off. "Do what?"

"Dude, where have you been for the past twenty minutes? Never mind. Just get your sorry ass out of that chair and come on!"

Rory wasn't up for whatever little scheme they had cooked up. Neither was he up for going a few rounds with J.T. So he swigged down the rest of his beer before following his crew and one other gentleman he didn't recognize out the door. The group huddled in the alley as the man he didn't recognize disappeared around the back of the building.

"Who is that guy?" Rory's instincts kicked into full throttle. He was in the middle of something that reeked of no good.

Sampson, a fellow soldier from the Mississippi bayous, piped up. "That's Leroy. He runs a towing business here in town, so therefore he owns a tow truck. It's parked around the back. J.T. paid him two hundred bucks to haul off the sergeant's car while he's eating."

"Uh uh, no way." he snagged J.T by the shoulder and whipped him around. "You are crazy if you think that I'm going in on this. You're gonna get us thrown out of AIT!" he hissed.

J.T. rolled his eyes. "Dude, you're getting me all choked up. Now quit your bitching."

Just then, light pierced through the dark, flashing on and off twice. That was their signal to begin the next step. Filing down the alley, they passed the bar, a dry cleaners shop that was closed for the evening, and the Chinese restaurant where their drill sergeant was eating sub gum chow mein.

Without understanding why, Rory helped them hook the sedan to the back of the tow truck. Two others kept a look out. Fortunately, the streets were dead at ten-thirty. They had ample freedom to carry out their plot. The drunk tow-truck driver hopped into his cab and slowly pulled away from the curb. Everyone stifled their exuberant laughter and decided to get well away from the scene of the crime.

The next morning, rumors about what had happened spread rampantly through the compound. Everyone placed bets on who it must have been and what their punishment would be once they were caught.

The drill sergeant was exceptionally rough on them the day after their twenty-four hour pass was up. He kept eyeballing everyone to see who would crack. He had not been too pleased when he and his coworkers had stepped around the corner to find their car missing. Apparently, the State Troopers had called the Fort's headquarters to notify them that one of their cars had been located behind an adult only club.

Rory and J.T. kept their faces straight and their heads down as the information filtered through the camp. The culprits were never discovered.

# CHAPTER FOUR

# Family Dynamics

With the last week of training finally upon them, Rory eagerly anticipated the week of leave they were allowed before graduation. J.T. hadn't mentioned anything about his plans.

"So, are you flying back to Montana to see your family for the week?" Rory asked.

J.T. shrugged. "Nope. I don't really have any plans yet."

Rory narrowed his gaze. "Why not? Don't you want to see your family? Aren't they coming back with you for graduation?"

With a neutral expression J.T., stretched back on his bunk, crossed his arms over his chest and looked up at the ceiling with an air of indifference. "My family wouldn't come to see me if I won the Nobel Peace Prize. As long as I follow in my dad's footsteps and become a stellar soldier, they are happy enough with that. There are no accolades for mediocrity in my family. Graduating from M.P. training is nothing. I have a lot to prove before they'll even think about acknowledging my achievements."

# The Complexity of a Soldier

Rory picked up his scuffed boots and began to polish them. He tried not to pass judgment but was quietly thankful for his own parents and upbringing. "Wow, that sounds harsh," he said.

J.T. snorted. "Dude, my childhood was a boot camp. Now that was harsh. This is nothing. I'm glad my family won't be around to point out all the little shit I'm probably doing wrong."

Rory was silent as he picked up the other boot. Then an idea occurred to him. "You should come back to Oregon with me. I'd love for you to meet my family and I know that they'd love to have you."

J.T. turned a speculative gaze toward his friend. "I couldn't do that. You haven't seen your wife and kid for nearly five months. You need some alone time."

Rory gave him a devilish smile. "Don't worry about my alone time. Emily and I will be just fine. Besides, if she finds out that you stayed behind and I didn't bring you along, she'd bust my chops. So that's it, it's a done deal. You're coming with me."

~~~~~~~~~~~~

Later that night, when the barracks hummed with the sounds of soldiers with bone-deep fatigue, Rory found himself staring wide-eyed at the ceiling. He was thinking about his life waiting back home. His earlier discussion with J.T. had inspired thoughts of his own family. Obviously there were some complex dynamics in J.T.'s family situation. It caused him to realize just how rich an environment his parents had raised him in.

Thinking of his parents instantly triggered one of his favorite memories…the day they had surprised him with a new truck. On Rory's high school graduation day his father, had purchased a beat-up classic as a gift. Not only had Rory's love and passion for restoring classics made him ecstatic he'd also been, shocked. His father had not personally given him a present since...well, for as long as he could remember.

Justin Nichols was the type of father who woke every morning at four-thirty to begin his monotonous routine. Tending their one hundred and twenty-five acre ranch meant he wouldn't show his tanned, sun-wrinkled face at the house again until early in the evening. Because his days were full of back-breaking labor, he left the household duties to his efficient and loving wife, Sarah. He taught his two sons by example to earn a living by working hard and being as self-reliant as possible.

Since Sarah ran the house just as efficiently as her husband ran the ranch, she tackled all of her duties with a zeal that left others, tired simply by having watched her. Her responsibilities encompassed all things except the business of running the ranch and included the imagination and consideration that went into planning holidays, celebrations and any other family event. This meant all gifts were planned, purchased and wrapped by Sarah without Justin knowing exactly what they were giving until the recipient opened the treasure. The arrangement suited both of them.

So when the family returned to Nichols Acres early in the evening of his high-school graduation ceremony, Rory immediately spotted the Chevy pickup sitting in the drive. He pressed his face to the glass to check it out, assuming the car belonged to his Uncle Travis.

That uncle had initially sparked Rory's interest in classic car restoration. Uncle Travis lived on the other side of the mountains. He worked in insurance but spent most of his free time and spare money on his obsession restoring Chevy models. He refused to focus on anything built later than 1972 because after that, "they just weren't made like they used to be."

# The Complexity of a Soldier

One summer, Sarah had packed up Rory and Rodney then headed over Meacham Pass to visit her brother. The two had been close while growing up but rarely saw each other as adults. She had too many responsibilities between the ranch and raising the boys.

One Thursday morning in June, she had wakened with the vague memory of a dream trickling into her consciousness. She and Travis, both children, had waded through the creek that ran behind their childhood home looking for crawdads.

The dream had dissipated but the feelings from it lingered. She missed her youngest brother and the closeness they had shared while growing up immensely. She'd made a last-minute decision to take the boys over the mountain for a quick visit. Tackling the most immediate errands and obligations allowed her to squeeze in a rare weekend trip.

Rory had just finished seventh grade and was beginning to develop the tough-guy attitude other boys in his class had recently donned. He had sulked in the back seat of his mom's Ford Taurus for most of the drive. He would miss his friend's paintball birthday party because of the trip.

Uncle Travis engaged Rory from the moment they poured themselves out of the hot car. Although their seven-hour drive had been exhausting, Travis had dragged him into the large shop where his current restoration project was under way. As Sarah and Rodney kept themselves occupied indoors, Rory discovered his true passion. He instantly loved the smell of oil and grease that permeated the shop. Thumbing through the classic car magazines scattered throughout the house, he asked a barrage of questions. His uncle was only too pleased to answer, thrilled that his nephew was so interested in his hobby.

From that day on, Rory read everything he could get his hands on about classic cars and how to restore them. Sarah ordered a subscription to Classic Truck magazine and often found him passed out on their couch after a day in the fields with a magazine spread across his scrawny chest.

Once Rory was in high school, he joined every shop and automotive class that was offered. He couldn't wait to get his hands on a project of his own. He saved nearly every penny he earned working for his dad, hoping his little cache would help him move off of the ranch and purchase his first solo restoration project.

Rory had attended the senior breakfast the morning of graduation, so he had missed Uncle Travis's arrival. As he followed his fellow seniors in the procession, he spotted his favored uncle sitting next to his parents in the football stadium bleachers.

After the ceremony, they all piled into his mom's new SUV. Rory was sitting in the back seat with his brother and uncle, talking about his post-graduation plans to join a police academy. They drove into the gravel lane and around the barn. As the lane opened into a large circular drive, Rory focused in on the battered up yellow Chevy.

"Whoa, Uncle Travis, is that your newest project?" He peered out the window and gawked at the truck.

His uncle merely grinned. The car wasn't at a full stop before Rory jumped out and sprinted to the truck. He circled it while taking in every detail. His parents stood back as he rattled off the wear and abuse on the vehicle. After mumbling his assessment, he gave his uncle a sideways glance.

"The body is pretty beat up, Uncle. How is the engine?" Without waiting for an answer, he continued, "It looks like a pretty big project. That passenger door is obviously a replacement. It doesn't even sit on the frame right. It must be a different year. Whoever did it, had no idea what they were doing."

Prowling around the truck, he said, "I bet you're gonna have a pisser of a time finding a better replacement." He was proud of his assessment and waited for his uncle to confirm his observations.

Instead, his dad piped in. "Well, if it's going to be too much of a pisser then maybe you're not up for the challenge."

Rory furrowed his brow, wondering what the heck the old man was talking about.

Justin sighed and tried again. "I'm sure the guy I bought it from would be nice enough to let me return it. I can just tell him that my son was too much of a numbskull to appreciate his graduation gift." He delivered his statement with a bland stare.

Rory's brain kicked into high gear. His heart raced, as excitement filled him. He was about to jump into the air with delight but caught himself at the last moment. He didn't want to cause an emotional scene. He straightened his spine and threw back his shoulders. Meeting his father's direct gaze, he thought, *screw it!* and took a few brisk strides to close the gap and embrace his father.

"Thanks so much, Dad! I love it!" he said in his deep baritone. They gave each other a quick slap on the back and stepped back.

Rory's father beamed. "I'm proud of you, son. I know you'll fix her up real nice."

He dipped his right hand into the pocket of his starched slacks. He usually wore worn jeans and looked uncomfortable in the unfamiliar attire. He'd only worn the new pair of slacks one other time. "Here's the key. You go ahead and check her out with Travis while your mom and I get ready for your celebration dinner."

Rory could sense his father was a bit awkward and emotional. He watched with a knowing smile as Justin spun on his heel, put his arm around his wife's shoulders, and led her toward the house with his familiar bow-legged gait.

As Rory gave a long stretch, the hard bunk under him groaned. With an absentminded smile tugging at his mouth, he remembered his beloved truck. It was his pride and joy, other than Emily and Callie of course. He was wise enough now to know that his emotional ties to the truck were not solely because it had been his first restoration project. It was also a symbol of his relationship with his father. He wasn't exactly sure why, but every time he thought of that truck, he thought of his father.

Justin Nichols was one tough son of a gun. Rory had grown to have great respect for him. He still pondered why he had rebelled against the idea of following in his father's footsteps. He spent most of his adolescence fighting against his father, who had only tried to raise his sons as upstanding, strong men.

Only weeks after his father had given him the truck, Rory had been mired deep into the restoration. The sun had been unforgiving that day. It beat down on his back as his arms contracted and strained to loosen the rusted lug nuts on the front driver's side tire. He bit his bottom lip so hard he tasted the metallic flavor of blood as skin broke and it trickled into his mouth.

Rory crouched down and put his full weight into the task. The July heat and the direct rays of the afternoon sun made him sweat heavily. He fought with the tire iron, swearing under his breath as he willed the damned lug nuts to give.

Rory had been driving down the dirt road to the house when the truck swerved violently. He'd had to wrestle with the steering wheel to navigate safely to the side of the road without going into the ditch. Though he was only a mile away from home, he didn't want to push his luck by driving on the rim. He'd stopped immediately to assess the damage.

The tire was completely blown. It dawned on him how lucky he was that it had blown at thirty miles per hour on an empty dirt lane rather than at sixty on the highway. He was just about to give up and allow himself a quick fit of rage when the tire iron jerked. He felt the give of the lug nut as it finally loosened its grip. *Sweet,* he thought and his red face relaxed as he continued the job. It wasn't until the other vehicle was near that he heard the crunch of gravel under its tires. His dad pulled up next to him with a bemused expression pinching his face.

"How's it going, son? Having some trouble?" His dad gave him a sly grin as he leaned his brown forearm on the window ledge of his truck peering down.

Rory decided not to let his father's smug attitude rile him any further. He turned his attention back toward the grueling task, hoping the rest of the lug nuts wouldn't be as stubborn as the first. "Nope, I'm just fine dad," he said in an attempt at nonchalance. "Where are you headed to?"

"Gotta run to the feed store to get some more salt blocks for the number four pasture and some salve for the calf that had a run-in with the barbed wire fence last week." He talked in a distracted tone as he continued to watch his oldest son. Over the previous year Rory had filled out and left the last remnants of boyhood behind. Just the week before he had overheard his father tell his mom how odd it was to look at his son and see a full-grown man. He was also eerily aware of the uncanny resemblance that mirrored his father's looks. Rory was proud that his father was taking note of the fact that he was an adult now.

Really though, he was pulled in two directions when it came to his dad. Rory wanted his approval but always seemed to be starting arguments as he asserted his opinions and desires for the future.

He wondered...no, dreaded the possibility that his dad would offer to help with the flat tire. It would lead to another useless altercation that had plagued their relationship since Rory had been about ten years old. That's when he'd begun to express that ranch life was not for him and that he would do something greater with his life.

## The Complexity of a Soldier

Justin always let him know he respected Rory's aspirations. He didn't hold it against him that he wasn't particularly fond of the hard work bestowed upon his sons at an early age. But the fact remained that, there was a lot of work to do. He firmly believed his sons needed to feel the weight of responsibility as well as the reward of doing their part in the family's lifestyle.

He consistently expressed the staunch position…his two boys didn't need to enjoy the work but they did need to experience the life lessons the work would bring. He loved his sons very much and made sure they had plenty of free time to do the things young boys do. He also ensured they understood his clear expectations of how they were to conduct themselves as boys and eventually as men. It was a lesson Rory understood yet resisted just for the sake of resisting.

Swiping away the salty perspiration dripping into his eyes, he prepared to brush off his dad's offer to help. He was surprised when no offer appeared.

"Well, looks like your doing a fine job there, boy. I'll just be on my way. Make sure you get done in time to do the milking for the evening." He settled back into the cab of his truck and pulled away.

Rory strained against the last lug nut with a ferocity that had the vein on his left temple popping out. His hand jerked from the release just as the tire iron slid off. He scraped his knuckles against the metal. "Shit!" he swore and threw the tire iron on the ground.

He stood up to allow the blood back into his legs.

He paced in a circle and rubbed the sting out of his knuckles. Wanting to vent his frustration, he shouted down the road as his father's truck disappeared into a wake of flying dust, "Thanks for the help!"

He rolled his shoulders to work out the kink that was slowly forming between his shoulder blades. He took in the low rolling fields that stretched as far as he could see. The only foliage was the sage brush that peppered the foothills. The only trees on his parents' property were a group of large oaks clustered about fifty yards down the hill from his house. A little oasis had been created by a thin creek that filtered down from the mountains. His parents had loved the home instantly because of how it lay in the barren fields backed by brown foothills melding into the heavily forested mountains behind them.

Rory and his little brother Rodney had spent their entire childhood roaming the one hundred and twenty-five acre ranch as well as the land surrounding it. There they had played cowboys and Indians, and run Army battles. As they'd grown older, they had packed enormous lunches into their backpacks whenever their dad let them off the hook from their daily chores. They'd take their four -wheelers into the mountains for a day of hiking and exploration .

Rory took in a deep breath filled with the smell of sage and freshly cut wheat. He forced his anger to dissipate before turning toward his truck. He was just about done with the worst of it and was determined to finish the task quickly and without any additional mishaps.

He wanted to see Emily that night, so he needed to get the dang tire fixed in time to do the rest of his chores, take a shower then head into town.

*Father's and their son's,* Rory thought as he lay in the quiet barracks. The complexity of his emotions towards his father and the town he'd been raised in still perplexed him. The memory had been so vivid he was rubbing his knuckles as if the pain still lingered. Shaking his head, he willed his mind to shut down for the night and allow him at least a few exquisite hours of reprieve. But there was no end to the engrossing flashbacks. He could only surmise he was anxious to get home and clung to hints of the past to close the distance between himself and those he loved.

His growing friendship with J.T. was oddly similar to the endearing and sometimes brutal relationship he had with Rodney. Closing his eyes, he sifted through the memories involving his brother. He settled on one particular altercation only months before he'd moved into the house he and Emily shared. Rory had been shaving before his next outing with Emily. He'd been mentally going over how he would bring up the subject of their relationship when the Nine Inch Nails song Closer blasted on the other side of the wall. The interruption startled him. His hand jerked, and nicked his jaw. "Damn it!" he swore under his breath.

Rory and Rodney were only two and a half years apart. For the most part they got along quite well but once in a while Rodney would grow cantankerous. He would poke and prod making it his primary goal to irritate his brother until Rory finally broke and gave him a thorough beating. Rory resisted as long as possible but Rodney knew all of the right buttons to push.

Neither Sarah nor Justin could understand why Rodney would purposefully instigate these senseless interactions but figured it was his way of getting his older brother's attention. He usually laughed throughout the entire violent resolution, as if he was having the time of his life being pulverized by his sibling.

Rory liked the song but for some reason he hated the way the angry music grated on his nerves inside his home. It felt wrong to send the loud and disrespectful lyrics booming throughout the house. He often resorted to brute strength as he coerced Rodney to turn down the volume.

"Turn it down, Rodney." His voice bellowed in an attempt to override the blaring music. He had a lot on his mind and the last thing he wanted was to have to deal with Rodney's immature antics. When there was no response he slammed his razor down on the sink. Wiping the last of the shaving cream off his face, he'd flung open Rodney's bedroom door.

"I said turn it down!" His jaw was set in the way it did when his ultimatum was meant to be taken seriously, instantly, and without question.

Rodney was just as tall as Rory but at sixteen had yet to fill out. He was gangly and awkward. He was sitting on his bed with two drumsticks pretending to play to the music.

"What was that? I can't hear you." He grinned wickedly as he continued to beat out the rhythm.

Rory didn't feel like messing around with his punk brother any longer. He took three stiff strides across the room and turned the volume down so they could barely hear the music. He was stepping back out the doorway when the volume shot straight back up to maximum level. A shiver shot straight up his spine and his fists curled tight. Rory spun on his heel and stared his brother down.

Rodney held a remote above his head with a sly grin on his face.

"Remote. Sweet, huh?" he said. Then he yelled out the next lyrics along with Trent Reznor. "It's the only thing that works for me. Help me get away from myself."

"I'll help you get away from yourself, you half-wit!" Rory darted toward his brother intending to tackle him and confiscate the remote.

Rodney's face broke into an ear-splitting grin. Before he had time to think it through, he chucked the remote straight at his brother's head. Rory was stunned for a second as the impact hit him straight under his left eye. It had immediately begun to water from the assault. His cheek throbbed in perfect unison with the blood coursing through his veins.

## The Complexity of a Soldier

Rodney laughed in a frantic, hysterical way. He knew he'd crossed way over the line. "Oh, crap, dude!"

He jumped off of the bed and scurried toward the window. He hoped to somehow get around his brother and out the door in one piece. Rory was going to have a shiner for his date with Emily. His fist landed square between Rodney's shoulder blades as he was trying to escape. Rodney's arms flailed as he went face-down on the hardwood floor. Rory straddled him and put him in a sleeper hold showing no mercy. The fact that he was laughing the entire time only caused Rory's anger to flare even more. He dug an elbow into Rodney's back and was trying to figure out his next move when he felt a hard slap against the back of his head. He turned to see his mother glaring down at him her eyes flashing their wrath.

"Get off of your brother now! Don't you think that you two are getting too old for this nonsense?" She was mad, but only a little. She secretly loved these little brotherly spats. They were generally harmless and once Rory moved out, there would be a large hole left behind for all of them. Rodney would probably miss him the most. Rodney rolled onto his back with a huge sigh. His laughter slowly died out and his brother stood up.

"Sorry, Mom," Rodney said. "It was my fault. I was giving Rory sh....umm, a hard time." Profanity was something his mom definitely wouldn't tolerate.

Rory grabbed Rodney's hand and briskly pulled him to his feet. His anger was already dissipating and being replaced with a shared brotherly amusement. "Yeah, sorry, Mom."

Sarah looked at Rory's shiner. "You better get downstairs and put some ice on that right away."

Rory gave a crooked grin and winced as he gently touched the tender flesh. Then he flipped his brother the bird as their mother turned to chastise Rodney. That day, he realized how much he would miss his little brother when it came time to move out. Who else would pound on him and keep him in line? It had been the first time he'd felt a tug in his gut, an inkling of sadness as he thought of future plans away from home. Now he was far from everyone he'd grown up with. It was an epiphany to realize how much he longed for home.

The next morning as Rory hauled himself out of his bunk for morning P.T., he couldn't remember exactly which memory had led him into a sleepy oblivion. He spent the rest of that last week of basics feeling stronger and more optimistic. The comfort of those memories lingered, reminding him of everything he was soon going back to.

# CHAPTER FIVE

# Welcome Home

Rory stepped off the twin engine 414 Cessna charter flight from Boise, Idaho to Baker City's small airstrip. He never imagined he would be so happy to return to his hometown. *Guess absence does make the heart grow fonder,* he thought.

As his feet hit the tarmac, he spotted Emily. She rushed forward with one-year-old Callie bouncing in her arms. Rory dropped his gear and enveloped both his girls in a bear hug. He pulled them tightly to his chest, relishing the way their soft, warm bodies felt against his own.

His heart plummeted to his stomach when Callie's bottom lip began to tremble. Fat alligator tears welled up in her hazel eyes as she tried to pull away. Rory stepped back.

"She doesn't remember me," he said as his precious angel clung to her mommy.

Emily stroked Callie's hair, crooning in her best mommy voice, before responding, "She'll be okay, Just give it a little while. She's been doing this to everyone lately. The pediatrician says it's normal at this age to have stranger anxiety."

"Stranger anxiety." The bitter truth of the term hit him like a brick wall. He was a stranger to his little girl because he had been gone for so much of her short little life. She'd forgotten who he was to her.

Emily instantly reeled him back in by shifting the focus. "This must be John Thomas." She reached out to shake his hand. Rory recovered quickly and made proper introductions.

On the drive home, Emily said, "Your parents are planning a welcome home dinner tonight. Rodney has been beside himself waiting for your return."

Rory absentmindedly nodded, registering only about half of everything Emily said. All he could do was stare at her, marveling at how she seemed more beautiful to him than ever. Then he looked back at his daughter in her car seat. He was just as awe struck. Five months had been too long.

In some ways it felt like he had been gone for an unforgivable expanse of time. He felt a chasm between them and feared that he might not be able to reach over the gap. Then he would look into his wife's eyes and the rest of the world would disappear. Staring into each other, they communicated in a way only they could understand. The gap would close and seal away his trepidation.

By one in the afternoon, the jet lag and radical change in time zones had both men rummy and lethargic. Rory rubbed his bloodshot eyes. Succumbing to huge yawns, he sat on the couch and shared the details of their infamous prank on the drill sergeant. He enjoyed the way Emily giggled with amazed delight.

"I cannot believe you were able to wrangle Rory into something like that," she said to J.T. "I'm amazed anyone could convince him to participate in something that wasn't his idea or that he was against. You guys could have been permanently removed from the program."

"Yeah, well, he can act like he was an innocent bystander if he wants," J.T. said, "but he was into it just as much as the rest of us were."

Rory snickered. His eyes closed and his head tipped back against the couch as he gave in to the fatigue.

Emily gave him a pitiful look. "Come on, Soldier, I'm putting you and Callie down for a nap. You're gonna need your rest if we're going to make it out to your parent's place this evening."

She picked up Callie and turned toward Rory with her free arm outstretched.

"You okay down here, dude?" he asked J.T.

J.T. pulled off his boots. "Just so long as you don't mind if I make myself comfortable on your couch."

"Go for it. Make yourself at home. Feel free to dig around the kitchen if you get hungry."

He felt bad about leaving his friend to fend for himself but his brain had shut down. Emily's suggestion sounded too good to pass up and was probably for the best.

He dragged his long frame off of the deliciously decadent couch and followed Emily and Callie up the stairs. He forked off toward their room as Emily steered toward Callie's. Stepping into his bedroom, Emily's familiar scent teased his nostrils. He closed his eyes and relished how the comfort of being home settled his soul.

*Now I'm starting to sound like J.T.,* he thought. Either that or he was deliriously tired. With that last coherent thought, he shuffled toward the bed and lay down without pulling back the blankets.

He settled into the sanctity of his home, his room, his bed. With his right arm flung over his eyes to block out the sun filtering through the window, he fell into a deep, tranquil sleep.

~~~~~~~~~~~~

As Sarah sat next to her husband in their spacious dining room, she scanned the cherry wood table that had been passed down from her mother. Her heart swelled with pride as she looked upon her eldest son and his lovely family.

Although Rory had always seemed reserved and had kept most girls at arms length except for a few casual dates, she had always known he would one day find that perfect fit and would never let go. Now she wondered if he had been holding out the whole time, somehow subconsciously waiting for Emily to come into his life and unwilling to settle for less in the interim.

Emily couldn't have been a better daughter-in-law. It didn't matter that she came from a family of money. She maintained a humble and open attitude toward life, and had a flair for running her home and raising Callie that closely resembled Sarah's. That made her even more endearing.

The entire five months Rory had been away, Emily drove out to the ranch at least once a week so they could see Callie. She was always sure to dig right into the never-ending list of chores. Justin warmed to Emily quickly. He was so wrapped around his granddaughter's little finger he often came in from the fields early just to spend extra time with them.

Rodney had taken a little longer to relax around Emily. He tended to be loud and obnoxious around his friends and family but terribly shy whenever girls were added to the mix. Emily had been relentless with prodding him to open up. He'd eventually warmed up to her joking and teasing as if she were the sister he'd never had.

Sarah glanced at her son's new friend and smiled knowingly.

# The Complexity of a Soldier

She'd been smitten with J.T.'s charm the moment she'd met him. He enchanted her, greeting her with a tight hug and instantly addressing her as mom, which she loved. He was a perfect addition to their cozy little family.

She wasn't surprised at how well he blended into their home. By the end of the night Rodney had shown him his entire C.D. collection, triggering a heated argument over their favorite rock bands. Rodney convinced J.T. to spend the night at the ranch so they could head out early in the morning for a bit of fishing. J.T. readily agreed, happy to let Emily and Rory have their home to themselves for their first night back.

*That's a good boy,* she thought. Just like her son was a good boy.

~~~~~~~~~~~~~~

Emily was happy to spend time at Rory's parents' house for dinner but as the night progressed, she noticed the subtle transformation he had undergone. He still looked like her Rory but he was somehow more mature. His physique had filled out dramatically. His intimidating good looks had her body responding. It had been too long.

When they got home, it was already ten o'clock and little Callie was sound asleep. She let Rory scoop her up and carry her into the house. She watched as he nuzzled her soft little cheeks, inhaling the sweet baby scent that no one could resist, before he gently settled her in her crib.

Emily didn't waste any time. The minute Rory walked into their bedroom she all but jumped him. She leaped into his arms, wrapping her legs around his waist, and showered him with kisses.

God, she'd missed this! She felt him respond with equal and

unabated enthusiasm. He held her firmly to him, kissing her neck and her earlobes until he reached her mouth. He took in her kisses as if he was dying of thirst and she was the only water left on earth.

They fell to the bed without missing a beat. Ravaging every inch of each other, they branded their taste into memory forever. Their lovemaking was almost frantic as Rory pulled her to him, refusing to let her get more than a few inches away.

Emily was lost in her own passion. When he claimed her, she bit down on his shoulder. She wanted to hurt him for making her love him so much. For going away and leaving her waiting, wanting.

Rory pulled her mouth to his, covering her full lips with a deep kiss. He took her breath just before she cried out for him. There would be no surrender for either. They were determined to go over the edge at the same time. When the fall came it was simultaneous, it was absolute, it was rapture.

~~~~~~~~~~~~

Later that night as they lay in the quiet blanket of darkness, Emily asked, "So what's next? What happens after your graduation ceremony?"

Rory had drifted off in a sleepy haze. He forced his mind back to consciousness. "Well...you and Callie will come back with me for graduation. Then we will come home for another week before our official transfer papers are processed."

Emily leaned on her elbow. "Do you have any idea where they might send us? It just seems weird that they would keep us in the dark up until the last minute and we're just supposed to up and move at the drop of a hat like that. It's not very conducive to family life."

## The Complexity of a Soldier

Rory sighed while rubbing her soft back. "It's just how it is, Em. I think we'll get transferred to either Texas or Washington. I'm hoping for Washington. Even though the weather is terrible, we'll still be closer to our family."

Emily heard the fatigue in his voice and lay off of the questions for the rest of the night. She curved herself into the crook of his arms, enjoying the feel of him. As long as they were together, it didn't matter where they lived.

# CHAPTER SIX

# Memory Lane

A couple days later, Rory drove Emily, Callie, J.T. and Rodney up the mountain behind his parent's house to the lake. Rory had been itching to get up to his favorite spot since he stepped off the plane. Although it was "their place," Emily convinced Rory to invite the others. It wouldn't feel right to leave them behind.

At first he was reluctant but after a few moments he decided he would like to share it with his best friend.

Rodney had already been there plenty of times. The brothers had discovered it together and had spent many hot summer days throughout their childhood swimming in the cold waters. And he'd always known he would one day share it with his children, so the only one left was John Thomas. He would be able to appreciate the sanctity of the spot just as Rory did.

As he drove the Chevy, his wife sat in comfortable silence directly to his right and little Callie drifted off in her car seat. J.T. rode in the truck behind them with Rodney. Their trip reminded him of the first time he'd brought Emily up to the lake.

After their day at the job fair, their relationship progressed faster than either one of them could have predicted. It soon became apparent their interaction was taking on a life of its own. It didn't occur to them to resist it. They just followed their instincts and enjoyed the ride.

Their first date to the movies had been simple and innocuous. Emily chose the comedy Austin Powers and they had both laughed at the slap-stick humor and chomped on heavily buttered popcorn while sipping sodas.

Two hours later, they stepped out of the dark theater and into the lamp-lit streets. Rory took Emily's hand and led her around the corner so they could stroll through town. They followed Auburn to Main Street, winding up in the Rainbow Records store. They rifled through the vast collection of music comparing interests. They both admitted they were unabashed fans of music more common in their parents' genre such as Clearance Clearwater Revival, Led Zepplin and The Beatles.

A week later, they started out at the old-fashioned burger joint off Tenth Street and wound up in the park sitting on swings just as twilight reached its prime. Rory knew how ridiculous his long frame looked in the child-sized swings but Emily was struggling to keep a straight face so he started clowning around in an effort to crack her up.

Rory enjoyed nothing more than making her laugh. He loved watching her whole face light up as she lost herself in the moment. Her eyes crinkled at the edges as she tipped her head back. It caused something in his gut to clench with anticipation. *God, she's beautiful*, he would think every time he had the pleasure of seeing her lost in laughter. He was constantly intrigued by his reaction to her.

# The Complexity of a Soldier

Later, Rory scored big points when he offered to treat them both to the local ice cream parlor. Emily's one true weakness was chocolate ice cream. The conversation stayed on light small talk, covering how their graduation ceremony had gone the week before and stories about family members who had traveled a good distance to help them celebrate.

"That's why I can't stay out too late tonight," Emily explained. "My grandma and grandpa stayed an extra week to visit but they're heading out tomorrow morning. My mom and dad are hosting a huge breakfast real early before they leave. My mom wants me home so I can be up and at 'em early to help her set up. She's kind of anal retentive about stuff like that."Rory licked his Rocky Road ice cream cone and chuckled. "Sounds like our moms might have something in common after all." He leaned in and touched his napkin to the corner of her mouth to dab off a spot of ice cream. "Let's make a day trip next time, okay?"

Emily self-consciously licked the spot he had just wiped. "Okay. What did you have in mind?" she asked in a breathy whisper.

"I was thinking we could go for a ride in the mountains. I can show you my favorite spot. It's hard to get to so we have to ride the four-wheeler but it's definitely worth it." He wasn't sure how a city girl would handle tromping through the forest but he figured if she just gave it a chance she would be glad that she had.

"That sounds great. I will pack our lunch."

Rory was pleased she seemed so enthusiastic. They agreed he would pick her up the following Saturday around eleven after he had finished his morning chores. That night as he dropped her off in front of her parents' house, she surprised him once again. Shifting the truck into park, he had barely turned toward her when she took his face into her small, slender hands and kissed him full on the lips.

# The Complexity of a Soldier

It was the last thing he had expected so it took him a second to catch up with her. Once his brain engaged and he felt her about to pull back, he replicated her move. He cupped her face with his large, calloused hands. Emily responded by opening her lips to allow his tongue to sweep her mouth and graze her teeth. She kissed him back just as thoroughly, gently nibbling his bottom lip before she pulled away.

She slid across the bench seat with an innocent smile. "I'll see you next Saturday, Rory. Good night." Then she swung open the heavy door, hopped out with a wave, and rushed up her sidewalk and into the house before he could do anything other than wave back.

Rory sat dumbfounded. He was bewildered that she had been able to side-swipe him like that. She kept surprising him and although a part of him liked it, he wasn't sure what to expect from her between one moment and the next. The kiss had floored him. She'd been so unattainable to the other guys in school he'd been sure he would get the same rejection. Before he had made his first move, she'd swooped in and knocked him off balance with a move of her own.

The following Saturday, Rory pulled in front of Emily's house a half hour late. At the last minute, his dad had decided he needed help fixing a section of fence on pasture three. Reluctantly he'd driven out to help for an hour. They ended up bickering as his father grilled him about whether or not he had started applying to police academies yet.

Justin focused on the tactile job. After lifting the broken section of fence off the ground, he examined the extent of rot to determine if he could simply hammer it back into place or if he needed to completely replace the board. "So?" he asked. "What's the scoop, son? Where's it going to be?"

# The Complexity of a Soldier

Rory was rifling through his dad's toolbox for nails. "I don't know yet, Dad," he answered in a curt, annoyed tone. He hoped his dad would get the hint and leave the topic alone. "I've been kind of busy lately doing stuff like this, if you haven't noticed."

Justin gritted his teeth to keep from responding to Rory's poor attitude and thick sarcasm. He'd filled out only one application and had yet to send it in. He wasn't sure why he was dragging his heels. He wasn't usually the type to put anything off but something kept nagging at him to wait until after summer was over. The academy in Colorado had a session starting in the fall then another one starting the next spring.

He felt like he owed it to his mom to give her a little more time before he completely uprooted and moved away. At least that's what he kept telling himself. He knew his dad assumed he'd been all talk the last few years and would end up staying on the ranch after all. He really didn't feel like getting into a knock down, drag out with him about it, so he clenched his jaw, hammered in the last nail, and excused himself for the day.

Back at the house, he quickly loaded the quad into the back of his truck before rushing inside to wash off the dirt and grime. As he pulled up in front of Emily's house in her immaculately groomed neighborhood, he spotted her silhouette pacing back and forth across through front window. Once again, he cursed himself for being late.

He hopped out and rounded the pickup figuring he would officially meet Emily's parents. But she was already rushing toward him down the sidewalk. Grabbing the cooler, he placed it directly behind the cab next to his quad. As she hopped in, he noticed she was dressed appropriately in hiking boots, jeans, a periwinkle blue v-neck t-shirt, and a sweatshirt tied around her waist for the cooler mountain air.

# The Complexity of a Soldier

As they began the ascent up the mountain, he was elated. When the road got too narrow and dangerous he parked off to the side and unloaded his four-wheeler. After he strapped the cooler onto the back, he straddled the seat and waited for Emily to climb on behind him. She pulled her sweatshirt over her long straight hair and wrapped her arms tightly around his thick, strong torso.

*This wasn't a good idea,* he thought as he felt her pressing against him. *This was an incredible idea!*

Because the terrain was rough, Rory started out slow. About half a mile out, he tested Emily's courage when he accelerated over a fairly flat stretch. She squealed with delight rather than fear. He smiled, realizing he had a little daredevil on the back of his quad. He took the longer way to their destination, giving her a more exciting ride with hills and turns to give her heart a little jolt.

Finally, he reached the spot where he preferred to park. He let Emily crawl off the back before he slid off and snagged the cooler. He enjoyed watching her take in their surroundings. He'd always admired the seclusion and comfort of the forest, and how incredibly beautiful and peaceful it was out there with not another human being for miles. He was sure she would appreciate it just as much.

"It's wonderful here," She said.

Rory held out his hand with a sideways grin. "This is nothing. Come on."

Emily grasped his hand and let him lead her down a thin path covered in pine needles. The path grew fairly steep as they followed it down into a ravine. Rory paused. Emily had been carefully watching her feet and was unaware that they had stepped into a clearing. She looked up to see why they had stopped.

Rory watched her face as she took in the most beautiful place either of them had ever seen. She put her hand to her mouth as she stood in awe. They had stepped out onto a ledge just above a pristine, crystal-clear lake in the bowl of the canyon. The lake was surrounded by rocky, jagged mountains. Their majestic beauty was reflected in the motionless waters. It was as if they had discovered one of the only places yet to be touched by the hand of man. It was God's finest creation, and it was theirs for the afternoon.

"Do you like it?" he asked. He had never brought a girl to his secret retreat before. Now he was thrilled to share it with her for reasons he wasn't yet sure about.

Emily jumped into his arms and hugged him. "Like it? I love it! It's the most beautiful place I've ever been." Then she stepped back and looked up at him. "Thank you so much, for sharing it with me."

Rory had guessed she would respond that way but he had underestimated his response to her.

*She is mine.* The thought leapt into his mind before he could question it. It wasn't like him to feel so possessive but he wanted to make her his, whatever that meant, and he had no intention of letting her go. Leaning down, he gave her a soft kiss with a brush of his lips. Then he guided her down to the lake. On flatter ground, they set up their picnic next to the mossy shore.

Rory was impressed with the spread Emily had prepared. She'd made fried chicken and potato salad as well as deliciously sweetened iced tea. She had brought napkins, small plates and forks as well. It was all planned and organized in the same fashion he'd seen his mother do so often before.

Rory drifted back to the present as the road began to grow rough. They were near the spot where they would park and transfer to the quads. He felt as if he were the king of his universe and was so glad to be home. He wanted her to share his reverence for the fortuitous events that had been the makings of their relationship. With a cocky grin, he gave her a sideways glance.

"Remember when I brought you up here, Em?"

## The Complexity of a Soldier

She peered up at him lovingly. "Which time? I remember them all. But I do have to say there is one particular instance that stands out more than the others."

Rory flashed another glance her direction, guessing which memory she meant. He knew she would be blushing. He searched his mind to recall the sequence of events. "I remember now. I didn't have anything like that in mind. I was just planning to ask you to be my girlfriend."

Emily looked shocked then burst out in delirious laughter. When Callie stirred, she cupped her hand to her mouth. "What do you mean?"

Rory shifted gears. "Remember? It was the week after I met your parents. Man, that was stressful! I'd always avoided parents until then because I could never stand the tension. You know, the kind where you know the father is imagining all of the ways he can rip you apart if you hurt his daughter?"

Emily gave a hearty laugh. "No, I don't know but I can imagine!"

~~~~~~~~~~~~

Rory's trip down memory lane triggered Emily's memories. As she stared out the window of the truck, she looked past the familiar scenery to the images flashing through her mind. The evening she had introduced him to her parents was one of her favorite memories. It had been the beginning of a series of events that had led to their engagement.

When Rory stood up to shake her father's hand, Emily practically shoved him out the door. As soon as they hit the road, they drove just east of town to join a group of their schoolmates at the river. A bonfire was blazing and a wood barrel had been filled with fruit, rum and vodka. Emily had only been to one other party like that since she had moved there and even then had only hung out for an hour before heading home.

This time she was proud to be on Rory's arm. She even decided to allow herself to drink some of the fruit punch. She'd been surprised that she actually liked the tangy, fruity taste. She scanned the group huddled around the fire as she sipped from a red plastic cup and let out an obnoxious squeal when she spotted her best friend Abby. Hearing a sound like a dying chipmunk, Abby turned to see her friend scurrying around the large fire.

"Oh, my God! What are you doing here, Miss Priss?" she teased lovingly. She always ribbed Emily for being such an upstanding citizen and the quintessential good girl.

Emily left Rory talking with the twins, Jaron and Jason, on the other side of the fire. She glanced his way when Abby began her inquiry.

"You're here with Rory? The last time we talked, you told me about your first date but then I went on vacation with my parents. I just got back into town last night. I had no idea you two would be here together. That's so cool." She leaned in further. "So what's the deal? Are you two like official or what?" she murmured as if she were asking for top-secret information.

Emily blushed and shrugged. "I don't think you could really call us a couple or anything yet but we have been hanging out a lot lately." She paused, nervous about her next question. "Do you think he might ask me? I mean, like officially?"

"I don't know. To tell you the truth Em, I have never seen Rory date anyone for very long. He just kind of keeps to himself a lot of the time."

Emily's hopeful expression faltered.

"But I can say, it is blatantly obvious that he likes you," Abby said. "Lots of girls in this town would sell there soul to the devil to have Rory Nichols look at them the way he's looking at you right now."

Emily's eyebrows rose and she looked across the fire at Rory. Her gaze instantly locked with his. A shiver ran up her spine as he narrowed his eyes. His jaw clenched as he became aware of the heat not from the fire but between the two of them. It sizzled across the gap.

~~~~~~~~~~

That night had only further convinced Rory he was ready to take the next step. He decided Emily would find it romantic if he took her up to what he considered their spot to discuss their relationship. It was a hot July day and he knew a dip in the icy waters of the lake would be the perfect way to cool off.

He had told her to wear her swimsuit underneath her clothes, and to put her hiking boots on. When she skipped out of her house, Rory took in the sight of her. She wore denim shorts and a white spaghetti-strap tank over her yellow bikini. Her shiny blonde hair was pulled into a long ponytail. Emily jumped into the pickup and rubbed her hands over the new upholstery he had just finished.

"Wow, this looks great!" she said. "Did you do it yourself?"

Rory looked from her face to the seat and back to her face again. "Yep. It was a pain but I like it. You look great, too!"

They made their way up the mountain with the quad and descended back down into the ravine on foot. By the time they plopped their things down on the calm shore, they were both sweaty and overheated. They immediately took a quick dip, each of them only able to stay in for a few minutes. Although the temperature was a good seventy-eight up on the mountain, the lake was fed from snow melting off the peaks above.

Emily's teeth chattered as she toweled off. They both sat in the sun, letting the rays seep into their flesh. The heat radiated into their shivering bodies. They ate lunch then took a walk around the small lake. Little critters made sounds as they went about their day oblivious to the intruders. Birds called to each other, squirrels and chipmunks chattered and the knock, knock, knock of a woodpecker searching for food sounded in the distance.

When they had made a full circle, Rory decided to ask Emily about her college plans. He'd realized that their relationship would be affected by his plans to go to Colorado and any plans she had for school. He was hoping they would be able to work something out so they could continue with what they had going.

"Have you decided on a college yet?" he asked.

Emily grabbed a brush out of the small satchel she had slung over her shoulder. "Yeah, I am already set to join Eastern State. I was accepted to one in San Louis Obispo and one in Arizona but I decided it would be a lot easier to live with my parents and drive the forty-five minutes over the pass to school every day. If I get sick of it, I can just settle with dorm life and move over there."

Rory puzzled over this, trying to decide if it was a good thing that she was staying in town or not. Before he could comment, she broke into his thoughts.

"You know, my dad was just telling me about a police academy in Boise, Idaho," she said.

Rory raised his eyebrows, trying to recall if he had come across something in Boise during his research. "Really?"

Emily continued brushing the tangles out of her hair. "Yeah. I checked it out online. It is one of the smaller ones but they have high reviews for the graduation rate from the criminal justice program."

## The Complexity of a Soldier

Rory's interest was piqued. He wished he was in front of a computer at that very moment so he could check it out himself. "I'll have to look into it. I'm glad I haven't sent off my application to the one in Colorado yet. This might be better for my circumstances and it would certainly please my mom to have me that much closer."

Emily stuffed her brush into her bag. "Yeah, it's only like a two hour drive from Baker to Boise, so I figured that you could come home every weekend." She hesitated before adding, "If you wanted to."

Rory suddenly saw the moment for exactly what it was. This was the time they would look back on and know they had already committed their hearts and souls to each other. He had started the day planning to acquire a steady girlfriend but at that moment he was suddenly humbled. There would be no one else ever again for either of them.

Rather than fighting it, he decided to succumb. It was so much bigger than him. He should just go with it. Before he could analyze the ridiculousness of the impulse, he dropped down on one knee and bent his head. "I can't believe that I'm doing this," he whispered.

Then he grabbed Emily's hand and looked up into her face. "Emily," he said, "I know we haven't known each other for very long but there is something inside of me I can't begin to define, something that knows you're the one for me. I will do my best to offer you a life full of love and happiness if you would agree to marry me."

His heart was racing and his mouth had gone dry. Was he going insane? It was the most daring and romantic thing he had ever said to anyone. He was shocked that he had delivered it so well.

Emily's eyes welled up. Tears threatened to spill over as she tried to compose herself. Rory's logic kept telling him to slow down, that they were too young. But his heart knew he could wait a thousand lifetimes and never change the way he felt about her. He could only hope and pray that she felt the same way.

"Yes! Yes! Yes!" she squealed.

Rory's heart filled. He wasn't insane. He had never felt more grounded in his life. With a beaming smile on his handsome face, he stood and lifted her off her feet hugging her tightly. He felt as if he had just won the world.

Now, sitting side by side with a new addition snuggled into the car seat, they were heading back to a spot that held so many wonderful memories. Rory took his right hand off the gearshift and pulled his sweet Emily in for a quick kiss.

He turned back to the task of driving as they neared their destination. It was the very end of August and temperatures were beginning to get cooler after the sun went down. But the days were still hot and sticky as the eastern side of the state enjoyed the typical Indian summer that would last through September.

Rodney put Callie in a child carrier strapped tight to his back. He took the quad slowly to avoid any accidents. Rory and Emily followed close behind. Although they trusted him with his niece, they still kept a close eye on his driving. J.T. straddled Justin's four -wheeler and followed at a close third.

Once they parked the quads, Emily followed Rodney down the steep trail toward the lake. Rory and J.T. gathered the two coolers, a couple of blankets and were only minutes behind.

Rory stepped onto the ledge overlooking the lake just as he had two years before with Emily. When J.T. scanned the breathtaking scenery, his jaw slackened. He recited the first stanza of a Robert Bridges poem. "I love all beauteous things, I seek and adore them; God hath no better praise, and men in his hasty day is honored for them," he said in a gentle, heartfelt tone.

A deep, grumbling laugh bubbled out of Rory. "Jesus, J.T., would you like a tampon to go with that little emotional outburst?" He was completely unsurprised by his friend's reaction but had to give him a hard time nonetheless.

J.T. ignored the jibe and continued gawking at the terrain while taking deep, cleansing breaths of the mountain air.

While they enjoyed their picnic, Callie slipped into Rory's lap to show him a pretty rock she had found. Rory was ecstatic enough to jump over the moon but remained calm. As long as no one made a scene, he hoped she would stay comfortable where she was.

After awhile he plopped her on his shoulders and tromped around to point out birds, squirrels, and any other wildlife that might delight her. He felt J.T. watching him with his wife and child. He wondered if his friend ever intended to settle down and have a family of his own. He would have to ask.

Emily must have also noticed John Thomas' longing expression. As they gathered their picnic supplies for the return hike, she asked, "How old are you J.T?"

J.T. furrowed his brow. "Twenty-two. Why? How old are you two?"

"I turned twenty-one two weeks before Callie's first birthday in late July, and Rory's twenty-first birthday happened while he was away at basics in the beginning of May." Emily shifted her gaze toward Rory. "I was thinking it would be fun if mom would babysit tonight. We could take your friend out for a few drinks so he could get a taste of the night life in Baker City." Rory noticed her suppressing a sly smile. *What is she up to?* he wondered. He gave her a sideways glance.

"Not much going on in a town this size, Emily. I doubt J.T. wants to go kick up his heels in some po-dunk dive."

## The Complexity of a Soldier

J.T. jumped in. "I'm sure it's just like the ones I'm used to back in Montana. I haven't had a night out on the town since that one night in basics. Come on, Rory, it sounds fun." Then he looked at Rodney. "You down?"

Rory said, "Uh, Rodney's still under-age. He's only nineteen."

Rodney jumped up. "That's okay. We'll just go to the Lodge Pole tavern. I've been in there plenty of times, they never card anybody." As his older brother stared him down, Rodney smiled and nodded. "I'm down."

# CHAPTER SEVEN

# Match-Maker

Later that night, Emily shooed the guys out the door. She claimed she would run Callie over to her mom's then meet them at the Lodge Pole Tavern. She'd already called Abby to demand that she be ready to go out for a few drinks. She of course hadn't filled her in on the details. She didn't want to project anything or create an expectation, she just wanted to provide an opportunity and see if there would be a natural spark.

She was hoping so. She could tell J.T. was a great guy. The fact that Rory trusted him spoke volumes. Abby's eclectic taste for the bad boys would draw her to J.T.'s rugged good looks before she had any idea about his soft interior.

Abby seemed to be a magnet for every bad boy within a sixty mile radius. She was probably one of the sweetest girls Emily had ever known. They had become friends shortly after Emily moved into town when she had joined the cheerleading squad.

Abby was gifted with an athletic build and gorgeous, dark

auburn hair. Emily had always considered those traits physical reflections of Abby's spunky, vivacious personality. She tended to be the life of the crowd and got a little ahead of herself after a few too many drinks. She loved a good time and the guys flocked to her whenever she stepped into the room. Emily was probably one of the few people who knew that Abby really wanted to settle down with a stable guy and have a family of her own. Then they could call each other and swap mommy stories.

Unfortunately, Abby was the worst judge of character and fell head over heels with the town pothead, the traveling musician with a string of girls throughout the Northwest, and the guy trying to land himself in prison for running a chop shop out of his garage. Eventually Abby would figure out that her current beau was a loser. She would call Emily in tears, berating herself for yet another 'pick of the year.'

Between J.T.'s tough-guy looks, his Celtic tattoo and his military background, Abby would be attracted to him before she figured out he was actually a very nice guy with romantic inclinations and a poetic nature. Bubbling with excitement, she listened while Abby fervently relayed how brutal her paralegal finals had been the week before.

"I am so proud of you, Abby, and how hard you've been working over the past few years, I know that it hasn't been easy doing it all on your own," Emily said. "I officially proclaim this a night of celebration. Drinks are on me!"

"I like the sound of that! But I'm staying away from men tonight. I don't need their drama."

Emily pursed her lips. She'd heard her friend proclaim such things before.

~~~~~~~~~~

# The Complexity of a Soldier

Emily and Abby sauntered through the front door. The guys were toward the back of the packed bar at a table next to one of the pool tables. A local band played at an unnecessarily loud volume as they wound through the hazy smoke of the crowded dance floor.

Rory and J.T. were concentrating on their pool match. Rodney lounged at the table waiting to play the winner. She and Rory exchanged glances. She could tell by his inquisitive expression that he had her figured out. Her match-making efforts had been discovered. She answered his curious smirk with an innocent smile and a bat of her lashes.

J.T. was bent over, gauging his next shot when he glanced up. His tongue nearly dropped out of his mouth. It was the exact reaction Emily had been counting on. Her sultry best friend was perfect eye candy with dark red hair, wearing skin tight jeans, a sexy tank top that accented her trim physique, and a saucy smile.

She openly sized him up in return. Abby's gaze was direct and unabashed. She took in the stocky, muscular build and the muscles that rippled as he gripped the pool cue. She gave Emily a sideways glance and murmured, "Slap me sideways."

J.T. finished the match, sinking the eight ball with authority. Although he was supposed to play Rodney next, he forfeited for the opportunity to drink his beer and chat with the girls. His motives were obvious.

"Hey, Abbs, good to see you," Rory chimed.

"Hey, Rory, glad you're back. Emily was a pain in the butt while you were gone," she teased.

J.T. approached in a not so subtle manner and waited to be introduced.

"Abby," Rory said, "I want you to meet someone I met in training. This is J.T. J.T., this is Abby. We all went to school together."

# The Complexity of a Soldier

"Nice to meet you, Abby. I'm glad you could join us." J.T.'s tone was smooth and gentlemanly.

Abby offered her thin, delicate hand. "Likewise."

Emily had predicted the match accurately. Within minutes, J.T had Abby cracking up as he described the day he'd acquired his tattoo. Apparently he had been in Vegas celebrating his twenty first birthday with a few of his friends from back home.

"I woke up face-down on my bed at the hotel room with a splitting headache. I was still wearing the clothes I'd had on the previous evening only there was now a white tutu around my waist. Don't ask, 'cause I have no idea. Anyway, another addition to my person was this tattoo." He pointed to his left bicep.

"Only it wasn't this particular tattoo yet. At that point, it simply read eat shit. Between the tutu and the permanent graffiti of profanity, I about died laughing. My head felt as if it would explode, though, so humor was not my friend. I tried to recall the night before but only snatched glimpses. Too much Seagrams and Seven. Honestly, I was just relieved that I didn't wake up to a wedding ring on my finger and a stranger in my bed.

"I thought about keeping the tattoo but it really wasn't my style. My mom would have freaked out if she saw vulgar profanity engraved onto her son. So I decided to have something else put over it. I wanted something Celtic because of our families' genealogy and after much deliberation settled on the symbol of the dragon because it means luck and power. Plus it looks pretty damn cool."

"The dragon's definitely cool but the story is what makes it legendary," Abby giggled.

Emily could tell the alcohol was working its liquid courage magic when Abby dragged J.T. out on the dance floor. Despite his claims that he couldn't dance, he had Abby all over the floor, breaking out tricky swing-dance moves and man-handling her with grace. By the look on her face, Abby apparently approved of his skills.

Emily watched with a smug little grin spread over her face. *Bingo!* She thought. It was a done deal.

Rory caressed the back of her neck and leaned in with a whisper, "You naughty little girl. Setting up our friends like that." She knew he was just as delighted to see the two of them hitting it off so well.

When the band took a fifteen-minute break, the lead singer announced that the mike was open. J.T. escorted Abby to her seat and, without saying a word, headed toward the stage. He looked as if he could take on the world.

"Oh my god," Abby said. "What is he going to do?"

Rory just shook his head and shrugged, "I have no idea but I can't wait to find out." J.T. had a few words with the band before they headed backstage and borrowed the lead guitarist's acoustic Fender. He proceeded to play two Eric Clapton songs back to back. His voice was thick and gravelly, an intoxicating caress that filled the bar with the fun Rock and Roll Heart cover. The crowd responded with enthusiasm, dancing and singing along to the upbeat tune. He segued into the slower, sexier melody Wonderful Tonight, without missing a beat. Couples swayed to the rich rhythm of his deep baritone. Rory, Emily and Rodney sat in awe of the surprise performance. Abby leaned over and said to Emily, "Yummy."

When J.T. finished, he gently placed the guitar in the hands of its' rightful owner before hopping off the stage. The entire bar whooped and hollered. Rory stood up and slapped him on the back.

"You never cease to amaze me, man. That was totally awesome. I had no idea you could play guitar and sing like that."

## The Complexity of a Soldier

J.T. was dangerously close to blushing. He brushed off the compliment with a grunt. Emily couldn't contain her delight.

When last call rolled around, Emily and Rory decided to call it quits and head home. "That's it for the two of us," Rory said. "We better call it a night."

"What? It's early yet," J.T. complained.

Abby piped in. "I had a great time tonight. Thanks for inviting me."

"Wait, where are you going?" Emily asked. "You're in no shape to drive."

"I'm doing what you guys are doing. Walking. It's only six blocks."

Emily shook her head. Her thoughts were cloudy with exhaustion and heavy drink. "No way. You can't walk through town by yourself at this time of night."

All three men agreed in unison.

"Oh, come on, you guys. It's Baker City, for crap's sake. Most people are asleep. Besides, the police are patrolling. I could use the cold night air to sober me up a little."

Rory said, "Listen, you can stay with us at our place. We've got room."

His tone suggested he was not to be argued with but Abby wasn't so easily bullied. She ignored his demand and changed tactics. Batting her lashes, she asked, "Maybe John Thomas could walk me home?"

Stupid was one thing J.T. was not. He knew an invitation when he heard one. "I will escort the lady home as she wishes," he said bowing at the waist as a gentleman would.

Emily and Rory were satisfied with the outcome and turned toward Rodney. "Well, you are staying with us, little brother."

He readily agreed. The last thing he wanted was a ticket for driving under the influence. Their mother would tan his hide no matter how old he was.

~~~~~~~~~~

Rory was amused at how inseparable Abby and J.T. were for the remainder of his stay. Abby had seriously considered purchasing a last-minute ticket to Missouri to watch the graduation ceremony. Unfortunately, she couldn't afford to miss work or the price of a plane ticket so she settled for J.T.'s promise to come back for another week while they awaited their transfer orders.

Rory wasn't looking forward to the long travel day with little Callie but he was glad that this time his girls were with him. They stayed in Missouri for only the few days needed to attend the graduation ceremony. They flew out late in the afternoon on the third day.

The graduation ceremony really didn't mean anything to Rory. He looked at it as yet another step in the right direction. His choice to join the military had proven useful but it had also challenged his relationships. Although his contract was only for four years, he imagined there would probably be more unexpected trials ahead.

He mulled this over on the flight home. His nerves frayed as Callie fussed and whined from discomfort and exhaustion. Her ears had bothered her for the majority of the flight. By the time they landed in Baker City in the middle of the night, everyone was spent, grumpy, and relieved to be home on solid ground.

~~~~~~~~~~

That first night, Abby was pleased when J.T. immediately took up where they had left off the week before. He was just as fatigued as Rory and Emily had been but they stayed up until the wee hours of the morning. They were determined to spend every possible moment with each other riding the rush of a new and promising relationship.

That night at the bar, Abby had suspected her friend was playing matchmaker. But since she; loved Emily dearly and found J.T. dangerously attractive in a rangy kind of way, she had decided to play the game to find out where it led.

She'd see what a hot military guy had to offer a small town girl like her. She was throwing caution to the wind and was sure to pay the price. Hopefully it would be worth the ride. So far, it already had been.

They enjoyed each other's company. They laughed until it hurt. And even though it was still early, she was elated that he truly seemed to be a good, honest guy. Still, she tempered her hopes so she wouldn't be disappointed yet again.

Later that week, Emily met Abby for lunch while J.T. and Rory took Callie to visit his parents at the ranch. Their blue heeler, Sydney, had given birth to a new litter of puppies six days earlier and Callie was anxious to see them. Emily enquired about how things were going between her and John Thomas.

"I don't know." Abby was unable to suppress a shy smile. Her heart fluttered as she wondered the same thing. "It's all so crazy. I mean, we barely know each other, yet I could swear he's the one. I know you've probably heard that come out of my mouth more times than you can count but I actually mean it this time. Those other times, I knew I was headed for heartache. This time…it's just different." She gave a pathetic smile, hearing how ridiculous she must sound. "Crazy, huh?"

Emily stirred sugar into her iced tea. "I don't think it's crazy. Rory asked me to marry him on our sixth date. I don't think I'm one to pass judgment on the timing of love. It seems to have a mind and agenda of its own. We silly humans are just along for the ride."

"Well, I don't think we are quite ready for the L word yet, but who knows what will happen by the end of the week." She offered a knowing grin, feeling as if she was still a teenager experiencing the rush of new love for the first time.

# CHAPTER EIGHT

# Orders Received

While in Missouri for the graduation ceremony, J.T. made arrangements to have his paperwork mailed to Rory's address. On September third, eight days after the pair returned to Oregon, Rodney drove into town to the feed store. He stopped at the post office before heading home. When he saw the official-looking envelopes addressed to his brother and J.T., he decided to make a quick detour past Rory's place. He found them in the garage hunkered over a 1957 Chevy Justin had bought from a junkyard.

"Apparently an elderly gentleman passed away," Rory said. "His disgruntled son gave the truck to the junkyard, to be rid of all things related to his father. Must have been a nasty dynamic between them but it's a score for us."

Rodney joined the conversation about the state of the engine before remembering why he had swung by in the first place. "I picked these up on my way home. I figured you might want them as soon as possible."

# The Complexity of a Soldier

Both Rory and J.T. recognized their order packets. Straightening their backs, they took them with an odd mix of dread and enthusiasm. They each gave the other a quick and wary look before tearing open the paperwork. Almost in unison, they announced, "I'm going to Washington."

They stared at each other. The chances they would be transferred to the same base had been high, so they'd been hopeful. They gave each other a fist bump as Rodney moved in to give his brother a hug.

"That's so awesome," Rodney said. "Now you won't be too far away. Mom is gonna be so relieved." When he excused himself to head home, he had a bounce in his step. He was reluctant to admit he was just as pleased that his brother would not be going too far.

"I've got to tell Emily." Rory rushed into the house.

J.T. couldn't have been more pleased with his orders. He was glad he would be in Washington with his best friend, and he was happy he would be able to visit Abby. They would only be a day's drive apart. He stopped short when he realized the truth of his silent admission…he wanted to be with Abby.

From the moment she had sauntered through the smoky haze of the bar with her auburn hair cascading down her back like some sort of Olympus Goddess, he had been intoxicated by her. He bit the inside of his cheek as he played with the idea that he was falling for her. Did he like this? Should he put a stop to it? His immediate response was an irrevocable No.

The realization made him take a step back. Something stirred in his chest. This feeling, this overwhelming emotion, was something he'd always longed for but had always managed to avoid. He'd been too concerned with living up to his fathers' dogmatic expectations. A relationship carried on while one was in the armed forces was a difficult feat and usually ended in bitterness and heartbreak.

# The Complexity of a Soldier

So did he like it? Hell no, he didn't like it, and hell no, he wasn't about to put a stop to it! Abby was amazing. She was everything. They would make it work, he decided with elated finality.

~~~~~~~~~~~~~~~~

Eight days later, on September 11th, 2001, Emily was feeding Callie breakfast and Rory was packing boxes, for the move. A news bulletin flashed across the television screen. The Twin Towers in New York City had a large plume of smoke coming out of a hole in the top of one of the buildings. Rory turned up the volume and caught the tail end of the report. A plane had flown into one of the legendary towers.

"Hey, babe, come check this out. This is crazy," he called as he watched the scene with morbid curiosity.

Just as Emily walked into the living room with Callie on her hip, the camera panned to a different angle. As the reporter went over the few details known at that time, another plane came into view. To everyone's horror, it flew directly into the other tower.

"Oh, my god." Emily put her hand over her mouth.

Rory's face fell as the seriousness of the situation escalated beyond comprehension. There was no way two large commercial airplanes would accidently fly into two buildings right next to each other. The buildings had been targeted purposely. Although he didn't know the details, he knew it must be an attack on the country.

His suspicions were quickly confirmed. Reports began to come in verifying that four planes had been hijacked. Two had been flown into the Twin Towers. One had been flown into the Pentagon, and one had crashed in Pennsylvania on route to the

# The Complexity of a Soldier

White House.

Only moments after this was confirmed, cameras caught the surreal sight of one of the towers collapsing in nearly free fall speed. The devastation was unlike anything America had ever experienced. Rory's first thought as he watched the building fall would later strike him as odd.

"Buildings don't fall like that," he said. A sense of numbness surrounded him as he imagined the unity of the moment for the entire population.

Emily started to cry as the television screen filled with panic, white dust and mayhem. "This can't be happening," she said. "This is just too awful to comprehend."

Rory pulled her close to comfort her but a part of him knew his country would never tolerate such violence. It would retaliate against whoever had implemented such an evil plan. The first line of defense was the military and he would be called upon to defend the nation.

~~~~~~~~~~~~~~

By September 21st Rory, Emily and Callie where settling into a small duplex on base at Fort Lewis, just south of Tacoma, Washington. Rory was impressed. Even though they lived on the outskirts of the sprawling city, they were surrounded by luscious green foliage. Every type of deciduous tree grew there as well as tall, majestic evergreens. Dense bushes and brambles crowded their trunks. Washington was famous for its relentless torrential rainfall but it was also known for its endless beauty, carpeted in vast shades of green.

Only two weeks after their arrival the rainy season began. It lasted for the next seven months and Emily was vocal about her dismay. Rory listened patiently one gray, rainy day when she said, "I know how this god-forsaken place developed such beauty. Anywhere it rains this much is going to be green. So what? It's not like you can enjoy it when you're stuck inside all the time." He knew a large part of her agitation was being homesick.

The cold, damp weather left few options for getting her and Callie out of the stifling confines of their small home. By the time spring hit, they were both going stir crazy. Whenever the rain let up, Rory gathered his family to venture outdoors, itching to feel the rare sunlight hit their pale faces.

Meanwhile, he and J.T. were acclimating to their new jobs on the military police force.

This was exactly what he had been working so hard towards. Every morning he prepared to report to duty, to the job that he loved. It gave him a sense of pride to wear his uniform, to protect and serve the civilians he had sworn an oath to. It filled him up to know he was providing for his family and setting a stellar example of service and dedication.

He and J.T. patrolled the base, carried out basic duties, ran security at the entrance checkpoints, answered domestic disputes among military families, and investigated anything that came under their authority. They were also regularly updated on the prospects that were evolving if President Bush decided to invade Iraq.

Shortly after the devastating September 11th tragedy, Bush announced his new War on Terrorism during a joint session of the U.S. Congress. The action was later termed the Bush Doctrine. Rumors of a link between Iraq and Al-Quaeda began to seethe throughout the media hysteria, and soon more than half the country believed that Saddam Hussein had actively been harboring and supporting terrorists within Al-Qaeda forces.

Throughout the entire year of 2002, the United States focused less and less on the initial villain believed to be behind the attacks, Osama Bin Laden, and more on Hussein's reign and power in Iraq. The looming threat it posed to America's security suddenly amplified.

Government officials and the media began to insist that the Iraqi government had an intensive nuclear and chemical weapons program. The United Nations Security Council passed resolution 1441 calling for Iraq to cooperate with United Nations inspectors. The officials would verify that they did not have any weapons of mass destruction or cruise missiles within their possession.

Much to every American's dismay, after the invasion of Iraq, the U.S. led Iraq Survey Group concluded that Iraq had ended its nuclear and biological programs in 1991. The United Nations of Monitoring, Verification and Inspection Commission also was unable to find any evidence of weapons of mass destruction.

Meanwhile, an entire nation was hurt, scared and angry. Citizens were eager to believe and support their government in the pending invasion as long as it made their world a safer place for their innocent children.

Both Rory and J.T. were flown out in November of 2002. The nation prepared to join the multinational force setting up for the impending military maneuver. When Rory received his orders, he sat Emily down in the quiet of their bedroom to break the news. Before he uttered the words, she spoke.

"I know. Don't even say it. You don't have to. I can see it written all over your face."

She paused for a heartbeat. "How long? A year?"

He wasn't surprised she was taking it like champ. "Yeah. A year."

She sighed. "I figured. I've been thinking it over and I want to move back home while you're gone. Callie and I need our family, our friends if we're going to get through this. It will make it a bit less unbearable."

"That's fine, Em. Whatever you need to do. We'll get everything worked out before I have to leave."

A new feeling crept in over the next week as he helped her pack. At first he couldn't identify the sensation tugging at the back of his mind and wrenching his heart. Then he pegged it. It was fear. He was afraid and unsure how he felt about identifying his weakness. He wasn't afraid of what he would have to face on the battlefield of war. He was afraid of what his wife and child would have to face without him by their side. Who would to protect them while he was gone?

These new thoughts were unsettling and uncomfortable. He pushed them aside hoping the paralyzing sense of helplessness would dissipate.

~~~~~~~~~~~~~~~

Emily had known it was coming but the day he received his orders she sat on the soft pillow-top mattress, knee to knee with her handsome husband, and couldn't bear the thought of him actually going to war. An unimaginable fear wrapped around her and cloaked her in an anxiety that would last the entire twelve months he was away.

While she focused on preparing for his departure, she kept only the bare minimum of her and Callie's essentials with her. She would stay up until the day his unit flew out. She was also overwhelmed by a sense of having lost control of her own destiny. Everything about the situation was a cluster of unknowns. She wouldn't be able to know any real details about her husband, the father of her child, for an entire year. Their communication would be minimal and his wellbeing would always be in question. His very safety would always be on the precipice of disaster.

The only thing that was a minor comfort was that J.T. was in Rory's unit. They would be able to fight off the loneliness together and they would have each others' backs. The day the men were scheduled to leave, Emily went down to the Army base's airstrip to say her final goodbyes.

Abby and J.T. had maintained a long-distance relationship over the last year. Just before the men had received their orders she had considered a move to Washington so they could see where their relationship was going. When their orders came in, the idea was put on ice until after J.T. fulfilled his deployment. Much to their mutual disappointment.

Now Abby stood by Emily's side. She watched the person she believed to be the love of her life prepare to go straight into ground combat while still trying to support her friend. Emily was immensely grateful she didn't have to go through this moment alone.

She was trying her best to maintain her calm and collected presence with a sick smile pasted onto her face. Unfortunately she could feel herself cracking as Rory and J.T. began to gather their gear. They were handsome and formidable in their ACU's. She stood dumbstruck, gripping Callie's two-year-old hand as if the child were her life support. Her lip began to tremble and she turned her back so her husband wouldn't see she was about to lose her composure.

~~~~~~~~~~~

Rory had been dreading this moment. A huge ball of nerves settled into his gut, weighing him down until he felt imprisoned by it. He hated to see Emily upset but as soon as tears were involved, his resolve would buckle. He would do anything in his power to wipe them away.

*God, I didn't want to leave her,* he thought, feeling pulled in two directions. His sense of duty pulled directly against his commitment to his wife and child. But he couldn't fix it. Everything revolving around this situation was completely beyond his control. He felt powerless to do anything other than calm her with his soothing words. He dropped his gear and enveloped her from behind. "Please don't cry baby," he said. "I promise everything is going to be okay."

Emily broke at that point. She simply turned into him as her hot tears soaked his uniform. "Promise? You're going to war. You can't possibly make a promise like that."

"Shush, now. I am going to promise that. I can feel it in my bones. J.T. and I are going to come home to our girls." He stroked her honey-colored hair, needing to convince himself just as much as he needed to convince her.

Then the intercom announced it was time to start boarding. He gave her one last squeeze. Emily hastily wiped her tears and held Callie up so Rory could kiss her goodbye. "Bye, bye daddy. See ya later, alligator," she said in her cute little voice.

Rory's heart squeezed and a lump in his throat threatened to choke him. "After awhile, crocodile," he answered. Then he gave Emily one last heartfelt kiss before he turned, snatched his gear and walked across the terminal with determined strides. He was eager to leave, rather than drag out the painful goodbye any longer.

J.T. finished his lingering goodbyes with Abby, placed a smacking kiss on Callie's cheek and hugged Emily before following suit.

Both men departed with very heavy hearts.

# CHAPTER NINE

# Amped Up

Stationed just outside of Bagdad at what was in the process of becoming Camp Cropper, Rory and his unit reported to the 115th Military Police Battalion. When finished, the camp would be the central booking station and a temporary holding facility for detainees.

Rory and J.T. had multiple roles as did many of their fellow soldiers. They were officially members of the security team but unofficially they did any odd job to prepare the system for full functionality. They worked long hours and bided their time until further orders came in.

Up until March 18th their days weren't too dissimilar from their lives back home. Their time was filled with tedious though exhausting work. The one big exception was the drastic change in climate. The temperatures were a brutal shock to their systems and at first it was all they could do to keep themselves adequately hydrated. They learned to look out for one another, watching for symptoms of heat exhaustion after they'd witnessed far too many of their teammates lose consciousness or vomit as a result of the unforgiving heat.

On the 18th, in the bowels of the underground bunker where conversations were safe from high-tech microphones, their commanding officer announced that President Bush had signed official orders that were effective immediately. They had all been expecting the announcement. Rory listened to the ominous declaration and took a deep breath. He felt as if he would not be able to let it out again until he stepped back onto American soil, safe and with his family.

On the evening of the 19th, two F-117 Nighthawks from the 8th Expeditionary Fighter Squadron dropped four enhanced Bunker Busters on the palace compound. That was followed by nearly forty Tomahawk missiles fired from the ships located just off the coast. The very next day, Special Ops commandos throughout Iraq responded. At 10:15 p.m. EST, Bush announced his "attack of opportunity" orders. All troops were on standby to cross the border and begin ground combat.

Rory and J.T.'s responsibilities kicked into full gear. They processed groups of detainees brought in and were shaken by their condition. Many were injured and were taken directly to the medical facility before being placed in detention. Throughout the first few days, their commanding officer kept them updated. He reminded them to be ready if orders required them to join combat forces in the city.

Everyone did their part, keeping up with the pressure of the steady pace. It was a full two weeks before Rory was finally able to contact Emily, telling her he was safe but busy. He had contemplated not telling her he would likely be required to engage in ground combat but his conscience won out.

# The Complexity of a Soldier

He could only imagine how it would feel to be on her end of the phone, helpless and disengaged from his reality. To her credit, she kept her discomfort close to the vest and changed the subject. She would not want him to regret having told her. He understood and respected that. If he were in her position, he would rather be terrified and know her whereabouts than be left completely in the dark.

On one particularly long day, Rory pulled a double shift when a bout of dysentery hit a majority of their men. They were dangerously short of staff. The illness was likely contracted from one of the detainees and wiped out a large part of the staff. All able bodied men were required to fill in and work overtime to ensure the facility had the required security.

As Rory wrapped up the last of his reports for the day, one of the Corporals entered his station. Word had just come in that Saddam had emerged from his underground bunker the day before, April 9th, to greet the public before disappearing as a fugitive. The U.S. Marines dispatched three companies to locate him.

Over the course of the next week, the Battle of Bagdad settled as the last of the resistance stopped and America claimed the city. With this news, the atmosphere in the camp calmed down despite the long, tiring days. The prospect of joining the battlefield had dissolved significantly. Everyone was relieved with the idea of sticking to the confines of the camp.

~~~~~~~~~~

Only a week later, on the evening of April 28th, 2003, several hundred residents of Fallujah defied the U.S. implemented curfew. Although it was one of the more peaceful cities, protestors marched down the streets past soldiers at the Ba'ath party headquarters to protest the military presence. It was reported that U.S. forces fired into the unarmed group, killing seventeen and wounding seventy. That triggered the insurgents to retaliate.

Two days later, the 82nd Airborne division was replaced. It soon became evident that larger force was needed, so the 2nd Brigade was called in. Rory and twelve other men, including J.T., joined the 3rd Infantry Division to help settle the escalating unrest.

Rory and J.T. were flown out in a Chinook helicopter carrying its limit capacity of thirty- three troops and two High Mobility Multipurpose Wheeled Vehicles. Later that night they entered the city with a group of soldiers packed into a STRYKER tank. The tank had been designed to easily maneuver in close urban settings while protecting its passengers.

The small team would secure the perimeter of a specific area in the market district. Once they were in place, they would provide other units with maneuver and mobility support so they could secure areas further into the city.

Rory sat inside the body of the tank thinking of his wife and child. He felt removed from his body, like he was watching someone else's life from a distance. He held his M-16 rifle against his chest and waited for the okay to evacuate the vehicle.

*This has to be the weirdest day of his life,* he pondered.

He stole a glance at J.T. to gauge how he was handling the situation. J.T. was quietly reciting a Yeats poem when their team leader announced, "Thirty minutes until we reach our destination point. Time to amp it up."

"Amp it up?" Rory was perplexed until the team leader reached out a closed fist. Rory cupped his hand and the Corporal dropped a small yellowish pill into it. Rory was about to decline when everyone else tipped their heads back and swallowed the undefined medicine. Most of the other men had already seen the battlefield and had apparently expected the pill.

He was still mulling it over when a red-head with glasses next to him said, "It's not really an option. Besides, you don't know how many hours you're going to need to stay awake once we're in there, and you'll be glad that you had it."

J.T. gave an indiscriminate shrug then swallowed his yellow capsule. Rory figured he was the last person to question pre-battle practices. Throwing his into the back of his throat, he choked it down with a dry swallow. Just then the driver blasted a Rage Against the Machine song.

Within minutes, Rory's skin began to flush. His cardiovascular system reacted to the increased blood flow and his heart raced wildly. He was suddenly filled with an insane and indescribable feeling of strength and energy. It pulsated throughout his body as if it were being pumped by the loud, angry music. He suddenly understood what the team leader had meant by amping it up.

J.T. was flexing and contracting his fists. He too was beginning to feel the effects of the pill as it took hold of his system. The vibe within the vehicle evolved from anxious and wary to a blood-pumping, action-seeking team of soldiers looking to release their superhuman power on the battlefield. Now he knew this was the weirdest day of his life.

By the time the men reached their destination point and the STRYKER navigator had deemed the area clear, the team leader gave the order to evacuate. The majority of their team spilled out to secure the area. Rory followed J.T. and instantly caught the ominous sound of a Howitzer discharging repeatedly in the distance. He inhaled the sharp odor of gunpowder as it filtered throughout the streets in a smoky haze. Everything was happening fast but his body and mind were alert and ready.

As his team broke off into pairs, he was relieved that the

immediate area seemed to be deserted. They were to go through each building checking for hideouts and disarming booby traps. Most of the structures were still intact but a few had been struck by bombs or grenades. These would require extreme caution due to the risk of collapse.

Once the area had been secured and they had established a perimeter, the team leader contacted command and reported their status. They were instructed to keep their area tightly locked down so they could assist the crew that would arrive within the hour. When the following team arrived, new orders were given. They were to infiltrate the residential neighborhood, which required going door to door to perform random searches for obvious insurgents. When found, they would be relieved of their weapons and detained.

Rory did not like the idea of dealing with innocent civilians and had to bite his tongue. This was not the time or place to voice his concerns. *Just follow orders,* he chastised himself. Be a team player. This was not a game with simple rules. Lives were on the line if he decided to go against the grain.

*God damn, it's hot,* he thought as he accepted the water bottle being passed around. Hot didn't even begin to describe the stifling temperature. It took a conscious and proactive effort to replace the vast amount of water loss caused by the extreme heat and the effects of the drug.

Their commanding officer called out. The team came together as instructed, strategically placing themselves in positions both offensive and defensive.

Looking out for oncoming forces, they surrounded the first civilian home. They secured the house quickly but the little Iraqi woman inside screamed in her native tongue as tears streamed down her face. She held a picture of what must have been her husband. She was distracting, disturbing. Her six young children screamed and cried along with her. Their fear was tangible as the soldiers scoured the place.

Rory's stomach turned as they marched out and on to the next home. He felt like a monster. Those children would see his face in their dreams at night. Their innocent minds would always recall the way strange and foreign men had destroyed their lives. To everyone's relief, the next few houses were empty. It appeared the inhabitants had fled the moment the city became violent.

When they reached the sixth residence, they heard shouting from inside. Then a warning shot was fired into the streets. The soldiers posted themselves in secure positions before bursting into the small house from multiple entry points. J.T. and Rory both entered through the back door. They filed through the home, hitting the bedrooms first. Rory changed direction and rushed to J.T. when he called out for back up.

He stepped into the room and assessed the situation quickly. They had walked into a particularly precarious situation that could easily turn into an epic disaster if they didn't handle the matter delicately.

A small, disheveled man stood in front what Rory assumed was his family. He looked frantic and held a US issued MK19-3 he must have swiped off a soldier in his skinny arms. He was screaming at them. His face was red and spittle flew from his mouth. His speech was too rapid to be coherent. Neither man could understand what he was saying but knew he was frightened and wanted to protect his family.

"He's scared," Rory said quietly so as not to cause further fear. "They are all scared. We have to show them we mean no harm."

They both pointed their weapons downward, indicating that they had no intention of hurting them.

# The Complexity of a Soldier

They were trying to calm the man down and convince him to drop his weapon, when a series of shots rang out, possibly from the street in front of the house. A few men from their unit, unsure where the shots were coming from, burst into the bedroom. The commotion sent the already fragile man into hysteria.

*No,* was his only thought as Rory spun around and threw his hands into the air but it was too late. The frightened man was determined not to let a bunch of radical American troops hurt or kill his family, even if it meant committing a horrific act. He called out a command in a loud, shrill scream. His wife and children closed their eyes and covered their ears. He pointed the automatic weapon at them and fired. He mowed them down with a downpour of bullets that left only blood and death in its wake.

Both soldiers witnessed the atrocity as if it were playing out in slow motion. J.T. tackled the shooter to stop the massacre. Rory leaped forward and grabbed the weapon as the thin man fell to the wood floor under J.T.'s weight.

Neither of them expected the man to fight but he rolled to his back with a wild look and swung a large knife. He struck J.T. in the shoulder.

Rory cringed as he heard the tearing of uniform and flesh. He saw the jarring impact as the blade entered his friend's body. He guessed J.T. mustn't have felt the sting because his face indicated no pain. He looked into the crazed eyes of the man in his grip. Before Rory could react, bullets struck the man in the chest. His eyes went wide and he slumped back to the floor.

"J.T.? Are you okay?" Rory was barely able to hear himself above the ringing in his ears.

He pulled his friend away from the slack body. The man had been their victim and their attacker. His entire body shook as adrenaline spiked and coursed through his system. Both of them were dazed by the realization that J.T. had almost been killed. Both of them could have been killed.

Rory was appalled at the scene and terrified for his friend. He grabbed J.T. by the shoulders and helped him to his feet. J.T. took one look around at the ugliness and slumped back to his knees, his lips losing color.

Four children ranging in age from about fourteen to three and a black-haired frail woman, lay together on the bed in disarray. Their father and husband must have believed he was enacting a mercy killing. Rory felt ill but he could still hear rapid gunfire outside. No one was sure who or where it was coming from. He and another team member hauled J.T. to his feet again and convinced him to focus. They needed to evacuate the premises.

"Come on, man," Rory said. "We've got to take cover. Let's get you outta here."

The team was about to go out the back door when they looked down the alley. A group of Iraqi insurgents pushed a towed howitzer over the dirty lane in their direction. The group spotted each other at the same time and Rory's team retreated back inside.

Two of their best shooters bolted upstairs to the roof. They would pick them off one at a time. The rest of the team took cover and prepared for a direct attack. Rory heard the Howitzer begin its wicked regurgitation of rounds. He peeked out of the bathroom window as a young boy of about seventeen came into view. He was looking straight ahead and didn't see Rory poised at the small window. Rory hesitated, doubtful he would be able to shoot the boy.

*Please don't make me shoot you, kid,* he pleaded. *Just run home to your parents.* But he didn't have a home anymore, did he? Not one that was safe.

A gunshot from above rang out as one of his own men hit the

insurgents one by one. The boy pulled out a grenade, gearing up to pull the pin before throwing it into the house. Rory hesitated no more. He riddled the boy with bullets.

His heart raced, his tongue felt dry and swollen but he kept firing as the opposing group fired at him with their hand-held weapons. Rory's skin flushed with heat and adrenaline but everything inside of him went frigid. It was as if the blood flowing through his veins had turned to prickly shards of ice.

Meanwhile, the soldiers on the roof had taken out most of the men that had been operating the Howitzer. The group suddenly realized they were vulnerable and outnumbered. They began to flee.

"The front is clear," J.T. reported as he joined Rory and the rest of the team in the kitchen. His color was returning but the look in his eyes was distracted. The commanding officer called out orders. They were to get back to their section in the marketplace. It took about an hour to move about the neighborhood without drawing attention but they made it back reasonably unscathed.

Rory and Jeff, who had the most experience with medical situations, cleaned up J.T.'s wound. It was only a surface injury and required minimal stitches. J.T. couldn't take his eyes off the cut as they cleaned it, and Rory could only guess that the gravity of his near-death experience was still surreal. He was lucky the guy had been so distressed and had only made a slicing motion rather than a stab. A knife of that size would have caused considerable damage had it impaled him straight on.

"Whoa, I've been stabbed," he murmured.

Rory caught the thickness of shock in J.T.'s voice. Light humor was best for the moment. "Don't be so dramatic," he said. "You weren't stabbed. You were...what would you call it, Jeff?" A slice?"

J.T. peered up at him. "Slice, cut, stab, call it whatever you want, asshole," he growled. 'It frickin' hurts. Now get your filthy hands off me before I get some kind of wicked infection and lose my arm for good. How's that for dramatic?"

Rory backed off as a devilish smile played over his features. J.T. would be fine.

That same evening the men were instructed to rest but all where still suffering the lingering effects of the pill and their own adrenaline. It left them twitchy and raw, restless and off balance, which made sleep evasive. Even when their bodies finally gave in to exhaustion, it was a fitful and pathetic parody of rest. The hours were riddled with dreams as gunfire and the sound of explosions filtered in from the distant city.

~~~~~~~~~~

The days of the following week overlapped as the days and nights rolled into and over each other, making it difficult to distinguish time. Their activities never ceased to require one hundred percent of their effort and energy. They woke every morning and amped up before heading back into the streets. There was a complete lack of routine or order so what was once up now felt down. They slept whenever the situation permitted and moved forward at a relentless and unforgiving pace.

One evening they marched down an alley not far from their section of town. Their heads were muddled with fatigue and exhaustion. Their mouths were parched from the dust that permeated the air. The day had been fairly quiet until a deafening explosion reverberated in the air. They felt it under their feet and knew it was close by.

Instantly alert, the unit took cover as best they could. They plastered themselves against the nearest building, grasped their weapons and prepared to face whatever awaited. The team leader poked his head around the corner to analyze the situation. He gave orders to follow. They fell in step as he rushed out into the street.

Rory was particularly lethargic that day even with the aid of the little yellow pill. Still he was the second on the scene. As he scanned the area to size up the situation, a new flush of adrenaline gave him new vitality.

An armored Humvee had driven over a makeshift land mine. The explosion had erupted up through the floor of the vehicle and the impact had flipped it on its side. The driver had been thrown from the vehicle and was literally blown in half. The lower part of his body lay approximately fifteen feet away from his torso.

*He's gone, don't give it another thought,* he reprimanded as thoughts of the soldier's family tried to seep into his mind. It wouldn't fix the situation to think of the loss. He just needed to focus on the now. He could think later.

Rory avoided the corpse's blank stare and ran to the other side of the vehicle. He might be able to help anyone still inside. He and his team leader reached the roof and saw three people inside. The two in the back appeared to be unconscious. The one in front was awake but in such a state of shock he was blinking and glancing around, disoriented and whimpering.

J.T. and the others were right behind. Everyone moved quickly to remove the other three as quickly possible. If enemies found them vulnerable and in the open like that, they would be in as much trouble as the men they were trying to help.

Three soldiers climbed onto the upside of the Humvee in an effort to pry open the doors. They were able to open the back door because its hinges had been blown loose from the impact of the blast.

A mix of unfavorable smells rose up as Rory reached into the body of the vehicle. He grabbed one of the injured men's shirt collar and gave a great heave. As soon as he had him part way up, the other men got a good grip on him. They hefted him out together. He was still unconscious and other than a nasty red and purple knot on his forehead he looked to be fairly unharmed. Rory assumed the head wound was his only injury.

"This one's out but seems okay," he called. "Give him a look."

Glancing at J.T., he read his desperation to find life as clearly as he felt it within himself. They had seen enough death and had been the cause of some of it. Now they were leaping at the opportunity to do some good, to save a life.

He leaned into the truck to retrieve the other man. He was crumpled against the window and also looked to be fairly unharmed. He was just coming to when the man in front let out a shrill, spine-curling scream.

"My leg, I can't feel my other leg!"

J.T. and Private Johnson ignored his cry as they continued their efforts with the man in the back. He turned toward them, revealing that he had also hit his head. Blood from a large gash washed into his eyes as he blinked his way back to a scene that was unfathomably real.

Rory and two other men jumped off the Humvee and rounded the front, desperate to find a way to extract the distraught soldier through the shattered windshield. The soldier was thrashing about and screaming. He would hurt himself worse if they didn't get him out soon.

Rory shouted, "The best way to get him out, is through the broken windshield. We'll clear out the shattered glass the best we can so we don't cut ourselves or him."

They nodded and set about the task, willing to do anything to stop the chilling screams. Their team leader was on the satellite phone barking out orders to their closest medical unit. Private Rhea snagged Rory's arm and hauled him to the underside of the vehicle. He pointed at the gaping hole in the underbelly.

After a second, Rory spotted what the private had been anxious to show him. He could see into the front of the vehicle through the floorboard and saw oil pooling up and dripping out. *Not oil,* he thought. Blood. He realized he was looking at the stump of one of the man's legs. It was bleeding profusely and the blood gathered on the dirt road in a growing puddle.

Rory choked back bile as the metallic smell of blood hit his nostrils. He forced himself to look farther into the truck to assess any further damage to the soldier. The man's other leg appeared unharmed but was pinched into a tight spot. They would have to be very careful when pulling him out. Rory rounded the vehicle and discreetly apprised everyone of the situation.

They spent the next ten minutes wriggling the screaming man out through the windshield with as much finesse as they could manage. All the while J.T., who had finished assisting the other soldier, talked in a strong, encouraging tone to calm him down.

The team leader said, "I've radioed command and control to report our emergency. The medic helicopter will meet us in the open field just a few blocks south."

When they had the soldier halfway out the window, he suddenly stopped screaming. His eyes rolled back and he lost consciousness.

"No, damn it. Don't you die." Rory didn't realize he'd spoken out loud. He reached over and felt for a pulse, praying for a miracle. He found a thin, thready rhythm and everyone picked up the pace. They put a makeshift tourniquet around the meaty stump and ducked into the violent winds of the approaching helicopter.

# CHAPTER TEN

# Emily's Retreat

On March 20th, 2003, Emily was working the drive-through window at her dad's bank when television reporters announced that the United States of America had officially declared war. The night before, they had skillfully executed an air invasion on the Iraqi Presidential Palace. Operation Iraqi Freedom immediately ensued and the media propagandized the mission with the "Shock and Awe" buzz term.

Up until that point, Rory had been able to communicate with her more often than she had initially hoped. With access to a satellite phone, he was able to use it once a week. So far he'd been able to report that his tour of duty had been fairly uneventful. *Now, who knows how long it will be before he can call again,* she thought despondently.

That evening as she put Callie down, her vision blurred and she felt woozy. She realized she had skipped both lunch and dinner that day. She'd made sure to feed Callie, of course; actions like that were carried out almost without thought. She was engrossed with Callie but was almost equally engrossed in thoughts of Rory and his well being. Her concern for how the year apart would affect their relationship plagued her.

What if he came home different? What if he didn't want her and Callie anymore?

In her heart she knew he would always love her. They had something special, something worth believing in and waiting for. Despite that knowing, she had bad days. Days like the one she was having right now. On those days, the knowing did nothing to soothe her loneliness. It felt necessary, almost therapeutic, to simply wallow.

As a military wife, she was supposed to keep a positive attitude and show her unwavering support to her military husband as he fought for their country. And she did. Usually. But once in a while in the quiet of her room or in the solitude of her mind, she would allow other emotions to rise up and have their moment. She wanted her man home regardless of the ugliness in the world. In fact, because of it. The feeling that precious time was being wasted as their little one reached milestones and created memories that he wouldn't share while he fought an opaque enemy in a foreign land.

Then there were darker emotions, like her ever-growing anger and resentment. Toward who, she still wasn't sure. Her government, her president? She didn't know. She just knew she wanted to blame someone for taking him away from her and placing him in danger, risking everything they had promised one another in front of their family, their pastor, their creator. For what? Why?

But those thoughts were considered selfish. She knew better than to let them overwhelm her. Still, she had to recognize them every so often, and she did on only the rarest, weakest of occasions.

# The Complexity of a Soldier

Then she would force herself to think of the good times. She would make an exercise of bringing his face or the sound of his deep voice to mind. She would close her eyes and pray that just for a moment, she could escape into those memories so completely they would become real, tangible.

As she finished a makeshift meal of cheese and crackers, she decided this was one of those days. She would erase the realities of her stress, close herself in her bedroom, and pretend the outside world had stopped spinning its relentless motion.

She wrapped her hair into a messy knot on top of her head and stepped into a hot, steamy bath. She sank in up to her neck, rested her head against the wall and let herself remember. She traveled back to a time when things had been simpler, when she had felt centered in her own universe rather than aimlessly floating about.

After their unplanned engagement, they decided to keep their pledge to themselves. Their parents would only freak out and lecture them about their youth and their future.

That September, Emily began her first year courses. She and Rory spent most evenings together as well as every weekend. Their parents knew they were quite smitten with each other and easily imagined where it would lead. So one October evening when the couple gathered Rory's family in the living room to announce their engagement, neither seemed surprised. Sarah and Justin were wary about the rapid pace of their relationship. Emily was grateful when they merely congratulated the pair and hugged her to welcome her into their family.

The announcement wasn't received as well by Emily's father the following Sunday. As soon as the words were out of Emily's mouth, her father turned four shades of an angry red, marched out of the room, slammed the front door behind him and headed to his car.

## The Complexity of a Soldier

Rory rocked back on his heels nervously looking at Emily's mother to gauge her reaction.

Charlene pressed her fingertips to her mouth and her eyes were wide with shock. Then she put both hands on her knees and sat on the edge of the Victorian fainting couch.

"Don't worry about your father, dear," she said in a prim, businesslike voice. "He always gets like that when he doesn't know how to deal with something. He will take a drive and come back when he feels ready to proceed calmly."

She stared at her daughter with a neutral expression before sliding her gaze over to Rory. He seemed to be handling himself very well, given the circumstances. Charlene looked back at her daughter.

"I won't lie to you two. I think you are both much too young for this serious step but I cannot say anything more without being a hypocrite. I was only a year older than Emily is now when I met her father. We were engaged only six months later. And as you know he is six years older than me. The only reason my parents approved was because of his family's prestigious background."

Charlene looked at Rory again. "Luckily, neither I nor Emily's father, are as snobbish and pretentious as our parents were. As long as you make an honest and honorable living, which we believe you will, we are happy to have you as a son in law." With that, she offered a thin smile.

Emily saw the instant relief pass over his face. He shocked Charlene by embracing her. "Thank you so much, Mrs. Nelson. I promise to take very good care of your daughter and any future grandchildren."

Charlene cackled with delight, pleased at the show of affection and his obvious dedication to Emily. "Grandchildren? Let's not get too carried away, young man." She turned to hug her daughter and gave her a bittersweet smile. "I will talk with your father and everything will be fine."

Emily couldn't have felt more pleased. She had expected her father's response and knew as well as her mom that, he would eventually come around. Her mom had been the unknown. When she was also willing to respect their decision, it was a huge relief. She hugged her mom, peering over her shoulder to see Rory giving her a knowing wink.

Plans for the wedding commenced and the two found themselves swept into a whirlwind of details. One weekend in mid-November, Charlene and Jacob Nelson left town to celebrate their twenty-fifth wedding anniversary. They initially had asked Emily to stay over at a friends' house. After a drawn-out conversation as Emily argued that she was nineteen, a legal adult and old enough to stay home alone, they gave in.

Emily was their only child. She knew it was hard for them to admit they were holding too tightly. They refused to adjust to the fact that she was an adult and would soon be married and living in her own home. She pressed the issue until they conceded they were being ridiculous. They consented to leave her alone for the weekend.

Charlene left instructions for running the house, meal choices, and contact numbers in case of an emergency. Emily assured them she would be fine and shoved them out the door. She had invited Rory to spend the night with her. Even though she felt ready, part of her was tempted to back out. She ignored the prepared meals left by her mom and tried on the role of being Rory's wife.

For the next hour, she simmered a basic red sauce for linguine, tossed a fresh salad, and prepared a loaf of French bread. As she worked, she danced around the kitchen singing with the radio. At one point she glanced around the kitchen then down the front of her sauce-splattered shirt. *Crap,* she thought. What a disaster! Rory would surely think she was a complete bobble head. The thought struck her as hilarious. She laughed hysterically, in the wake of her mess. Then she gathered her wits. She'd better clean up if she didn't want him to think she was completely inadequate in the kitchen.

As soon as the meal had been prepared, she had only twenty minutes before Rory showed up. She rushed upstairs to freshen up and change her clothes. After much anguish, she settled on a light pink summer dress that accentuated her figure. She put her hair up but at the last minute decided to leave it down. It fell past her shoulders the way Rory liked it.

At the sound of the doorbell, she calmed her nerves and walked to the door. She hoped to portray the casual nuance of an adult welcoming an anticipated guest. No matter how hard she tried, she couldn't shake the odd sensation that she was shrinking as the immensity of her situation loomed.

"I am not going to vomit, I am not going to vomit!" she chanted quietly.

She took a deep breath and opened the door. Rory stood under the porch light looking devastatingly handsome in a dark blue polo shirt and slacks. He held a dozen red roses. She forgot all intentions of being sensible and grown up, and even her fear that she might puke. She rose up on tiptoes to kiss him before taking the flowers. She bubbled with excitement and nervous energy. Their rattled nerves kept conversation stiff through dinner.

After they finished their meal, Rory leaned back in his chair. "That was delicious. I had no idea you could cook like that."

"Oh, sure. I have a few dishes I'm good with. I get it from my mom."

"Okay, well, since you made dinner I'll do the dishes."

## The Complexity of a Soldier

"What? No way. This is my mess, I'll clean up."

But Rory would hear nothing of it. He made Emily sit in the bar stool at the counter while he cleared the table and did the dishes. "I can pull my weight around the house," he said. "If there's one thing mom drilled into our heads, it's that although there may be men's work and women's work, there are times the two come together."

Emily initially protested but she enjoyed their conversation as she watched him move with a fluid grace she found surprising given his height. She loved to watch him move. Did he watch the way she moved? When they moved to the living room, Rory stoked the fire with a few large logs.

They sat on the couch with Emily's feet propped in his lap for nearly two hours. They shared stories from their childhood and eventually segued into details of the upcoming wedding.

"Who is going to be your best man?" she asked. It had only recently occurred to her that Rory had many friends but none she would consider a best friend. He spent most of his time working on the ranch and a great deal of his spare time with her.

"Rodney's going to be my best man," he said. "I asked him last week. We were out breaking ice in the water trough for the cows and it occurred to me that I would need to have a best man."

Rory chuckled. "That little twirp turns to me and says I need to ask him proper. I was like, what the heck is up with this turd? He tells me it just didn't feel like I meant it or anything, asking him in the middle of a herd of cows out in the freezing cold weather. Like he was my girlfriend or something. He was just trying to give me a hard time, so I acted like a hard ass and told him to forget it. I didn't want him to be my best man anymore. Oooh, that got him all kinds of mad. He stomped off and wouldn't talk to me for the rest of the day."

"Rory!" Emily playfully slapped his arm.

# The Complexity of a Soldier

Rory flinched with a devious laugh. "Hold on. I told him I was just joking but he was still in a tizzy about it, so I told him to stop being a princess pouty pants, which happens to be the worst thing I could call him. He hates it! Before I knew it we were in the middle of another one of our wrestling matches rolling around on the snowy ground."

Rory rubbed his jaw. "That jerk managed to land a solid right hook on my jaw and sent me flying back on my butt. I have to admit, I was stunned for a second, but obviously my little brother needed to be reminded who was boss. So I picked him up and threw him into the water trough." A huge grin showed nothing but love for his brother.

Emily had been laughing throughout the entire story. "Oh, you two never stop, do you? I feel sorry for your poor mother. You know what's going to happen, don't you?" she asked with raised eyebrows. "You're going to have two sons just like you. It's the mother's curse. It happens every time. People have children that act just like they did."

Rory's face grew serious. "I never thought of that before." He grinned. "I better hope they end up more like their mother."

Emily laughed again then broke into a huge yawn. Rory stood up and scooped her off the couch and marched her up the stairs. She rested her head against his shoulder as her insides fluttered with anticipation.

Rory was the perfect gentlemen and offered to sleep on the couch downstairs but Emily pulled him down to the bed with her. Her room was decorated in almost pure white with only touches of light blue. As the moonlight filtered in through the lacy curtains, it bounced off of the bright interior and gave them a soft light to see each other by.

They slowly helped each other undress. She felt hindered by

her shyness and was comforted when he took everything slow. He allowed her to warm slowly rather than burning too hot at once.

She lost all self-consciousness as her body answered his. He awakened new sensations. She caressed his cheek as he leaned over and looked into her face.

"You're the first person that I will ever be with," she whispered.

Rory brushed back a strand of hair back from her face. "And I intend to be the last."

The memory was still so vivid she could almost taste him as she sat in the steamy waters of the tub. Thinking of him that way had awakened her flesh. She tempered her desire because he was so far away. She didn't want to think about that yet. She wanted to keep thinking of him here with her. So she closed her eyes and drifted back again, knowing she was avoiding her pain but not caring. Just for a moment, she didn't want to care. Just for a moment she wanted to go back.

They had initially planned to wait until after the New Year. After considering it further, they decided to be married on New Year's Eve moments before the countdown. They would time their first kiss as man and wife to precisely midnight. It would mean a late wedding but Justin was friends with a Justice of the Peace and had already made arrangements for him to be their minister.

Rory was baffled, grouchy even, by the number of details involved with planning a wedding. He got twitchy every time Emily asked for his opinion on what he considered inconsequential and frivolous things. She was understanding and didn't take it personal.

One day as she was going over the swatches of colors for the bride's maid's dresses, his hands were jammed into his pockets as he desperately tried to figure out which one he was supposed to say was the best. He probably didn't give a crap what the bride's maids wore. She had to admit that fussing over something as trivial as a specific shade was fairly ridiculous. It occupied her mind space but for him, red was red. Still he was being a good sport, pondering the choices as expected.

Her heart squeezed. What a sweetheart, putting up with all of that nonsense. She couldn't imagine why he was being so supportive. Even she was beginning to feel a little overwhelmed. She had to remind herself that the wedding day wasn't as important as all the days to follow. She would try to be the best wife she could for Rory, which included being able to step back and evaluate situations like these. She giggled and reached up to give him a big kiss.

"Forget about it," she said. "I'll figure this stuff out later. Let's go get some dinner before I chew off my own arm."

Rory chuckled as appreciation skimmed his features. "Are you sure? I thought you wanted this figured out by the weekend so you could put the order in first thing Monday morning."

"I do, and I will, but it's not fair to drag you through this bridal hell with me. I don't really mind it and I can see that you hate it and I don't really blame you. So unless you want to keep doing something that makes you want to stab yourself in the eye then I suggest you take my offer to let you off the hook."

"Thank god! It's a done deal. You don't have to twist my arm."

The wedding went off without a hitch. The Legion Hall was filled with members from both sides of the family. The ceremony felt festive since it was coupled with the New Year's Celebration. At eleven-forty, Emily's father walked her down an aisle lined with gorgeous red roses and puffy white carnations. The flowers went unnoticed as she walked the path to her future husband.

Her heart was in her throat. Oh god, she hoped she could

actually go through with it! She pleaded with herself to keep it together. "Please help me get through this without passing out or making a fool of myself," she whispered.

She felt beautiful in a simple gown with a high neckline that followed the curve of her collarbone before sweeping low down her back. The bodice was fitted, hugging her frame past her hips then gently fanning out around her legs. A small train trailed behind. Her glossy, smooth hair was pulled away from her creamy face and ringlets fell in the back under a thin veil.

Her mind raced and her heart sang when she saw Rory in front of the congregation looking down the aisle waiting for her. This was it. This was the moment she would become his wife. She had waited for this day for as long as she could remember. Her dad gave her a light kiss on the cheek before placing her hand in Rory's.

Their vows were straightforward and followed by a prayer. Then they lit a unity candle while the song, *From this Moment* played. Emily heard a sniffle and peeked at Abby crying softly into her white handkerchief.

Seconds before midnight, the minister wrapped up the ceremony. "Now you may kiss the bride," he said. The entire room began the countdown. Emily looked up into Rory's face, eagerly anticipating their first kiss as man and wife.

Rory beamed as he joined in. "Four, three, two, one," he said, then he leaned down. He kissed her in the first few moments of their marriage and the first year of the new millennium.

~~~~~~~~~~~~

By two in the morning everyone was yawning and beginning to fade, so the bride threw the bouquet and the groom threw the garter. Details were quickly wrapped up so everyone could escape to the

# The Complexity of a Soldier

sanctuary of their homes and the comfort of their beds.

Rory had secured a small, partially furnished, rental home the week before. He had told her about it but had forbidden her to see it. He and his mom rushed about, preparing for their wedding night.

Even though it was pitch black outside, Emily wore a blindfold. She squirmed in anticipation as Rory drove across town. He led her up the sidewalk and took off the blindfold so she could see the outside. She took in a sharp breath. Their first home was a white, narrow two-story with a small covered porch and a sweet little swing Rory had purchased to give it a cozy feel. It was just perfect. She giggled with delight and flung herself into his arms.

Rory swung her up so he could carry her over the threshold. Once inside, Emily was touched at the obvious thought and deliberate care Rory and his mother had taken to ensure their home had the comfy, warm touch of a woman. The lacey curtains were in her favorite shade of blue, and the Oriental rug and the throw pillows were perfectly matched to give the living room balance.

She immediately felt at home and was near tears when Rory put her down. Rory tried to flick on the lights but she pulled his hand back from the switch. "Later" she said, and pulled his head down to hers.

With their rare privacy, Emily felt daring. She reached out to bolt the front door. Looking directly into his face, she eased her wedding dress off her shoulders and down her body until it pooled around her feet. He clenched his jaw as his eyes roved over her with a possessive caress. She reached out to invite him into her arms. He carried her upstairs to the four-poster bed his mom and dad had bought as a wedding gift.

They explored each other as if they had never seen or touched the other before. By the time Rory took her over the first peak, she was trembling in full surrender. When she could take his deliberately slow teasing no more, she wrapped her legs around him and brought him to her in an embrace he was unable to resist. They were joined as husband and wife for the first time.

That memory would never fade or lose its essence. Emily patted herself with the oversized bath towel Rory normally used as she continued to indulge in her memories of their courtship. She was using them as a sort of brick barricade, a fortress into which she could at least temporarily escape the relentless heaviness she carried in her heart.

She spread a creamy lotion over her toned body, brushed out her honey blond hair and slipped between the cool sheets of their bed. Still clinging to the sanctuary of her mind, she hoped it would carry her into a peaceful night's sleep.

# CHAPTER ELEVEN

# A Friendship Tested

Time was inconsequential in battle. For Rory, seconds, hours and days morphed into one another as survival instinct took over and blocked out all other priorities. Things he once believed to be important when tucked away in the safety of home became a fleeting concept. He thought of Emily and Callie, his parents and brother, and whether or not he had been kind enough, good enough, appreciative enough while he'd had the time. Those obsessive worries permeated his mind space even in the most dire scenarios.

Thankfully, things finally began to settle down in the third week. Most of the violent sectarian groups had fled the city. Rory and J.T. stayed with their team for an entire month before the corporal reported that they would return to Camp Cropper within forty-eight hours.

When they returned to the MP camp, it was already June second. Rory was anxious to contact Emily, assuming she would probably be beside herself with her own anxiety. He couldn't get to a phone fast enough, he couldn't hear the sound of her voice soon enough. When she answered, he tried to visualize her and Callie in their home safe, their lives uninterrupted by ugliness and violence. He needed to picture them that way to cleanse away his inner disease.

"Hello? Emily, is that you?" The line was a bit sketchy and he wasn't sure if the call had gone through or if someone had in fact picked up.

"Rory, it's me. I'm here. Can you hear me?"

"Oh, baby, I'm so glad to hear your voice. God, I miss you so much. How are my girls, how's Callie?"

"I miss you too, honey. I wasn't sure when you'd call. I was getting so worried. They say so many crazy things on the news and it gets me so scared. I finally had to stop watching. "Are you okay? Are you back at the camp?"

"I am. Both of us are, me and J.T., but I don't want to talk about that. Tell me what baby girl is up to."

"Well…I started potty training her. She is so excited about her pink potty chair and big-girl panties. She's had a few accidents but we're making progress."

Thinking of his little girl growing up without him around caused his throat to tighten. "Tell her that daddy is so proud of her. Tell her I love her. How are my parents, your parents?"

"My parents are great, nothing new. Your dad hurt his back pulling a calf a few weeks back. Rodney's been picking up the slack with one of his buddies who needs extra cash before he hits the rodeo circuit. Your dad was going nuts laid up like that but he's getting around pretty good now. I think your mom had the worst end of that deal, though. He was driving her crazy."

Rory chuckled. His heart warmed to hear of his family. "I bet. Is she hanging in there?"

# The Complexity of a Soldier

"She's fine, you know her. She's tough. She misses you terribly, though. Hey, Abby says to tell J.T. he'd better hurry up and come back to her. That goes for you, too. I miss you. I want you home."

"I miss you too, baby."

Rory clung to the sound of her sweet voice teasing his ear. The gap between the realities of their vastly different lives was immense. He was glad his family was far away from the travesty surrounding him. No matter how hard he tried, he could not reconcile the opposing situations.

"How about you, Rory, how are you doing?" she asked.

"I'm pretty tired. Hot. It's not really something you can put into words, Em. It just is what it is." His answer was vague but he really didn't know how to talk to her about what he was going through, nor was he sure he wanted to. He doubted he ever would. Now wasn't the time or place.

With heavy hearts they said I love you and got off the phone. Rory headed to the showers to wash away the month of grime and emotional fatigue weighing on every cell in his body.

After a blissfully hot shower he felt surprisingly refreshed. He headed to the sleeping quarters and found J.T. bent over a small desk writing ferociously. His head jerked up as Rory entered and looked almost shocked to see him. Tapping his pencil in a quick rhythm, he asked, "What do you think that stuff was they kept giving us in the field?"

Rory stretched out on the stiff single bed. "Not sure. Must have been some sort of upper or something. I didn't like it though. It made me feel like I was crawling out of my skin."

J.T. snorted, "I think it was like a medical-grade speed. It made me feel like I could run a marathon and win this war by myself."

Lifting his head off the pillow, Rory gave a warning glare. "Just remember it's supposed to make you feel like that, so you forget you're not actually invincible. That way you'll perform the way they need you to rather than doing the sensible thing and running for cover to save your own hide."

John Thomas stared off into the distance before eventually turning back to his writing. Rory drifted off to sleep.

~~~~~~~~~~~~~

Rory slept hard that first night back at the compound. He woke in the early morning hours of his first official day off in over a month. Slightly disoriented as he came to, he tried to recall if he was still in the field. The feel of the bed under him rather than the hard cement of the building they had slept in along with the deafening quiet of the room, rather than the relentless sounds of a city under attack reminded him they had returned to MP headquarters.

He heard the familiar sound of pencil scratching paper and rolled on his side to see J.T. sitting just as he had been hours before.

"What the...dude, have you been at it all night? Did you go to bed at all?" His voice was thick with sleep, his lips dry.

J.T. appeared irritated at the break in his concentration. He shrugged and didn't bother to glance at Rory. "Umm...yeah, I slept for a little while but woke up early and roamed before I came back to the room."

Rory sat up. Why was his friend so restless? He was dead tired even after a hard nap. He rubbed the back of his neck where a kink had taken up a permanent residence at the base of his skull during their month in the field.

"You hungry? You want to get some breakfast?" He watched J.T. closely. Something felt off, something wasn't right.

# The Complexity of a Soldier

J.T. sat back in the wooden chair and looked at Rory for the first time. "Uh, no...yeah...I mean, I guess I could use some food. I don't really feel very hungry, though." He absentmindedly ran his fingers over his short hair.

Something was definitely going on. J.T. never turned his nose up at the idea of food. He was like a non-stop eating machine and had shamed every other man on the compound with his ability to take in staggering quantities of food. Rory always teased J.T. saying he must have worms.

Rory took a closer look. He noticed how disheveled and strung -out J.T. looked. His eyes were so bloodshot it made his own eyes water just to look at them. His clothes looked slept in and he had a day's worth of stubble on his face. That was a big-time foul in their occupation, where hygiene was one of the highest priorities. A thought crossed Rory's mind.

"I bet some of the guys know where to get their hands on more of those pills," he said.

J.T. was hunched over his paper, writing with staggering speed. His knuckles were white from the tight grip on the pencil. "Yeah, I know. I was talking to one of the guys in the kitchen about it this morning and he hooked me up. It's not exactly difficult to get your hands on that stuff even though we are out in the middle of the freakin' desert."

Rory's anger spiked. "What the hell, J.T. I don't care if they pass it out like god-damn candy. They're drugs, and you don't need to be taking it anymore." He stood up and loomed over his friend.

J.T. ignored the loud outburst. That only angered Rory further. He snatched the paper and tossed it into the garbage. "I'm talking to you and I expect you to respond, damn it!"

J.T. shot up so quickly he toppled the chair. He stood with his legs spread, squared off and ready to take on his friend.

# The Complexity of a Soldier

*Whoa!* Rory thought. He had instigated what could easily turn into a brawl because he'd let his temper get out of control. John Thomas stood with wild eyes and his chest heaving with rage. Rory knew his fun-loving, sensitive friend had been replaced by a tired, strung-out version. He wasn't sure he knew how to deal with this man.

Taking a side step toward the waste basket, he gracefully leaned over and retrieved the paper keeping his gaze on J.T. the entire time. "Hey, man, I'm sorry. I shouldn't have done that. I got out of hand but now I'm going to give this back to you," he said calmly, hoping to diffuse the situation.

He glanced at the paper before handing it back to J.T. It looked much different than anything else his friend had written. Rather than organized stanzas in a neat and heavily slanted script, a mess of words had been scribbled in an almost incoherent fashion. Phrases crowded the margins up and down both edges.

J.T snagged the paper but didn't change his defensive stance. He gave Rory a look that dared him to take it to the next level. Rory put his hands in the air. "I said I was sorry. We'll talk about this later."

He turned and walked out. As he walked through the doorway, J.T. mumbled something under his breath. Rory ignored it, hoping J.T. would get some sleep if left alone. He wanted to sort through the situation but J.T. needed to be cohesive and rational.

It was probably the first time he'd ever walked away from a fight but his friend was in an altered frame of mind. Rory was also keenly aware that the drug could give the user superhuman strength. He was unwilling to put it to the test in his tired and worn-out state.

A few hours later, Rory decided to head to the makeshift gym. A bit of exercise would loosen up his stiff muscles and joints. At the very least, he hoped to burn off the lingering tension over J.T.'s recent behavior.

Some of the soldiers had set up a basketball hoop in the covered area just outside the weight room. There they could play out of the sun's intense rays on days when it wasn't too hot. He spotted J.T. playing with a small group and decided to join them.

"Ahh yeah, boys, ready to play some real ball?" He taunted. He was suddenly feeling ornery.

The guys had just been messing around, but now they had an even number and split into teams to play three on three. They played as men do, talking smack as they made baskets and showed off their skills. Within minutes, they were all dripping sweat. It soaked through their t-shirts and stung their eyes. Rory's height gave him a huge advantage over J.T. and one of the other men. He couldn't resist slam-dunking the ball more than once.

"How do ya like me now?" he goaded, enjoying the first real release of stress in over a month.

Normally J.T. was a good sport, taking the jibes as well as he could dish them out. But he revealed his lingering anger as he clenched his fists. He was itching to put Rory in his place.

Instead of responding with a quick quip, he picked off the ball the next time Rory had it. He took it over the boundary line before bringing it back to the hoop for a slick lay up. His team high-fived him but J.T.'s jaw stayed clenched. His expression was taut with aggression.

The next time Rory had the ball and it looked as if he might dunk it, John Thomas side-swiped him. He plowed his right shoulder into Rory's side just below his ribs as he jumped toward the rim. Rory fell with a huge thud. His left shoulder slammed against the floor at an awkward angle and he felt something inside pull beyond its limits.

# The Complexity of a Soldier

J.T. ignored the fact that he had probably just really hurt his best friend and simply scooped up the ball for another lay up. The pain in Rory's shoulder was agonizing but the flash of his temper was much more intense. He shot to his feet, gripping his sore shoulder while he ran down the court, his vision focused only on his target.

The other men were initially stunned as they watched the scene unfold. They tried to decide if the two friends were just messing with each other in good fun or if things were truly getting nasty. They caught a glimpse of Rory's unhindered fury as he picked up his pace in pursuit of J.T. They stepped in to keep the altercation from going from bad to worse.

Rory made it to J.T. and pounced, delivering a solid punch to his jaw as he straddled him. Before any real damage was done, he was pulled off. As he was lifted away, J.T. kicked out. The toe of his shoe struck his temple.

"What the fuck, J.T! What in the hell is your problem?" Rory bellowed as he lunged again.

The other four put all of their combined physical strength into keeping the two of them apart. Rory was fuming mad as he struggled to get out of their grip and wrap his brain around how to deal with J.T. The drugs were an escalating problem and were altering his personality.

Taking everyone by surprise, he suddenly started to rant incoherently.

At first, no one could understand him as he growled through gritted teeth, spittle spraying from his strained lips. Then his speech became clearer. They listened as his torment surfaced over and spilled out in a torrent of blame and accusation.

"No one has even spoken a word about it since it happened," he shouted. "I mean what the hell does that say about us? That guy shot his entire family with an automatic weapon, just to keep us from harming them." His voice was raspy from fatigue.

"We are supposedly over here to fight terrorism but who are the real terrorists? That was a family trying to live their lives and we go busting into their home, their home for Christ sake!" His fury turned into a desperate sort of plea, confused with pain. "With guns and bombs going off all around them, a husband and father takes one look at us with our agenda and rifles, and decides to take matters into his own hands rather than let his family be subjected to us for another second."

He managed to break from their grasp. Rather than charging Rory again, he pushed his shoulders back defiantly, daring anyone to challenge his next statement. "Not one of you assholes has even mentioned that day but I can't seem to get it out of my damn head. So obviously something must be wrong with me, right? Well, fuck that and fuck you!"

With that he turned and stormed out of the covered area and into the building, without glancing back.

Two men still had a grip on Rory and he shook them off. He should have known what had been eating J.T. It still weighed heavy in his own mind. Coupled with the drugs, it didn't surprise him J.T. had finally snapped. He scanned the faces of the other men.

"Who has been giving those pills to J.T.?" he asked.

No one spoke up. Stepping forward aggressively, he snarled, "I want to know who gave him that crap."

Finally Josh offered, "Chad gets it from one of the higher ups but no one knows who. You can talk to him about it."

Rory's posture relaxed slightly. "I'll be sure to do that."

Later that evening, after Rory had politely informed Chad that if he ever gave J.T. those pills again he would rip off his arms and shove them in an extremely sensitive area, he grabbed dinner.

## The Complexity of a Soldier

Rather than eating in the cafeteria, he headed to his room. J.T. was passed out face down on his single bed. His body had finally shut down from physical and emotional fatigue. He stared down at him and felt as if he were staring at a brother. *He's family,* he thought and slowly backed out, relieved that J.T. had finally wound down enough to fall asleep.

~~~~~~~~~~~~

J.T. passed out around five-thirty in the afternoon. He woke thirteen hours later, at six-thirty a.m., feeling nauseated and jittery. He slowly sat up and tried to recall the last time he'd eaten anything and assumed his blood sugar was low.

"Ugh, I feel like crap!" He mumbled and dragged his hand over his stubbly face.

He needed to report to work in half an hour, so he dressed and shaved quickly. He hoped to grab something with protein before starting his shift. Rory was nowhere to be seen. Embarrassing flashes of the previous day's events slowly trickled in. He felt ashamed of his actions and relieved he could put off facing his friend for the better half of the day when he would feel better, stronger.

After reporting to his superior officer, he found somewhere to sit, still shaky and covered with a clammy sweat. His body was having a hard time coming off of the drugs and he knew it would probably get worse before it got better. He had been popping the little yellow pills for most of the past month, enjoying how strong and powerful it made him feel.

Now that he looked back, he realized it was a crutch. It allowed him to feel tough when what he really wanted to do was crawl into a hole and cry. Ever since the incident with the family in the village, he had been unable to get the bloody vision out of his mind. It haunted even his dreams. He couldn't shake the queasiness that had settled into the pit of his stomach and the last thing he wanted was for everyone to know how poorly he was dealing with the stress. It was hard for him to admit even to himself.

Rory was right. He needed to stay away from that stuff. And he was determined to do so, but first he needed to face his friend and own up to his childish behavior. Unfortunately, his body had a different opinion about it. His thoughts were disjointed and scattered all day. He began to obsess about getting his hands on more of the feel-good so he could get rid of the shakes and the cramps clenching his gut.

By the time his shift was over, he had passed the worst of it. When he felt inclined to hunt down Chad, he steered himself in the opposite direction. He wanted to find Rory, who would be leaving his post soon. If he didn't do it now, he never would.

~~~~~~~~~~~~

Rory spotted J.T. just as he was reporting off. He still had a nervous look but it wasn't the same wild-eyed, drug-induced frenzy of the day before. J.T. approached warily, still in his uniform.

"Hey, do you want to go get a beer or something?" he asked.

They obviously weren't going to be addressing the incident from the day before just yet. Slapping him on the shoulder, Rory said, "You look like you could use a beer. So could I."

They marched to the canteen, picked up two beers and settled themselves on the back stairs of their barracks. Rory sat on the top stair with his long legs stretched out. J.T. took the second and propped his elbows up on his knees. They enjoyed the cold, yeasty drink as it slid down their throats. There was still plenty of light left in the long June day but the air cooled rapidly as the sun dipped low in the sky.

"Hey, man, I'm sorry about wigging out on you yesterday," J.T. said. "This place has been getting to me."

Rory knew he was purposely avoiding the pills but also recognized it was unnecessary to state the obvious. "It's okay, dude. I probably deserved it for being so cocky during the game." He shifted then added, "You know you're not the only one struggling with the things we've seen or done."

He cleared his throat. Talking like this had never been one of his strong suits.

"I shot that young boy only minutes after that man killed his family. I didn't want to shoot him. He looked about the same age as my brother but he had a grenade in his hand and hate in his eyes. I had no choice. I can't forget the way his body went rigid from the impact of the bullets then went limp and fell to the ground as life left him. I did that."

His voice trailed off as the images played before his eyes. He was back there once again. It wasn't the first time, nor would it be the last. He desperately wished he could take that moment back and recreate it so the end result would be different, so the boy would still be alive. J.T. perked up as his best friend admitted his personal struggles with the things they were doing and had witnessed in the desert.

He too cleared his throat. In a hushed voice he asked, "What the hell are we doing here, Rory?"

Rory knew the question was meant two ways. He was wondering why the two of them were there instead of living different lives, different careers, different paths. And he was questioning why their country had sent American soldiers into Iraq when supposedly the 911 terrorists were hidden in remote caves in

# The Complexity of a Soldier

Afghanistan. Most soldiers were beginning to feel antsy. They had yet to find any evidence of weapons of mass destruction, their primary objective toward removing Saddam Hussein from power.

No one questioned whether Saddam's regime had been terrible. But now that he had fallen from power and was on the run, the country was in a complete state of disarray close to complete anarchy. Because the upset had been initiated by the U.S. invasion, the soldiers would have to remain in the country for an extended period of time to stabilize the unrest until they could reestablish some form of a democratic government. All of that, though true, left them hollow inside. They found no concrete answers to justify their role or their sacrifice.

Rory sipped his beer even though it was no longer cold. "I don't think we're supposed to question the why, J.T. We just need to keep our noses to the ground, watch each others' backs, and finish out our tour of duty so we can get home to our families."

J.T. blew into his bottle and listened to the deep sound that echoed out. "That's the problem. I'm starting to realize that I might not be the type to just go with the system because I'm told to."

"Well, then you're in the wrong business, J.T. That's the military mentality, their code. Follow orders, don't ask questions. It's weird because that's the exact modus operandi our founding fathers were adamant about breaking away from. We weren't supposed to depend on a military industrial complex economy." He shook his head.

"But that's where things are at now and who's going to change it? It would take a major movement, a revolution, but that's not going to happen. People are too busy trying to keep their heads above water, a roof over their heads, maybe put their kids through college so they might not have to do what we're doing.

"I'm just as bad as the rest of them. I don't want to rock the boat by asking a lot of questions either. I know that sounds terrible but I just want to get back to see my little girl grow up. I think most of these men feel the same way. They know something is rotten in Denmark but don't want to be the one to sacrifice themselves by calling attention to the real issues."

J.T. stood up and began to pace around. "Look, I hear what you're saying I'm just not sure I'm cut out for sticking my head in the sand like that anymore." He let out a raspy, half-hearted laugh. "My dad would kick my philosophizing rebel ass, and tell me I wasn't good enough to wear this uniform with this pretentious attitude, if he heard me right now."

Rory laughed. He had never met J.T.'s parents but he'd heard enough about them and their views to know John Thomas wasn't exaggerating. He felt compelled to lighten the mood and passed along Abby's message. He filled him in on how Emily and Callie were doing. Soon enough they were laughing as he relayed one of the recent stories Emily had shared.

The weekend before, Emily had decided she and Abby needed a girl's night out. Emily took Callie to her mom's house. They apparently had way too many Liquid Cocaine shots and ended up doing karaoke to *Like a Virgin*, in front of an entire bar filled with their old high school buddies. Much to Emily's chagrin, one of the girls they were hanging out with had a video recording feature on her cell phone. She'd spammed it to everyone they knew via email by the next morning.

Rory and J.T. could both picture Abby participating in such a scene. Both found it amusing to picture sweet, innocuous Emily singing her heart out to a bad Madonna song. It was just the sort of comic relief they'd needed.

"Oh, I gotta see that!" J.T. allowed himself to bask in the temporary stress release as he laughed with Rory.

# CHAPTER TWELVE

# Home Sweet Home

Life on the compound carried on as usual for the next five months. As the facility eventually exceeded its maximum detainee capacity by hundreds, it began to feel crowded. The staff grew and had to build expansions to facilitate the rapid growth and meet the demands.

Rory was still wary of how J.T was coping. Although he was clean and hadn't displayed any overt outbursts, he was uncharacteristically reserved and subdued.

Considering Rory didn't really feel much himself, he could empathize with J.T.'s struggles. His own mind was often distracted and wandered as he replayed shooting that young Iraqi boy. The memory would sneak up on him when he was least expecting it and an immediate, unshakable dread would fill his insides. The simple realization that he had ended the child's life felt unbearably final. He wished he'd had the mental wherewithal to have only injured the boy.

# The Complexity of a Soldier

He compared his own state of mind to the atypical and distorted way of life they were expected to adjust to. Their individual coping mechanisms were being tested, and it wasn't surprising that many soldiers exhibited obvious distress in their miserable situation.

Rory and J.T. both officially fulfilled their one year tour of duty on November 8th, 2003. They couldn't have been more ecstatic when they received paperwork reporting the exact day they were to be flown out of the compound on a Chinook. They would be taken to Camp Victory, one of the largest Army airfields located only about five kilometers from the Bagdad International Airport. The base could house up to fourteen thousand troops, making it a small city in and of itself. It even had its own man-made lake.

When they touched down, they were led to sleeping quarters. They would stay the night before catching the seven a.m. flight out of the country. While stowing their gear in the large barrack, another soldier told them the best place to grab dinner and drinks.

"Now, that's what I'm talking about!" J.T. exclaimed.

Rory chuckled. "I can't get away from this place fast enough."

Both were clearly anxious to get home. A night out was the perfect way to pass the time. Otherwise their nerves would get the best of them and drag the night out endlessly as they watched the clock.

Around six o'clock they followed the soldiers' directions. The fairly large restaurant and lounge stood just slightly off the official base grounds. They were surprised when they walked in and found the place packed with soldiers and many of the locals. Rory surmised that since it was located just on the other side of the base, soldiers could go somewhere where their nightly activities weren't so heavily regulated but still be in a safe zone.

The restaurant was dark and blanketed in a heavy layer of smoke. American rock and roll played on the jukebox while dark-skinned waitresses flittered around in their short, butt-grazing pink skirts passing out drinks and Jello shots. J.T. took one look at the barely clad women and his dormant hormones kicked into overdrive. "Hot damn! Why didn't we have a place like this at Camp Hopper?"

Rory snorted. "Because of responses like that. Let's go sit down and get a drink so you can cool your jets, hot rod."

An hour later they were finishing up some of the best barbequed pork sandwiches either of them had ever eaten and polishing off their third beer. They were full and blissful as the alcohol coursed throughout their systems. A squat Iraqi gentlemen wearing a backwards Red Sox baseball cap, looking like a wanna-be gangsta, hopped up on a podium in the corner. He began to set up for the karaoke. Rory leaned back rubbing his full belly.

"You gonna sing for us tonight, Elton?" he teased, hoping his friend would give the place a show worth writing home about.

J.T. flashed a sideways grin. "First of all, this place could never appreciate a lyrical genius such as the great Sir Elton John. Second of all, I would have to be drunker than this to get up there and sing in front of this crowd."

Rory waived over one of the waitresses. "I'm sure that can be arranged." He was determined to leave the country with at least one redeemable memory.

He ordered two double Glen Fiddich scotch whiskeys and scanned the room while they waited for their drinks. The place was filled with soldiers who missed home. They were trying to drown out the experience of being enemies in a foreign land. They were men hoping they could, even if for only one night, pretend they weren't risking their lives for an agenda that at that point was arguable on many levels. As the waitress negotiated the crowd with her drink tray precariously balanced on her palm, J.T. leaned into Rory.

# The Complexity of a Soldier

"She's pretty, eh? I mean, look at her. She's incredible."

"We're gonna be home in two day's time. Abby's been waiting a long dang time for you."

J.T. growled, "I know, I know but dang, it's tempting." Then he eyeballed his friend. "Don't tell me you're not at least tempted, Rory. I know how much you love Emily but a man's a man. And like you said, it has been a long time."

Rory shook off the comment, refusing to give J.T. any fuel. He was grateful when the waitress finally headed their way, drinks in hand. When she placed the full tumblers on their table, she bent down and reached directly in front of Rory, all but sticking her cleavage in his face. J.T.'s jaw dropped. She gave Rory a sly smile before sauntering off with a perfected swing of her hips. "Oh, come on!" he practically shouted. "Now, how is a guy supposed to behave with that sort of thing going on right in front of his nose?"

Rory drug his gaze from the rocking motion of those teasing hips. "It's hard."

Instantly realizing the pun he had walked right into, he cringed.

"Yeah, I'll just bet it is! I'll ask again. How are we supposed to get through the night without pledging our souls to the devil?"

Rory tossed the amber drink to the back of his throat and swallowed it down in one burning gulp, "By drinking until we couldn't function even if we wanted to. That's how."

Though J.T. looked reluctant to completely rule out signing a deal with the devil, especially if she had a saucy smile and swinging hips, he followed Rory's example. Aiming for supreme inebriation, he chased down his own shot. He slammed the glass onto the table.

"I agree, and now that I am close to adequately intoxicated, I will sing a song in celebration of my love for women." He stood up to put in his karaoke request with the deejay.

# The Complexity of a Soldier

Thirty minutes and three more drinks later, he was called to perform the song of his choice. Rory turned to face the stage so he could watch his extremely intoxicated friend entertain the gregarious crowd. J.T. palmed the microphone in his virile grip, claiming the stage and coaxing the audience's attention as he waited for the introductory bars of the Aerosmith song to finish. The crowd was loose and carefree by the time he belted out the first lyrics.

"Pink, it's my new obsession, Pink it's not even a question," he sang in his best Steven Tyler impersonation.

Rory busted up. The song fit the evening's mood with its heavy sexual innuendos. He joined the rest of the bar to sing the chorus. "Pink, it was love at first sight, Pink when I turn out the lights."

He was completely wasted but enjoyed every minute of it. He would head home in the morning to his wife and child.

He watched J.T. give the performance of a lifetime. The audience ate it up. Rory was relieved that his friend seemed to be feeling better than he had for months. It appeared as if he was slowly melding back into the J.T. that everyone knew and loved.

~~~~~~~~~~~~~

*Why was it taking so long? This is physically painful.* Emily imagined that she was either going to explode or faint as she waited for Rory and J.T.'s flight to touch down. She was at the same spot she'd been when Rory had left one year earlier. Bent over a coloring book, she colored intensely as she tried to keep three-year-old Callie as well as herself busy.

Abby, had made the drive from Oregon with her the day before. She paced anxiously while sipping the cold coke she had retrieved from the vending machine. Emily knew how nervous she was to see

# The Complexity of a Soldier

J.T. She had convinced herself over the last year that his affection had most likely waned. He would be disgruntled to see her waiting for him and expecting their relationship to pick up where it had left off.

Emily repeatedly assured her that it wasn't true but had eventually given up. Abby had an annoying habit of tuning out anything anyone said once she got something into her head.

Suddenly a large group of the women and families that were also waiting rushed toward the far terminal. In a flurry of excitement, they'd formed a tightly packed circle of impatient bodies. Although Emily wanted to dash into the crowd, she kept Callie out of the pressing mass. She sat wringing her hands as her eyes darted around, looking for a familiar face.

From a distance she heard Abby whisper, "This is it! I shouldn't have come."

Then she stopped pacing and stood frozen for a long time. She surveyed the scene with alert and guarded vigilance. Suddenly she leaped forward and ran toward J.T as he emerged from a cluster off to the left. She stopped right before she reached him, her face apprehensive. When he threw out his arms and gave her a "where's my kiss?" look, she jumped into his arms and practically knocked him off his feet.

Emily stood slowly. Her heart thudded in her ears as she watched Rory's tall form emerge from the chaos. He was searching the crowd. When she locked eyes with him for the first time in twelve months, her heart stopped then started again.

She rushed forward. She couldn't get to him fast enough. When they finally embraced, she broke down and cried. The familiar feel of him was such a relief. He looked so handsome. She couldn't believe he was finally home. She only wanted to pull him tighter until they found a way to melt into each other.

# The Complexity of a Soldier

"Rory, Rory. I love you! Oh, I'm so glad you're home."

Callie stood up from her coloring book and slowly walked over to her parents. Emily had shown Callie her daddy's picture nearly every day he'd been away so she would recognize him. She wanted to avoid a repeat of the other time he'd returned home. She hadn't shared that with Rory. She could see by his hesitation he was expecting to give his little girl time to get reacquainted.

She watched him look down into Callie's face. For her, the daily changes in her daughter had been subtle but for Rory, the changes would be drastic. She had lost nearly all of her baby fat and now looked like a big girl with her hair in long pigtails. He only smiled. He wouldn't pressure her or make her nervous. He looked pensive, exhilarated, wary and amazed, as he processed how much she had grown.

Callie smiled shyly, and said in a small, sweet voice, "Hi, daddy."

His face betrayed his relief. He bent over and held out his arms. She slowly walked into them and allowed him to pick her up.

"Oh Callie girl, I missed you so much!" He smelled her wonderful shampoo scent as his heart melted.

Emily breathed as sigh of relief. She was just glad she had been able to help their reunion go smoother this time.

~~~~~~~~~~

After they spent the designated week being officially debriefed, evaluated, and counseled for signs of post-traumatic stress, Rory and J.T. were given a month-long leave of absence. As soon as their leave started, they made the drive to Baker City. Rory wanted nothing more than to see his parents and brother. Being home would help him shake off the past year.

## The Complexity of a Soldier

His mom was in the kitchen cooking dinner when she turned and saw her eldest son standing in the doorway. She nearly dropped the tea kettle. "My boy!" was all she managed to squeak out as she flung her slender arms around his waist and pressed her cheek to his chest.

He held her and asked, "Where's dad and Rodney? Out in the fields?"

He didn't wait for an answer. As he stepped out onto the front porch, he found himself standing face to face with his father. Justin took one look at his mirror image with a shorter haircut and gave him a firm hug. Slapping him hard on the back, he said, "Welcome home, son."

Rory heard the familiar sound of the snowmobile racing across the field. His brother didn't even bother to unhook the gate. He simply parked the vehicle, leaped over the fence and ran up the drive. With a huge grin on his face, he looked like a very tall little boy.

*Little brother,* Rory thought as he leaped off the porch and met him halfway. There was no awkward moment. There was only two brothers who had missed each other greatly and where glad to be standing together again on the land where they had grown up. They hugged briefly but Rory couldn't resist. He promptly put Rodney in a headlock, throwing his snowcap to the ground and ruffling his dark brown hair. Everything was still as it should be.

The women and J.T. had stepped out onto the porch to enjoy the reunion.

# CHAPTER THIRTEEN

# Unsettled

J.T. spent a full week at Abby's house before boarding a plane for Montana. He would spend the upcoming Thanksgiving holiday with his family. After Abby dropped him at the airport she drove to the tiny house Emily had rented for the duration of Rory's deployment. The couple had invited her to join them for dinner. Since she was itching to talk to them about a few things, she accepted. For most of her visit, she and Emily talked quietly while they watched Rory and Callie play on the living room floor. "It's so good to see them together again, Abby whispered. "I know you missed him but he had to have missed you just as much if not more. He was all alone over there except for J.T."

Emily stared at them with a wistful smile. "I know. At least we had our friends and family. At least I had you. I'm just so glad he's here. Sometimes I look at him and wonder how in the world an entire year has passed. I have to pinch myself."

She glanced in Abby's direction as her expression turned

157

serious. "I don't know if I could handle it if he ever had to leave for that long again."

"Well, with this war going on, you just don't know what's going to happen, Emily. But let's not think about. He's here now and that's what matters."

They sat down at the dining room table to enjoy the hot meal. Rory asked, "So, Abbs, we didn't see you much over the last week while J.T. was in town. How was your visit?"

Abby laughed. "It was pretty good. We stayed home a majority of the time." She blushed. "Anyway, we had a nice dinner down at the Geyser Grand Hotel. That place is incredible since they remodeled it. We caught a movie one night. I did have the hilarious experience of shopping with him for Christmas gifts for his mother. That guy couldn't make a decision to save his life and he hasn't got a clue what a woman might want. I finally led him to the jewelry department and he picked up a nice sapphire necklace. She's gonna love it."

She paused for a moment. "Did you guys drink a lot over there?" She looked at her plate, clearly uncomfortable with the directness of her question.

Rory grabbed the mashed potatoes for a second helping. "No, not really. Too busy for that kind of stuff. Why?"

Abby shrugged. "I don't know. It's just that he's been drinking pretty heavily every night since he got back. I was just curious if it was a habit he developed over the past year, or if it was just his way of relaxing during his first week back." She took a sip of her red wine.

Rory glanced at Emily. She peered at him expectantly, gauging his response, but he remained quiet. Something she couldn't quite identify passed over his face. "Maybe he's using it to get to sleep. Sometimes it's hard to adjust to a different time zone, and it is a radically different lifestyle here. In Iraq our schedules made it hard to establish a healthy sleeping pattern, to say the least. Most of us have had difficulty with insomnia. I'm not all that surprised he's struggling with it as well."

Abby gave him a look. It was clear that neither of them were satisfied with his explanation. She placed her wrists on the edge of the table as a solemn expression captured her face.

"Well, that's the other thing," she said. "He isn't sleeping well at all. He's having bad dreams and he tosses and turns, moaning and sweating until the sheets are soaked. I try to wake him up but he usually shoots up off the bed. When he realizes where he is, he just heads to the bathroom to splash water on his face. I asked him about it once but he told me it was nothing. He didn't want to talk about it." She sighed, feeling frustrated and confused.

"I'm at a loss. I don't know what to do. Should I just give him space to work it out for himself, or do I try to get him to talk about whatever is eating at him?"

Rory leaned back and gave her a long, contemplative stare. "I guess giving him space would be fine for now. But I want to know if this keeps up. The dreams and the drinking, I mean. Maybe I can talk to him." He paused then continued.

"Listen, Abby, the stuff that went on over there is nothing I would want to share with the people I love, either. I know that sounds backward but it was bad enough that it happened at all. The last thing I want is to spread it around for others to think about. I'm sure that's how J.T. feels, which explains why he won't talk to you about it. I don't want you to take it personal. Okay?"

His words struck her hard. Suddenly she felt sad for J.T and Rory and everything they must have gone through. But she also felt happy and grateful they were home safe. She swallowed around the lump in her throat and nodded. "Okay."

# The Complexity of a Soldier

~~~~~~~~~~

J.T. returned from Montana during the third week of his leave. He was distant and disgruntled, and Abby again voiced her concerns to Rory and Emily. "I'm keeping my promise to give him space but it's becoming increasingly difficult to see past his moods," she said.

Rory noticed his behavior right away. He figured it had something to do with the interaction he'd had with parents. He decided to snag the snowmobiles and took J.T. up the mountain. He claimed he needed to gather firewood for his mom, hoping the isolation in nature would allow J.T. to open up.

He hitched up one of the small trailers. After they wolfed down one of his mom's famously large breakfasts, they set out into the cold. An hour later, they had taken down a few small lodge poles with the chainsaw. Halfway through the chore of chopping them down to firewood size, they took a coffee break. They were both sweating despite the cold so as soon as they stopped working, the dampness cooled them off dramatically. They slipped into their jackets.

Rory pulled off his gloves and grabbed the thermos and homemade cinnamon rolls his mom had packed. His warm breath plumed into white puffs as it hit the icy air. He took a swig of the bitter coffee and reveled in the way it instantly warmed his insides. *Ahh, thanks mom,* he thought.

"Don't be stingy." J.T. snagged the thermos out of his grip.

Rory didn't waste anymore time. "So, how was your trip to Montana? How are your folks doing?"

John Thomas gave his friend a sideways glance as he capped the thermos and reached for a cinnamon roll. "My mom's fine. She was glad to see me and kept talking about girls she wants me to meet. She wants me to settle down and give her grandchildren in the worst way. I should probably tell her about Abby."

A small smile tugged at his mouth before it shifted into bitterness and resentment. "Dad," he sighed, "is dad. He's set in his ways and can't open his mind enough to even think about different perspectives, much less entertain the idea that someone else might be right."

*Here we go,* Rory thought. He kept silent and waited to see if J.T. would elaborate further, or if he would need to be prodded along.

J.T. swallowed a large chunk of roll and washed it down with hot coffee. "I asked him about his time in the Vietnam War and heard the same stories he always regurgitated while I was growing up. When I tried to talk to him about the politics surrounding it, he said it wasn't his place to question things like that. It was his job to defend the country at all costs. It really irked him the way the Veterans were treated when they got home. So I tried a different approach. I tried to get him to talk about the current administration and the war on terrorism in Iraq, but he switched gears on me real quick." J.T. clenched his fist.

"Then he got his smarmy little snicker going before he said, "There goes my know-it-all son. Thinking he knows more than everyone else and questioning authority. What do you know about life, son? You think you got it all figured out? You gonna write a poem about your enlightened knowledge so the rest of us can get a clue, boy?"" J.T's voice boomed out with anger as he mimicked his father.

"God, he makes me feel so small." J.T. blurted out. "He always has. What I wouldn't give to punch him in the face just once." He cleared his throat. "What an asshole!"

## The Complexity of a Soldier

He shoved his hands back into his gloves, grabbed the ax, and stomped off into the trees.

Rory wiped his mouth with the back of his plaid shirt sleeve and followed J.T. into the dense forest. Now maybe his friend would be able to shake it off.

~~~~~~~~~~~~

As Rory and J.T. drove back down the mountain, they spotted an unfamiliar car in his parents' driveway. They parked the snowmobiles and put a large tan canvas tarp over the wood to keep it dry until it could be stacked in the woodshed.

They entered the house through the back and stripped off their dirty top layer of clothing in the mud room. Rory strained to identify the voices in the living room. Emily and Callie had stayed at the house to help Sarah bake cookies and do her chores. Callie's high-pitched giggle brought a smile to his face.

Emily poked her head through the doorframe and whispered, "Your uncle is here."

Rory's eyebrows rose. "Really? Uncle Travis is here? That car doesn't look like his style."

Emily she shook her head, "No. It's the other one, your Uncle Tristian."

Rory's brow furrowed. "Uncle Tristian? We haven't heard from him since I was like seven years old or something. He's my mom's youngest brother and they're not very close. The last I heard, he had served some time in jail for stealing or drugs, I don't know, maybe both."

Emily was wide eyed as her husband mulled over the estranged uncle's sudden arrival. She shrugged. "Well, he's here now and your mom has been visiting with him for the past hour. Now that you mention it, she did seem a little awkward around him. I thought it seemed so unlike her. It makes sense now."

Rory stepped into the warm living room where his mother sat on the hearth of the blazing fire. His Uncle Tristian sat on the couch with his feet propped up on the coffee table. His hair was wavy and greasy. It needed a wash. His clothes looked clean but wrinkled. He appeared road weary but had a smile on his face. The men locked gazes as the uncle stood up and shuffled around the table to greet his nephew. He was only about five nine and Rory towered over him. He had a firm grip though.

"Damn, boy! You're the spitting image of your father, and got his height, too."

Even though Tristian seemed amicable, something about him made his skin crawl. He remembered the same feeling from when he was young. He pulled back and shoved both his hands into his pockets, stifling the urge to cringe. Sarah had risen from the hearth.

"Your Uncle Tristian was passing through on his way to the coast and stopped by to say hi," she said. "Isn't that nice?"

Rory heard the tightness in her voice. It was so different from her typically warm and inviting behavior he knew she was trying to hide her own discomfort around her brother.

Tristian said, "Yeah, I got a job offer over in Coos Bay. I'm supposed to start first thing next week, so I figured I'd stop in and see how my big sister was doing these days. Man, I can't believe how time flies. You were just a little squirt the last time I saw you."

*Why are you here now?* Rory wondered. He wanted to know more about his uncle's past.

"Where are you coming from?" He gave Tristian a direct stare. He knew he was being disrespectful, rude even, but couldn't stop the nagging need to establish his protective role in the family. He needed to assess how trustworthy this man was.

# The Complexity of a Soldier

His uncle offered a toothy grin. "Oh, you know. I was down south for a few years but I got a little burnt out on the dry heat and decided it was time to head for the ocean. So I got on the internet and started looking around. I found a job working for parks and recreation doing like landscaping and maintenance stuff. The pay is okay but it's right by the ocean so I'm gonna be sittin' fat and sassy right on the beach."

Rory noticed that he'd been vague about where exactly he had come from. It was weird that his reason for just up and moving was the weather but he clenched his jaw and kept his mouth shut. He reminded himself this was his mom's brother and not to jump to any paranoid conclusions just because he had spent some time in jail years ago.

Just then, Justin Nichols walked through the front door. He had stomped off his snowy boots before entering the house. "Hey, Tristian. I was wondering who's car that was outside. Man, I haven't seen you in, what, fifteen years or so?" His voice bellowed as he shook his brother-in-law's hand. He gave Sarah his usual peck on the cheek. "Rodney will be in shortly."

Sarah told him how Tristian had come to be there. Justin said, "You'll stay for dinner, won't you? You need a place to stay for the night, you can stay in Rory's old room."

"That would be fantastic. I could use a bit of rest before I hit the road again," Tristian said.

The men sat down while Emily followed Sarah into the kitchen to help with dinner.

~~~~~~~~~~~~~

An hour later, Rory still felt uncomfortable with his uncle's presence. He had to keep reeling himself in and refocusing as J.T.

and Rodney rambled about rock bands and concerts with Tristian. Apparently, his uncle had been something of a roadie. He bragged about all the famous concerts he'd seen during his lifetime.

Rory listened from a distance, thinking that although the stories of his exploits were fascinating, they were somewhat unbelievable. When he claimed to have been on the road with the Smashing Pumpkins for a short time, Rodney was hooked. He ate up the lascivious tales of wild parties. At one point, J.T. gave Rory a look that said he wasn't swallowing a word of it and was just humoring him. Rory smiled and kept his mouth shut.

After dinner, they gathered in the living room while Emily wrestled with Callie, trying to put her shoes on. She was tired and they wanted to get her to bed. Rory gathered their coats as his daughter pushed, whined and ignored her mother's demands. Tristian rushed over to Callie and swooped her little body up over his head. Just as quickly, he lay her back down on the carpet and began tickling her senseless. Callie was delighted. She giggled and squealed as she squirmed under Tristians fingers.

*Get your slimy hands off of my daughter,* Rory thought. Something unrecognizable twisted his gut and he swept Callie to her feet. Even he was surprised at his brisk and unfriendly behavior. "Come on, sweetie, it's time to go home now," he said.

Callie stomped her feet. "Aw, I don't want to go home yet, Daddy!"

Rory didn't want to argue with his recalcitrant daughter any longer. He picked her up, sat her on the couch and swiftly pushed her snow boots onto her feet before slipping on her pink jacket and lifting her into his arms. He kissed his mother on the cheek, said goodbye to his dad and Rodney then shook Tristian's hand.

"Good to see you again, hope you have safe travels," he said curtly then headed out the door with Emily and J.T. close behind.

# The Complexity of a Soldier

The first five minutes of the drive was silent. Emily could take it no longer and tentatively asked, "You don't like him, do you?"

*Not in the least,* he refrained from saying aloud, still perplexed at his own visceral reaction. He gave a heavy sigh. "It's not that I don't like him, really. There's just something about him I don't trust. I don't want you or Callie around him, okay?"

He rarely asked anything like that of her, and she was visibly taken aback by his demand but she agreed.

"Sure, honey, but I don't really think we have to worry about it anyway. He hasn't been around in nearly fifteen years and he's heading out first thing in the morning. We probably won't see him for another fifteen years."

She was restless as his uneasiness vibrated between them. Rory concentrated on navigating the icy roads. He was quiet for the rest of the drive as he tried to settle his nerves.

# CHAPTER FOURTEEN

# Nightmares

Abby was restless as Emily and Rory gathered their things for the drive up to Washington. Rory would report to his superiors and they would find a place to live off base. When J.T. offered to stay behind for another two days, they planned to make the road trip together during her days off. His offer soothed her anxieties a bit. He seemed committed to their relationship even though he was so clearly struggling inside.

Stepping out of the office where she worked at as a paralegal, she looked forward to an evening at home with her man. She decided to stop at the local grocer to grab a few necessities for dinner. She was pleasantly surprised when she got home and was greeted by the tantalizing scent of lasagna.

"Wow! That smells so good. Did you make that from scratch?" She planted a wet kiss on John Thomas' soft lips and caught the familiar lingering whiff of alcohol on his breath.

He smacked his lips. "Yep, it's my mother's recipe." He took a swig of the rum and coke he'd been sipping for the past hour.

*Don't say anything,* she warned herself, trying to squelch her rising frustration. It was his fifth straight night of drinking and her patience was wearing thin.

She sauntered toward her bedroom, stripping out of her pinstriped suit and kicking off her heels. *Give him time, give him space. Talk about something else.* She wriggled her sore feet and padded to her walk-in closet for her favorite comfy yoga pants and a sweatshirt.

When she returned to the kitchen, she was determined to relax and shed the worries of the day. She watched J.T. move easily about her kitchen and pulled the piping hot lasagna out of the oven. While he whipped the garlic butter, she sat on a high-backed stool at the counter.

"So, what's going on between us, J.T.?" she asked. The relaxed approach wasn't going to happen after all.

J.T. spread the butter thick over the long loaf without missing a beat. "Wow! You just get right to the point, don't you?" He sounded amused.

"Actually, I think we've both been skirting around the issue the entire time we've been dating, or hanging out, or whatever you call what we've been doing. I have just reached the point where I would like to know if this is going anywhere or if I should move on. It's been hard waiting this past year while you were gone so you could at least be honest with me about your expectations." Her hands trembled as she tried to maintain her composure.

John Thomas set the knife down and leaned against the counter. "Look, Abby, I really care about you--"

"Care about me?" she said incredulously.

J.T. sighed. "Okay, I love you. Is that better?" He stared daring her to say anything further.

# The Complexity of a Soldier

Abby blushed. He had never told her he loved her before. Her heart soared, but she nodded and kept her mouth shut.

He ran his fingers through his hair then swallowed down what was left in his glass. "I love you but I don't really see how we can take this relationship any further right now."

Her heart sank. "Well, how come?"

"Well, for one thing, you live out in the middle of nowhere and I am stationed in Fort Lewis, Washington. After I re-negotiate my contract, who knows where they will send me?"

Abby was confused. "Wait a minute. Why in the world would you sign up for another term? You hate being in the Army." She was overstepping her bounds with the assumptive statement but she didn't care. He had never said directly that he hated being in the military but it was obvious enough.

John Thomas awkwardly shifted his stance. "It doesn't really matter how I feel about my career. It's what I'm meant to do, and the only thing that I can do." His tone rang with defeated resignation.

"What the hell are you talking about? That sounds like your dad talking to me. You can do whatever the hell you please, and you don't need his permission to do it!" Her frustration seeped into her voice.

His anger flashed across his face with a quick spike but was almost instantly replaced by his earlier expression of fatigue. He sighed. She could literally hear the hopelessness engulf him. His desolation was palpable.

"Abby, I don't want to get into this with you. I love you and I want to keep on loving you but if you haven't noticed, I'm not quite right in the head right now. I need to think some things through before I can have this conversation, okay?"

Abby felt as if her heart were breaking. She looked into his sad blue eyes. Even though he had just told her he loved her, she couldn't help but feel like he was breaking up with her. She bit her bottom lip to fight back the tears. She couldn't stand the thought of losing him, especially to an unseen, intangible force.

She turned her back to hide her broken heart. She was relieved when he returned to preparing their meal. After a subdued dinner and after John Thomas had polished off the last of the rum, he passed out on the sofa. Abby put a soft blanket over his slack body rather than wake him. She turned off the lights and shuffled toward her room, still feeling rejected and confused. She wrapped her arms around herself to ward off the oppressive loneliness.

Around two a.m. she was awakened by the sound of a soft and tortured moaning. After a few moments, she realized J.T. was having one of his nightmares. Her mind groggy, she threw back the blankets and rushed to his side. It was one of the worst she had witnessed. His moans were guttural and his face was pinched and strained. Her gut clenched as she watched the man she loved struggle with hidden demons.

She remembered reading people should be woken from a dream slowly to avoid frightening them or causing them to lash out. She kneeled down and gently placed her fingertips on his brow. She crooned, "Shush now, it's okay, I'm here, J.T."

He bolted upright and grabbed her by the throat. She stared at him, wide-eyed with shock. His gaze was unfocused. His large hands choked her thin, fragile throat as her auburn hair tumbled over her shoulders.

It was unbearable to watch him grasp the situation. Raw, pure emotion slipped over his features. Shame was the most prominent. Then he broke. He simply caved, pulled her briskly to his chest and held her as he began to weep. He stroked her hair and kept repeating, "I'm so sorry, baby. I'm so sorry."

# The Complexity of a Soldier

Her heart was racing. She felt weak and helpless, and feared she would be unable to help him through the nightmares that plagued him. They felt so much bigger than she was, so much stronger, but she ran her fingers through his hair and tried to reassure him. "I'm fine. You just had a bad dream. I'm okay."

He gently took her face in his hands and looked into her pleading eyes. "I would never purposely hurt you, Abby."

"I know that, John Thomas." She kissed him with every ounce of her love, letting her soul pour into him.

"You're like an angel sent to heal my broken spirit."

"You're not broken, you're just wounded. It's going to take time to heal."

She showered him with kisses to chase away his pain. He melted into the open surrender she offered him. He ran his fingers through her thick, silky hair and took the kiss deeper. His passionate response told her what she meant to him.

"I love you, Abby. Everything is going to be alright." His voice was thick and betrayed his doubt. They made love slowly, tenderly, right there on the living room floor. When they were spent, J.T. took the last of his energy and scooped her up. He carried her to the bed where they fell asleep tangled in the sanctity of each others' arms.

~~~~~~~~~~~

Christmas of 2003 was both chaotic and wonderful. Rory and Emily rushed to settle into their new place before the holiday. They felt especially lucky to be spending it together knowing that thousands of Rory's fellow soldiers were still far from home.

Emily secured a job at one of the local banks and put Callie into a preschool. Rory went back to his police work on base just as he had before his deployment. Life started to feel normal again. Her parents drove up to babysit Callie so the couple could celebrate their fourth wedding anniversary. They stayed at the Four Seasons Hotel in downtown Seattle and watched the fireworks from the Space Needle. They spent money they didn't really have and relished every minute.

Throughout the following spring and summer, there was talk about how long American troops would be stationed in Iraq. The president's ratings had plummeted as the American public realized that their fears and emotions had been manipulated. There were no weapons of mass destruction to be found in Iraq. Osama Bin Laden was still supposedly hiding in a cave while American efforts to locate him dwindled.

There were many heated debates as to when and how to go about withdrawing troops. Although most wanted to pull them out right away, many realized that by being there in the first place, they had created a situation which was now much too volatile to walk away from. It slowly became apparent that America's forceful presence would have to remain for an indefinite amount of time.

Rory and J.T. saw many of their fellow soldiers sent off for their second tour of duty. It was only a matter of time before they too would go another round. So when their orders came in on a hot August afternoon just two weeks after Callie's fourth birthday, Rory stared at the paperwork with a weight of dread writhing in his gut.

He hated the thought of telling Emily. Although he had already prepared her for the inevitability, the feat still felt like too much to bear. His superior officer had warned his unit they would be called up before the end of the year. When he sat her down, her face was determined. She already knew what was coming. She was going to try her best to stay strong.

## The Complexity of a Soldier

"Well, at least it's only supposed to be nine months this time." She gave him a half-hearted smile.

Rory offered a thin-lipped grin in return. "That's true but they didn't give us much time to prepare. We're supposed to leave in just over two weeks."

Emily stood up and busied herself with folding the Winnie the Pooh blanket Callie had drug out earlier. "I know you're not going to be gone as long this time but I still want to go home until you get back."

"Whatever you need to do, Emily, I'll support your choice. I know this isn't easy for you or Callie, and Washington still doesn't feel like home. It's probably best for you both to have family around while I'm away."

He stood up and rubbed his hands down his jeans. He felt bad about leaving her just after delivering the news but he was anxious to catch up with J.T.

"I think I should go see how J.T. is taking the news. You know, feel it out. He hasn't been himself since we got back from the first deployment. I can't imagine he will be too thrilled about going back."

Emily agreed with a nod. "Yeah, I should give Abby a heads-up, too. While she was up for Callie's birthday, she asked me to keep her updated on any new developments, so I'll call her while you're out."

She crossed the living room with the blanket draped over her arm and gave him a goodbye kiss.

~~~~~~~~~~~~

At eight-thirty p.m., Rory rapped on the door of J.T.'s base apartment.

# The Complexity of a Soldier

"Door's open," his voice boomed.

Rory stepped into the dark foyer of the small downstairs unit. The room was dark and silent. As his eyes adjusted, he smelled what he thought was laundry detergent mixed with an overpowering whiff of whiskey.

*He must have put a healthy dose of liquor away already,* he thought as he closed the door. Stepping further into the living room, he spotted J.T. sitting in his Lazy Boy with his bottle of Jim Beam perched between his legs. The only light came from the low-watt bulb over the stove in the kitchen to the left. A few additional streams trickled in from the porch light through the sliding glass door.

John Thomas's drinking had only gotten worse recently. Rory wasn't surprised to see his friend two sheets to the wind. He stuffed his hands into his pockets and rocked back on his heels.

"I guess this means you're not real thrilled with the orders we received today?" he asked facetiously, hoping to break the somber mood.

J.T. chugged from the bottle then held it out. "Want a drink?"

Rory didn't think it would hurt to have one swig considering the situation. He palmed the bottle and enjoyed the fire as it slid down his throat. It burned almost as much as the thought of going back to Iraq did.

The two of them stayed silent.

Rory pulled the ottoman to the middle of the room and straddled it in an innocuous and open invitation for conversation. He patiently watched J.T.'s profile through the shadows, waiting for him to speak when he felt ready.

"I won't go back," was all he said.

Rory propped his elbows on his knees. "Okay," he prodded.

"I refuse to be another sheep in the herd," he gritted through

174

# The Complexity of a Soldier

clenched teeth.

The derogatory term was for people who went along with the status quo without questioning why. Rory remained neutral and waited for his friend to continue. J.T. stared at his blank television screen as if it held a hidden message. His voice was hollow when he spoke.

"You can look back throughout the history of man and see the exact same pattern over and over again. Each century has been filled with wars as kings, Caesars, and self-ordained divine rulers raped and pillaged in an attempt to own and control more people." His voice was raspy and haggard from the effects of the alcohol and lack of sleep.

"You think this is any different?" His dark eyebrows rose above the glassy sheen of his unfocused eyes, daring Rory to argue. A long heartbeat passed before he looked back at the television screen.

"Anyone too blind to see it is an idiot, and I refuse to be a pawn in another ruler's scheme to gain as much power and resources as he can. This war isn't about protecting the American people. There is oil in that damn country, and a holy war has been going on there for centuries. This is about a few elite men wanting more money, more land but most of all, more power.

"Between the overzealous infringement upon our own basic rights and freedoms from the genius of the Patriot Act, among other blatant constitutional violations, we are more vulnerable than ever to being terrorized. Except the danger isn't coming from outside. It's from our own big brother government as it looms over us in the name of homeland security." J.T.'s voice grew intense. He stared at a distant image playing in the back of his mind.

"Men like us, just want to raise a family and live an honest life but are living and dying while we wave the flag over our heads and claim to be patriotic heroes. In fact, you're labeled a traitor or a conspiracy theorist if you dare question the powers that be and their hidden motives.

"Well screw that! I refuse to go along just to get along. In my opinion, that's what it means to be an American. We didn't break from tyranny two hundred years ago just to fall right back into it again with blinders over our eyes."

As he finished, his hands shook. He gripped the bottle and finished off the last dregs.

"I'm not going back," he repeated. His anger consumed him as quickly as he consumed the alcohol.

Rory felt pulled in two directions. Part of him wanted to cheer his friend on as he voiced what so many soldiers had thought as they struggled with what it meant to be an American, a soldier, and the role they were playing in the future of their own children. Another part of him was scared and worried for the state he was in. He wondered how concerned he should be with J.T.'s well-being. He pulled in a deep breath and exhaled slowly. "Well, I could kick the crap out of you so they will release you from duty on medical leave," he suggested. The comment was meant for comic relief but he was half-serious.

It was hard to think of facing another deployment without his friend by his side, but it was also difficult to imagine J.T. tolerating it again and coming out of it stable. John Thomas let out a sick laugh. He shook his head as if shaking off the mood seething inside him.

"That's okay, Rory. I'll figure this out on my own. I just need to sober up and think it through. You go on home to that beautiful wife and child of yours, and let me finish wallowing for the evening. I'll see you first thing in the morning."

Rory knew it was getting late and he should leave, especially since J.T. was done talking for the moment and obviously wanted to be alone. He stood but was reluctant to leave.

"All right. I'll see ya in the morning." He walked to the door. "Hey, man. Get some sleep. We'll work it out."

"Rory," J.T. called out. "You're the best friend that I've ever had. I love you, man!"

Rory wasn't used to displays of affection but he simply answered, "Love you, too. Now get to bed."

He shut the door and tried to shake the feeling that he had somehow just failed his friend.

# CHAPTER FIFTEEN

# No Words

At four-thirty in the morning, one hour before Rory's alarm clock was due to go off, the telephone trilled into the dark of their bedroom. He knew before answering. He bolted upright, reached across Emily and grabbed the receiver off her nightstand. "No, no, no, no!" he prayed as he placed the phone to his ear. A deep sense of foreboding echoed through his body.

A police officer proceeded to tell him that at approximately one a.m., a neighbor in J.T.'s apartment complex heard the sound of a gunshot. They immediately called the police. Four officers entered John Thomas Jackson's unit and found him dressed in his Class A uniform sprawled out in his Lazy Boy with his M-9 pistol on the floor and a single bullet through the roof of his mouth.

Rory didn't have the wherewithal to realize he was white knuckled, rocking back and forth as he listened. He wanted to get off the damn phone. He wanted to crawl under the covers and go back to sleep so that when he woke, it would all have been just a

178

# The Complexity of a Soldier

horrible nightmare.

"There was a note found at the scene," the officer said. "It was addressed to you. When you come down to the station, you can have a look at it."

"Uh, yes, thank you. I'll be down as soon as possible."

He handed his wife the phone. His mind was still trying to reject reality but failed miserably. For the first time since they had been together, his wife saw the terrifying sight of her strong, resilient husband give in to grief as he broke down and cried.

~~~~~~~~~~~~

Rory wanted to go straight to J.T.'s apartment but of course the investigative team wouldn't allow it. He drove down to the station and was again debriefed on the current details. The lead investigator knew both Rory and J.T. well. "I hate to have to interview you, Rory, but it has to be done. Especially since you were the last person to see him."

Rory answered the questions as best he could. He felt like he was walking around in a numb haze. Every noise, every voice reverberated down his spine and set his nerves on edge. While his body felt over-stimulated by the sensory input, his mind was sluggish and dull. He was unable to sort through normal, everyday thoughts and activities. It was a dichotomy of self that left him reeling, vulnerable and unbearably raw.

After the interview was officially over, the investigator said, "I can't give this to you permanently because it's evidence but I will step out of the room and let you read it. Once the investigation is finalized, it's yours." He handed Rory a folded piece of notebook paper.

*What could you possibly have to say that would justify this?*

## The Complexity of a Soldier

Rory imagined that somehow J.T. could hear his frustration. *You were my brother, my friend. Why couldn't you just get it together?* But he withdrew those bitter questions, feeling guilty and remorseful at how he so quickly jumped to blame and resentment.

If he wanted to blame someone, he needed to blame himself. He had known his friend needed help and just couldn't step up to the plate. He walked out of that lonely, desolate apartment last night leaving J.T. alone with his despair. If he hadn't left in that crucial hour, if he had talked him through the hopelessness, he would still be here right now.

Again, he caught himself delving into toxic thoughts. He couldn't allow his personal blame and disgust to carry him further into depression. He gripped the note and played with the edges. He needed to read it. But he delayed for another minute. Reading the words would make it official. He waited until he no longer heard noises on the other side of the closed door. Then he unfolded the ominous note. His throat tightened. He dreaded reading the last few words his best friend had ever written. His heart clenched at the sight of the familiar, slanted scrawl.

*Rory,*

*Sorry no poetic words this time. I just don't have it in me. I want you to know that you, Emily, Callie and Abby mean the world to me. I know this departure is selfish but I know no other way at this point. Tonight I spoke of being unable to go along to get along but neither can I face those who expect exactly that of me.*

*I don't expect anyone to understand but I just cannot face my destiny any longer, nor can I fight it. I lost a battle*

# The Complexity of a Soldier

*tonight. Not one on the field of war but the one between my heart, mind and spirit. I truly love you all, and am sorry from the depths of my soul.*

*Love,*

*John Thomas*

*Damn it all to hell! Don't be sorry J.T. We are all the ones who should be sorry,* Rory thought as tears streamed down his face. He desperately wanted to crumple the paper up and punch anything within arm's reach, screaming until his chest burned and his voice gave out. Instead he sat there staring at the white wall across from him for what seemed like an eternity swimming in grief and anger. He wanted to get enough of it out so he could walk out of the room rather than crawl.

When he finally felt spent and began to embrace another round of simply being numb again, he methodically folded the note and composed himself enough to leave the confines of the small, windowless office.

~~~~~~~~~~~~

J.T.'s parents arranged to have their son's body flown home to Montana. The services would be held in the community he'd grown up with. Rory and Emily decided to have a small service of their own before he left. Abby arrived two days before the memorial. She and J.T's fellow soldiers would pay tribute and say goodbye.

Emily drove Rory insane with her incessant worrying. He was just as concerned about Abby making the long drive north in her terrible emotional state, but there was nothing either of them could do about it. Cell phones helped her keep in touch throughout the day. Abby seemed to be managing well.

As soon as she pulled into their driveway, Emily rushed outside to embrace her. Rory watched from the front door. Abby's entire being looked strained as if it had been physically painful to keep her emotions in check during the drive. She stepped out of the car with a rigidity that came from more than just road fatigue.

When Emily enveloped her in a welcoming embrace, her body relaxed. She leaned heavily into her friend. The intense wave of grief washed over her as she shed the last bit of strength she had clung to for the previous fourteen hours. Rory stepped out onto the porch. Her broken heart poured out of her eyes and spilled onto the sidewalk.

Abby stepped away from Emily and ran into his outstretched arms.

"Why?" she sobbed. "Why, Rory, why?"

Rory felt stupid and helpless because he hadn't any answers for her. "Come on, sweetie. Let's get you inside."

Rory and Emily forced her to eat a small portion of soup while she rambled on with stories about J.T. Her mood fluctuated rapidly. One moment she laughed as she reminisced about some hilarious adventure they had enjoyed together; the next she cried hysterically as reality again slammed into her with an unforgiving force.

Abby was so free with her emotions, it was impossible for Rory to run from his own. Her anger, her grief, her despair reflected his own spiraling emotions. He soon feared that he would drown in the whirlwind of them.

~~~~~~~~~~~~

Two days later, the three stood inside the small, bright chapel. The heat from the sun radiating into its small space left it hot and stifling. Friends of John Thomas took turns speaking on behalf of the man they were determined to honor.

Abby whimpered into her handkerchief. Her salty tears flowed freely as soldier after soldier told humorous and touching stories about how incredibly funny and generous John Thomas had been. They even quoted a few of his infamous poetic sayings.

Everyone kept looking to Rory, curious as to whether he would have anything to offer. He could feel their unspoken expectations. They wanted heartfelt, memorable words that would honor his friend's life and help them understand the senseless act. They wanted him to bring them peace.

He stood up and in a flat, hollow tone said, "I wish I could stand here today and put into words the impact J.T. had on me and my family. I wish I had powerful and worthy words that would pay adequate tribute to my best friend. But I'm afraid there are no words that will do justice. I'm sorry."

Unable to continue, he cut in front of the pews and strode out the side door. He had nothing to offer them.

# CHAPTER SIXTEEN

# Second Deployment

Despite his all-consuming grief, Rory still had to prepare for his deployment, now only a week away. He asked his commanding officer for two days off. He personally drove Abby, Emily and Callie home to Baker City so that they would be surrounded by family. The drive was somber and silent except for the sound of Callie playing in her car seat with her favorite doll.

The intense waves of grief seemed to dissipate into an all encompassing and debilitating numbness. They felt lifeless and spent. They stared out the windows and let the world pass them by.

Rory dropped his girls at Emily's parent's house and said goodbye. He promised to stay in touch as much as possible over the next nine months. When he walked out the door, he wanted to report to his commanding officer as soon as possible. For some indefinable reason, he found himself wanting to run away for the first time in his life. He needed to distance himself from those he loved. He wanted to work hard. He wanted to fill his mind with facts, details, drills and paperwork so there wouldn't be room to fret about anything else.

Abby dropped him off at the airport only twenty minutes before he needed to board the plane back to Washington. As the Cessna lifted off, he stared down at the landscape below. He prayed that he would be able to get through the next nine months.

He spent the next five days working, going over his assignment in Iraq, and lifting weights until exhaustion had his muscles shaking. He put all of his frustration into taxing his body to its maximum capacity. His thoughts turned inward and he began to think of all of the ways he could have and should have been able to prevent his friend from killing himself.

He would fall into bed each night spent, expecting the fatigue to finally overtake the emotions and incessant thoughts. But his mind would kick into overdrive. He spent hours staring wide-eyed at his ceiling waiting for morning to come. By the time he flew out with the rest of his unit, he was actually looking forward to a radical change of pace. He hoped it would distract him from the realities back home.

He landed at Camp Victory in early September of 2004. He would be stationed there the entire nine months as a member of the police force. The general attitude of the troops was upbeat. Most of them were seasoned soldiers on their second tour of duty and knew what to expect if things got intense. Meanwhile, they could keep their heads up.

Rory kept to himself most of the time, feeling less than sociable. When the guys invited him to the bar where J.T. had sung, he declined the offer.

Only a month after he arrived, another sectarian group of insurgents began causing unrest in the city of Fallujah. The U.S. forces sent in different companies, and Operation Phantom Fury

# The Complexity of a Soldier

was officially underway.

~~~~~~~~~~~~

On November 7th, ground operations began from the West and the South of the city. The 36th Commando Battalion and the 3rd U.S. Marine Light Armored Reconnaissance Battalion, reinforced by Bravo Company, captured Fallujah General Hospital and the villages opposite the Euphrates River. These diversion tactics confused the rebels defending the city.

Navy Seabees shut down the electrical power at a substation northeast of the city while two Regimental Combat teams launched their attack along the north edge. Rory was in one of the heavy battalion-sized Army units that joined four infantry battalions in the heart of the city. They penetrated the city perimeter as STRYKERs surrounded the area. In the early hours of November 8th, the initial intense bombing began. It was followed by a direct attack on the main train station the rebels used as a staging point.

The entire first half of the day was so chaotic Rory and his team spent most of their time negotiating a path through their assigned district. Shots were fired in all directions. More than once Rory was knocked to the ground by booby traps as they discharged. He would scramble to his feet as quickly as possible, spitting grit and dirt. He thought only to help his team move forward without triggering further explosions.

He knew it was wrong but he was feeding off of the destruction and the danger. The recklessness and chaos soothed his hopelessness. The screaming inside his head drove him forward as the battle around him competed with the battle inside.

Since April of that year, there had been no American presence in the city. The rebels had had plenty of time to strategically place tons of bombs and IEDs. They'd also placed snipers in fortified positions throughout the district.

Rory kept his head bent and his rifle close to his body. He tried to stick to their modus operandi of clearing out specific buildings they believed had rebel forces within. Many of the buildings were empty but they came across several that housed rebels. The groups were quick to throw down their weapons and surrender for fear of their lives. It was relatively easier for Rory's unit to apprehend them and collect their weapons.

One single-story building appeared to be more of a warehouse. It had no windows and only one other door in the back. Rory assumed that because it was so confining and left no room for escape, the inhabitants felt desperate. They were instantly aggressive.

The second Rory's team entered, the rebels fired random shots. The blasts echoed through the cement building as two of Rory's team members fell to the ground.

The rest took cover behind large, steel storage containers that resembled freight cars. They donned their M40 protective masks and prepared to set off military grade tear gas. Once the room was filled and their opponents were gasping for oxygen and temporarily blinded, Rory's team moved in and subdued them without further complication.

No one else in Rory's unit was injured. Three soldiers focused on assisting the two men who had been shot. Both had been lucky enough to have avoided fatal wounds.

Rory and two other men held the captives at gunpoint, until the reconnaissance unit could fly them to Camp Hopper for processing and detention.

As he hovered over them, listening to his own breath echoing within the vacuum of his mask, his aching, blistered feet rubbed inside his sweaty, damp socks. The awareness of his own misery was almost too much to bear. Yet he was infinitely better off than the prisoners who kneeled before him. His captive didn't seem to recognize the peril of his situation. Instead of looking fearful or anxious, he stared up at Rory through the alien mask. His hatred flowed freely between them and poisoned their souls.

Later that night, Rory's unit dug small individual trenches into the hard packed ground on the outskirts of the city. They tried to catch a few hours of sleep before they set out on their next mission.

As Rory lay in the shallow bed covered in dirt and sticky with sweat, thirsty and battle worn, his mind raced. He pictured his life and what he was doing from a disengaged perspective. He projected himself up and away from his body, looking down at the scene as if he were a bird soaring above. He had never felt so alone and distraught, or so far from the people who meant the most to him. He slowly began to understand J.T. and the inner struggles he had wrestled with. His own unquestioning acceptance of matters and 'go along to get along' attitude threw him into depression.

He lay in that trench for four hours as his body hummed and didn't close his eyes for a second. When he rose with his team as the first light of dawn began to streak the horizon, his world had shifted. Despite the persistent lack of sleep and the sickness in his heart, his mind was clear.

~~~~~~~~~~~~~~

By November 16th, most of the fighting in the second Battle of Fallujah had been isolated to small pockets of resistance. By the time it was officially over on December 23rd, it was considered the bloodiest battle to date in the Iraq War. In January 2005, most of the troops returned to their original stations.

# The Complexity of a Soldier

Rory's unit was one of the last to clear out. By the time they landed at Camp Victory, they had been awake for well over fifty hours with the help of the little yellow pill. Rory had initially pocketed the pill, thinking of J.T., but as the second day without sleep wore on him, he gave up and choked it down. His inability to avoid its necessity irritated him greatly.

As they entered the largest community area of the base, their heads were muddled while their brains begged to shut down. Their commanding officer gave them strict orders to meet him in the mess hall. There they were given a new pill. This one looked completely different and was light blue. They were told to take it, eat a huge meal then go to their rooms to sleep off the fatigue.

None of them had the wherewithal to question it, nor by that time did they care. So Rory and the others filled their bellies without noticing how the food tasted in their dry, chapped mouths before shuffling off to bed.

Rory woke up almost exactly nineteen hours later. He felt surprisingly alert and refreshed. He lay there as the sun set on another day, thinking again about J.T. and the last conversation they'd had in his apartment. He went over it time and again, pondering how true his statements had been and tried to reconcile what that meant for him. How would he move forward into his own future and apply those lessons rather than continue the social and conventional norms placed on him daily.

He was sick of following protocol. Not only standard protocol but the unspoken, underlying protocol of life in the military everyone diligently adhered to. The protocol demanded that you follow orders unquestioningly and prove your undying love for your country. Well, he had plenty of love for his country and he was sick of proving it in this violent, thoughtless manner.

*Who am I? What do I stand for?* Those questions haunted him.

# The Complexity of a Soldier

He wondered if he had the strength to truly dissect those questions and face the answers. Had he always been so afraid of being an insignificant, small-town country boy that he'd rejected the best parts of his upbringing? Had he forgotten what it meant to be self-sufficient and independent minded? Was he a free-thinking person of strong moral content the way his mother and father had intended him to be?

Who was he really fighting with? What was he really fighting for? He didn't want to invade civilian homes or infiltrate cities. He didn't want to eat dust and MREs. He didn't want to fight anymore unless it was just to pound on Rodney in good fun. He wanted to go home and play with Callie and watch cartoons and eat pancakes until his belly ached. He wanted to make love to Emily until he fell over from exhaustion then wake up the next morning and do it all over again. He wanted to go home.

Rory gave a bittersweet chuckle as thoughts of food triggered his body to respond. The silent room filled with hungry growls from his stomach. Life kept moving forward with the monotonous routine of...well living.

He rolled to his side and pushed out of bed to search for something to eat. He tucked away his relentless inner chatter for now. He would try to answer those questions later. They weren't going anywhere. They would be waiting patiently to be answered, to be explained.

# CHAPTER SEVENTEEN

# Called Home

It was May, and Rory was scheduled to head home the following month. He was pulling a double shift to investigate a crime that had taken place the day before. A group of soldiers had taken it upon themselves to beat another soldier unconscious because they thought he was a thief.

The man was in the hospital with a fractured skull, multiple broken bones, and a bruised kidney. He was refusing to rat out the men who had attacked him. This forced Rory to test his evidence collection skills for the first time in months. He reveled in the tedious nature of the work. It kept his mind from wandering to his own personal details.

Emily was still talkative and sweet when she told him about Callie's newest adventures but he couldn't help noticing that she seemed more reserved than usual. He finally resigned himself to ask her about it. He heard her sigh before she answered.

"It's nothing worth wasting our limited phone time on, Rory."

# The Complexity of a Soldier

But Rory persisted, determined to get her to open up. Something nagged at the back of his mind. "Are you in love with someone else?" he asked.

Recently he'd heard countless stories about soldiers who had returned home to a rude awakening. Their wives had been seeing someone else during their tour of duty to fill the gap and keep loneliness at bay.

Although he couldn't picture Emily doing such a thing part of him understood that a woman needed to feel loved and cared for. Since he was across the ocean and had only small fractions of time to talk to her, no matter how many times he said the words, they fell flat after so many months without physical contact.

Emily sounded stunned. "What? No! Of course not, silly. Ugh, it's just that you've been gone for nearly a third of our marriage and it gets hard. Plus I see everything Abby is going through and I get scared. I'm practically paralyzed at the thought of losing you. We miss you, Rory!"

Rory was relieved to have that little paranoid suspicion put to rest. "I know, babe, I miss you, too! Just think, I will be home next month and then my four years will be up in less than a year. We can live wherever we want and I won't leave either of you ever again."

His own heart lightened at the prospect. He thought about that last conversation as he wrapped up his paperwork for the day. He would head directly to the showers before joining some of the other guys for dinner. He filed the case folder and turned toward the door as a younger soldier he didn't recognize poked his head inside.

"Are you detective Rory Nichols?" he asked.

Rory assumed the soldier was dropping by in regard to his current case. He tried to keep the impatience and fatigue out of his voice. "I am but I was just leaving for the day. Is it important or can it wait until tomorrow?"

# The Complexity of a Soldier

The private straightened and stepped into the room. "Um, no, it can't wait. I am here to deliver an urgent message, sir. Your commanding officer has already been informed of the news and is making your travel arrangements."

"What travel arrangements? What's going on?" His body and mind were on instant alert.

"I'm not privy to the details of the situation, sir. All I can tell you is that there has been a family emergency and you will be leaving as soon as possible." The soldier's face revealed nothing.

Rory felt sick and panicky as a million possibilities rushed through his mind. He thanked the private as he brushed past to seek out his commanding officer. Even though it was already nine o'clock, he was surprised and relieved to find him still in his office.

Staff Sergeant McClain sat with his right hip propped on the edge of his desk wrapping up a phone conversation. He waved Rory inside and got off the phone. Rory saluted.

"At ease, there has been an accident concerning your daughter."

*Oh god!* Rory's eyes went wide and his face paled. Sergeant McClain rushed to continue. "I've been informed that she is doing okay, and is recovering in the hospital where she and your wife live."

"Oh, thank god! Do you know what happened?" His voice was shaky, but he was slightly relieved to hear that Callie was okay.

The sergeant pressed his lips together. "I think it's best that you get any further details from your wife, Private." He glanced down at his wristwatch. "It should be--"

"Eleven hours difference, sir." Rory said. "It'll be just after o'eight hundred." He always kept track of his hometown time zone. He imagined what his girls might be doing throughout their day to help him feel connected to them.

Sergeant McClain pointed to a phone located on a small desk

# The Complexity of a Soldier

just outside his office. "Feel free to use that one. Your wife said to call her on her cell phone because she is at the hospital with your daughter. I have made arrangements for you to leave first thing in the morning. Good luck to you and your family."

He escorted Rory out of his office, turned off his light and locked the door. Then he left him to deal with the situation in private.

Rory was distracted and anxious but he saluted the sergeant just as he departed. "Thank you Sir!" He was dismissed and quickly turned on his heel to call Emily. She picked up on the second ring. Rory's heart slammed into his chest from the sound of her distraught voice.

"Hey, babe, I called as soon as I heard. What's going on?"

"Emily was hurt pretty bad and needed surgery. She might need another one, but I want you to know that she is strong and the doctors say that she is stable and will recover."

The distress in her voice poured into him. He didn't miss the fact that she was deliberately vague. She was avoiding saying how Callie had been hurt. He wasn't about to let her get away with it.

"You still didn't tell me how she was hurt. What happened, Emily?"

There was an unendurable, eternal pause over the static-filled line. Finally he couldn't take it any more and his voice came out gruff. "Damn it, Emily, I'm her father. I'm clear across the damn ocean. Now tell me what is going on!"

Emily's voice cracked as she began to speak. "Callie and I were out visiting your parents. Your mom asked me to drive into town with her to get some things for dinner. Callie begged to stay with your brother, to help him clean the chicken coop. You know how she loves those dang chickens, she even named them.

"Anyway, Rodney said that it would be fine and encouraged me

194

to go. I told him she needed a nap when they were done if I wasn't back yet. He put her down in your old bedroom and headed back outside just as your Uncle Tristian was pulling into the drive. He said he was passing through again to visit some friends in Utah. Rodney told him to go on inside while he drove out to a few of the pastures to wrap up the day early.

"When Rodney got back, Tristian's car was already gone. As soon as Rodney stepped inside, he heard Callie crying. He ran up and found her bleeding and badly injured." Emily paused for a second. She took a few deep breaths before saying vile, horrific words.

"Tristian molested her, Rory. They think he actually tried to rape her but because she's so small, it didn't work. When he saw that he had hurt her so severely, he freaked out and took off. No one knows where he is."

A buzzing roar filled Rory's ears and his vision blurred. His world tilted while his stomach clenched. Sour, acidic bile rose in his throat. His knees buckled and he lowered himself onto the cold linoleum floor. Taking in gulping breaths, he knew he was about to hyperventilate and was precariously close to throwing up.

"Oh, god Emily, I'm so sorry. I should have been there to protect her." His voice came out in a strangled derangement of consonants and vowels that sounded so distant and foreign that he wondered if he had in fact spoken aloud.

"Stop that right now, Rory. We all feel responsible. Your mom blames herself for asking me to go to the store with her. I blame myself for leaving Callie behind. And your poor brother is devastated because he left Tristian in the house with her rather than finishing his work later. Guilt is a useless and destructive emotion, so just knock it off." Her voice softened slightly.

"We need to pull together as a family and help Callie get

through this the best we can. She had surgery immediately after she arrived at the hospital. They will wait a few days for the swelling to subside before they determine if she needs another one."

Rory forced himself to stay calm as he finished talking with her. He promised to be home as soon as possible.

When she hung up, he slammed the receiver onto its base then picked the whole thing up, jerked it from the wall, and threw it across the empty office. His entire body heaved with a rage so absolute he felt it would devour him from the inside out. He kicked the back of a leather chair next to one of the desks. He relished the sharp pain that shot from his toes straight up his thigh and prepared for another swing.

A violent nausea gripped his insides and sent him rushing for the nearest waste basket. He kneeled over the bin with sour vomit dripping from his mouth. When he was done, he fell back onto the floor and wiped his wrist across his numb lips. He wished that somehow he could make it all go away.

*God damn it all to hell! God damn this god damn war! My Callie baby. I'm gonna kill that bastard. I'm gonna come home to you Callie, just hang on.* His thoughts were disjointed. He needed to get off of the floor. He needed to go home. I'm coming Callie. He'd brought this ugliness onto his family. He shouldn't have shot that Iraqi boy. He should have saved J.T. Poor Callie, poor Emily. Hold on, I'm coming home.

He sat there for what seemed like hours wishing that he was suddenly home and holding his girls safe in his arms and that he would never have to leave them again. He contemplated everything Emily had relayed, and had to force himself to stop picturing the violation his daughter had endured.

He was filled with two extremely intense emotions that left no room for anything else. He was determined to be rock solid and guide his family back to safety and recovery. But just as strong as his love, was a hatred so powerful he knew exactly where it would lead him.

# CHAPTER EIGHTEEN

# Retribution

Baker City, Oregon was beautiful that May. Spring had already been going strong for nearly two months. The skies were a deep blue, the air was warm, and everything was new and alive, rejoicing after reawakening from the dark, cold winter.

Unfortunately, Rory was completely oblivious as he stepped off the small Cessna. He wasn't surprised when he was greeted by his father. Emily rarely left her daughter's side, and he wouldn't have asked her to. They hugged before heading toward the parking lot.

Once they were sitting inside the cab, both men were silent. Neither of them quite knew what to say. Justin pulled out onto the highway toward the back edge of town and the hospital before clearing his throat.

"I've seen Callie earlier this morning," he said. "She asked for you. We told her you would be home today and she smiled for the first time since the…incident.

"Emily is holding up incredibly well and has been the voice of reason, insisting that we all stay focused on Callie. I think she understands that if she doesn't stay focused on that then she will focus on negative emotions like anger, hate, and even revenge. That will make it hard to pave the road to Callie's recovery as well as her own." He kept his eyes on the road. "She is a smart and brave woman. We would be wise to follow her example."

Rory heard the subtle warning. He was sure his dad was aware of his vengeful, hateful thoughts. But he listened carefully, clinging to every word. It was the most he had heard his dad say at one stretch for years. He needed to hear whatever wisdom or perspective he could offer.

Justin gave his son a sideways glance before refocusing on the stretch of highway. "Your brother is blaming himself. He is afraid for Callie, and afraid of how this will affect his relationship with you. He would do anything to set this tragedy right, son.

"Your mother is angry at this point. She never did care much for her youngest brother. She said that he would do cruel things to her and your Uncle Travis, trying to get them in trouble in an attempt to bring their parent's attention to him, even if it was negative attention. She says he never did anything vile, just sneaky little stuff that taught your mom to steer clear of him and not to trust him.

"He started selling marijuana when he was in high school and he started getting in trouble with the law not long after. He eventually left home after a huge blowout with their dad. They didn't see him for a few years, only hearing of his status through the grapevine. Then he just popped up out of the blue one day, claiming that he was on the straight and narrow.

"Sarah's mom had been worried sick about him over the years and was angry with her husband for being so hard on him. She blamed him for her son leaving. She welcomed Tristian back into the house with open arms, and Sarah's father was reluctant but allowed it to please his wife.

"Sarah says Tristian did seem to be doing a lot better and actually held down a job for the next year, so she decided to lighten up and give him a chance. However, as time passed, people began to complain about some of their valuables disappearing. She and her father always suspected he was stealing from them but her mom refused to acknowledge the possibility. Because Sarah never had any proof, she let it go. She resigned herself to stay out of it, knowing that she would be moving out soon anyway.

"Then one day while Sarah was away at college, Tristian stopped by her apartment to borrow a hundred bucks. He said a friend of his was in trouble but he didn't have the means to help them himself.

"Sarah was uncomfortable helping him because she had no idea what he was really going to use the money for but she gave him the cash anyway. She hoped he would just leave and not bother her again for awhile. She was right. He disappeared again without a trace, not even a phone call to his mom, for a long time.

"Over the years, he would pop in and out of their lives, fill them in on his latest exploits, which Sarah suspected were only half -truths then would up and leave again without so much as a goodbye or an explanation of where he was heading. She always wondered if he was in trouble with the law but never heard anything to support her suspicions, so she let it go.

"She feels guilty that she ever let him into our home in the first place. She knew he was no good but never in a million years would she have guessed he could do something like this, Rory. We all desperately wish we had done a better job of protecting little Callie. We are all suffering and we are all here for you."

Rory clenched his jaw. "I don't blame anyone but myself, dad.

# The Complexity of a Soldier

It's my job to protect my family. Instead I've been halfway across the world fighting men I have never even met, in the name of protecting an entire country. It's completely backwards." He was frustrated at the cruel irony.

"I will take full responsibility for this, and I will rectify it in any way I can, so my daughter can heal and feel safe again." His tone conveyed that he was a man to be reckoned with. Whoever crossed him would have to answer to him directly.

When they arrived at the hospital, Rory's pace was hurried. His long strides drove him down the hall toward his wife and precious daughter. But as his dad led him to Callie's room, his step faltered. Panic seized him. He had to take a deep breath before stepping into the small hospital room to face the people he'd let down.

Emily was sleeping in a chair next to Callie's side. She was bent over with her head resting on her arms that were propped on the edge of the bed. Callie looked so tiny lying in the adult-sized hospital bed and was also asleep. One delicate arm was wrapped around her favorite teddy bear. Her other hand lightly rested on her mother's hair.

*My girls,* he thought possessively. The sight was both beautiful and terrible and he had to swallow the lump that rose in his throat. He wished he was seeing them for the first time in nearly nine months on better and happier terms.

His peripheral vision caught a slight movement. His mother had been sitting in a rocking chair in the corner next to the window. She rose and held out her thin arms. She gave him a broken smile and silently pulled him into the hallway. He was reluctant to leave, but needed to hear what his mom wanted to say. He took a quick and longing look over his shoulder as they exited the room.

Tears welled up in Sarah's eyes and she viciously wiped them away. "They gave Callie a pain pill about an hour ago so she will be sleepy for a little while. The doctor just said this morning that the first surgery was very successful. They won't need to perform another one."

Rory stuffed his hands into his pockets and forced himself to ask the hard question. "How bad was the damage?"

Sarah wrung her hands and looked away nervously before returning her gaze. "He tore her in two places, which required minor reconstructive surgery. She had a fair amount of blood loss, the most dangerous part of the whole ordeal, but they say she has recovered well and has normal blood counts now. Initially they were worried about internal damage. Since she's so small, they don't believe he was able to fully enter her."

Forcing her voice to sound hopeful, she said, "They believe she will have a full recovery and will be able to have children one day."

Rory's stomach revolted again. He had to fight down the wave of nausea. He was glad that his mom had been the one to tell him instead of Emily. That would have been too much. He held his mother to his chest. Her resolve broke and she began to cry.

"It's going to be okay, mom," he soothed in a tone that was in direct opposition to the turmoil of emotions raging inside him. They threatened to break through the wall of fortitude he was trying to maintain. He was deeply afraid that if he let it all go, he would never be able to rein it in again.

Sarah stepped back and looked up into her son's strong face. Wiping the tears from her chapped cheeks, she said, "Your father and I are going home for awhile to get some rest. Your family needs you now, so we will give you some space."

She put her palm to his stubbly cheek. "We love you son."

Then she turned to join Justin. He gently put his arm around her shoulders. They walked down the sterile hallway as the singular, strong unit that they had always been throughout Rory's childhood.

# The Complexity of a Soldier

He stared after them, truly admiring their bond and devotion. He and Emily would need to demonstrate something just as powerful for their own daughter.

As Rory reentered the room, Emily's eyes fluttered open. She looked confused as her brain registered that she was seeing flesh and blood rather than a hopeful dream. She looked wobbly when she stood up and rushed into his arms.

Rory held her tightly, letting their bodies remember each other before he gently showered her face with kisses. Tears flowed freely and it broke his heart to see her so vulnerable.

Without saying a word, they faced their daughter's bed. Holding each others hand, they were united. Callie began to stir. Her face squeezed tight in a painful grimace when she stretched her legs too far. Rory and Emily rushed to opposite sides of the bed.

Callie's face smoothed out as the pain subsided. She opened her eyes and focused immediately on her daddy's face. She reached out and gave a weak smile. "Daddy!"

"I'm here, sweet Callie girl. Oh, you're such a brave, strong girl. I missed you so much." Rory was afraid to hurt her. Even though he desperately wanted to scoop her up into his arms, he bent and gently hugged her soft, little body, moving her as little as possible.

Callie demonstrated the incredible resilience all young children possess and began to talk about all the ice cream she had been allowed to eat and the nice doctors and nurses who were now her friends, and how she even got to watch cartoons while in bed.

Rory found himself humbled by his little girl's strength. He managed to crack a smile as she pretended that her teddy was talking to him. He stroked the hair from her face and touched her pale cheek as they visited. *She looks different,* he thought. *This has changed her, altered her. She is already older than she should be because of that monster.* There was no way he could ever fix this. How could she ever forgive him?

After only about fifteen minutes, Callie's strength began to wane. The pain pill continued to have its effects. Her eyes began to close and she gave an open-mouthed yawn. Rory continued to whisper to her and caress her hair as she slowly drifted into the dream world again. Her body gradually relaxed into the soft bed.

He turned toward Emily. They spoke in hushed voices about trivial details, uncomfortable with addressing the difficult situation surrounding his return. Finally he decided it was time to address the matter at hand. The question burning in the back of his throat couldn't be avoided any longer.

"Has anyone heard whether the police have any leads on where he might have taken off to?"

Emily sighed. "Not that I know of. Someone reported that that they saw a car similar to his at the Texaco station on the west edge of town. The owner says he bought a bunch of canned food and multiple bottles of water. The authorities figure he might have headed for the mountains but don't know where to start looking. They are patrolling the outskirts of town but he could be anywhere, Rory. The Elkhorn Mountains are so big anyone could easily hide out without being traced."

Rory scanned her face. Dark circles hung under her eyes and her face looked hollowed out. He should be offering to help her with anything she might need. He hoped to step in and take care of her just like he should have been doing all along. "Have you had anything to eat yet today?" he asked. "It's nearly noon."

Emily shook her head. "I haven't been very hungry lately."

He rubbed her tight shoulders. "I know but you have to eat anyway. Why don't you run out to the house and take a hot shower."

# The Complexity of a Soldier

Emily opened her mouth to protest but Rory put up his hand. "Go home and take a shower in your own house. Get something decent into your stomach then come back. I will stay right here with Callie until you get back. She'll be fine."

His tone was firm and his face was set with determination. There would be no point in arguing with him. She needed a break.

"I guess that it wouldn't hurt if I stepped out for just a little while." She reluctantly gathered her things, kissed him and headed into the outside world.

Rory sat with Callie for over two hours just watching expressions cross her face as she slept and the slow rise and fall of her chest. The jet lag weighed his body down as if gravity itself was growing in strength and force. Eventually he leaned back and drifted off.

He woke when he heard whimpering. His eyes flew open and locked on Callie's face. She was still asleep but clutched her teddy tightly to her chest. Her lip trembled and she cried in her dreams. Rory reached out. With his soft, deep voice, he hoped to squelch her fears and chase away her nightmares.

"Shush now, sweetie, Daddy's right here and everything's okay now."

Callie instantly settled down. Her little body went limp as she resumed a more peaceful sleep.

Rory shook with fury. She had likely been dreaming of the incident. He slowly pulled his hand away from her so the intensity emanating from him wouldn't wake her. He knew the doctors were predicting a full physical recovery but he wondered if she would recover from the emotional and psychological trauma. How long would she relive the terror in the realm of her dreams? How many times would that monster visit his little girl after she lay her head on her pillow?

## The Complexity of a Soldier

He propped his arms on the side of the bed. The anger and grief were so intense that the only outlet, other than hitting something, was the burning tears that poured out. His body shook as the pain slammed into him and bounced off every nerve inside his body. It left him raw, jagged, and completely defenseless to the assault of his emotion.

Through the muddled haze of his own blind grief, a quick flash of clarity streamed into his thoughts. He strained to grasp the vague and amorphous memory his mind was desperately trying to seize. Something Emily had said earlier rang in his mind as he pieced together parts of a fragmented puzzle.

A car...on the west edge of town...figure that he headed into the mountains....

Her voice repeated in his mind. He slowly began to recall a visit from Tristian when Rory had been seven or eight. It was bow season, so his dad had taken him and Tristian into the mountains on the west side of town to go deer hunting. Rodney stayed home with their mom because he was still too young.

They had tracked through the forest on foot following a well-established deer path. Justin was determined to teach his son how to move through the terrain as silently as possible. They came across an old one-room shack Justin assumed had been built during the gold rush, probably not long after people from the Oregon Trail had settled the Baker Valley. Cabins just like it were scattered around the mountain. They'd been built at a time when young, ambitious men had needed shelter while they panned the rivers for gold.

They stepped onto the small porch. The boards creaked under their boots as they peeked inside the dusty windows to make sure it was empty. Once Justin determined that the shack wouldn't collapse on the top of them, they stepped inside. The small cobweb-filled room had the dank, wet odor of years of a leaky roof.

# The Complexity of a Soldier

Rory had thought the place was cool. He'd repetitively suggested they should camp there for the night. Justin and Tristian had no intention of staying the night anywhere on the mountain and had laughed off Rory's pleas. They prodded him out of the shack and resumed their hunting expedition. Rory and Justin had shown the little cabin to Rodney three years later when he was finally old enough to join the hunting trips. He'd thought the shack was a fantastic discovery, saying that it was a great hideout for bank robbers or other bad guys.

Rory's mind fired rapidly as he connected the dots. He instinctively knew that was where Tristian had fled. His head shot up as the realization settled with a distinct finality. "I know where he is."

Just then Emily tiptoed into the room. She looking refreshed with her hair newly washed. A slight color had returned to her cheeks. Rory stood up and rounded the bed.

"I have to go do something."

His voice was husky and his eyes darted as if he was distracted. Her expression showed that he was alarming her. He needed to stay calm to avoid involving her or causing her worry.

"Listen, babe, I'm getting really bad jet lag and need to just go somewhere and sleep for like two or three hours, okay?"

Part of him felt horrible because it was the first time he had ever blatantly lied to her. But he was resolved in his decision. Emily settled slightly. She dug through her purse, handing him her car keys and rattled off directions to the apartment.

Rory bent down and gave her a thorough kiss before bolting out to the parking lot. His mind was frenetic. He imagined finding his uncle hiding at the cabin and hoped he could remember how to get there.

# The Complexity of a Soldier

~~~~~~~~~~~~

Rory made the thirty minute drive out to his parents' ranch in a calculated and purposeful state. He was glad that his dad was out working with the cows. He only had to get by his perceptive mother without raising suspicion and alarm. He wasn't sure how he was going to explain needing to get into his dad's gun cabinet. He hoped he could divert her attention long enough that he wouldn't have to.

But a mother knows her children better than they know themselves. The minute he stepped into the mudroom, with an expression of defiance and resignation, his mission was clear. She was retrieving clothes from the dryer. She straightened and met his gaze with her own observant, all-knowing eyes. His face hardened. He sought no mercy, fully aware that she would see everything inside him for what it was and what it would be. He was her son, a boy who had grown into a man and who now was going to rectify a tragedy as a father.

She simply nodded and turned back to finish her chore.

She knew his intentions and she was looking the other way. Justice had a life of its own, and she would not intervene.

With purpose, Rory entered his father's den, took the key off the top of the six-foot oak cabinet, and opened it up. He chose the .357 Magnum. He shoved it into the back of his pants and headed back out to Emily's car. Not a single movement was wasted.

By the time he drove back through town, and headed out past the Texaco on the west edge, it was after six p.m. The sun sat low on the horizon. It was an hour drive into the Elkhorn Mountains. His life passed before him. He thought of his childhood with Rodney and the wonders of growing up on the land and under the stern but loving hand of their father. He thought of his mother and her guiding light. He ran through his relationship with Emily and his friendship with J.T. More than anything else he thought of his daughter, his life blood, and what it meant to be her father, to protect her in this world of uncertainty and insanity.

He pulled the car onto the side of the dirt road near the little path he believed would lead to the shack. He wanted to walk the rest of the way in. If Tristian really was there, he wouldn't hear his approach and try to bolt. As he stepped out of the little sedan, the cold night air hit his skin. The adrenaline pumping through his veins kept him warm.

He reached inside the car and palmed the gun in his firm grip. He closed the driver's side door gently until he felt the soft click as it engaged in the frame. Silently he followed the faint, overgrown path into the forest. He stepped lightly on crunchy leaves and pine needles.

He'd been hiking for about a mile when he finally spotted the cabin nestled in a circular patch of pine and lodge pole. His adrenaline spiked. He wanted to run forward and bust through the door, but the soldier in him kept him grounded. He needed to think and get his bearings before he made any moves. Glancing around, he sized up the surroundings. He hadn't seen any other cars on his way up but he got the sense that someone was definitely inside the cabin.

By this time, Rory figured it must be going on seven-thirty. It was completely dark outside. He could hear the night animals as they awakened and began their nocturnal routine. He crept up to the house. As he got closer, he saw a faint glow filtering out the one small window located left of the door. He listened intently but still heard nothing.

He peered through the window and scanned the room. At first

his heart plummeted with disappointment. It appeared that the shack was empty. Oddly, a small fluorescent lantern stood in the far back corner.

As his eyes adjusted to the sharp contrast, he spotted a form curled up in the opposite corner. A man lay underneath a small blanket. He had no doubt that it was his uncle. His body went rigid in anticipation. *This is it,* he thought. *There's nowhere to run now, Tristian.*

He made his way toward the door with the stealth of panther. A sudden calm came over him as he faced the reality of what he was about to do. He closed his eyes and focused on slowing his heart rate and his breath to a normal rhythm. He opened his eyes and shoved open the dilapidated door.

The form on the floor leapt to his feet and the blanket fell to the floor. Rory looked into Tristian's bloodshot eyes. He looked haggard and disheveled. His uncle made a desperate attempt to escape the freight train heading his direction. He lunged right.

*I don't think so,* Rory thought. Before Tristian could escape, Rory adjusted his trajectory and rammed his shoulders into his uncle's ribs with the full force of his weight. He knocked him to the floor. His uncle's chin slammed into the wood planks with a thud.

Rory grabbed Tristian by the back of his shirt and hauled him to his feet. Tristian turned and took a sloppy swing. While he moved in slow motion, as if he were struggling under water, Rory's senses were sharp. He simply ducked to the left, then immediately returned a powerful right hook to Tristian's jaw.

Rory heard the rewarding crack of bone. Tristian's eyes rolled back and he stumbled back from the impact. Rory felt only triumph as he prepared for his next assault. He grabbed the front of his shirt and landed another bone-breaking punch in the middle of his face. His uncle's nose was instantly shattered. Tristian screamed and covered his broken nose as blood spurted profusely from his face. Rory stood his ground, his chest heaving. He had barely broken a sweat.

"You sick son of a bitch. You like to touch innocent little girls, huh? Well, you're not going to get away with touching mine," he growled through clenched teeth.

Tristian cowered and slowly backed into the corner. He looked like he wanted to cry, to beg, just like his poor, innocent daughter had probably done.

"I didn't do it, Rory."

Rory bellowed, "Don't fucking lie to me, you sick bastard!" and took a step forward. He was disgusted with his uncle's revolting display.

Tristian put his hands up defensively. "Okay, okay, but God, Rory, I swear that I didn't mean to hurt her!"

Rory looked at his insufferable, pathetic uncle. The sight of him made him sick. His insides responded to his seething anger and drove him forward. "I don't care what you meant. God, I can't even look at you. My daughter is lying in a hospital recovering from surgery because of you. She could have bled to death."

He took another step forward, grabbed Tristian's shirt in his vise grip and pulled the gun out of the back of his pants. He jabbed the muzzle under Tristian's jaw.

Tristian began to shake uncontrollably. The cold steel of the gun pressed against his flesh while blood dripped from his nose. He pleaded for Rory to think about what he was doing. "Please don't do this, Rory! Think of your family. They need you. What would Callie think if she knew her daddy was a cold-blooded murderer?"

Rage flashed across Rory's face. "Don't tell me what my family needs, and don't you ever say my daughter's name again! Now just shut up, you pervert!"

## The Complexity of a Soldier

Tristian's own temper flared. "How dare you judge me! You don't know anything about me, you little piss ant! You and your little cry baby daughter can just go to hell."

His eyes gleamed. His true self was revealed in the heat of the moment. He wasn't remorseful. He was just sorry he'd been caught.

Rory's calm returned. He looked into the blackness of his uncle's soul. "I'm not here to judge you. That will come after I'm done with you by forces beyond either of us." His eyes narrowed. His grip tightened. "No, it's not my place to judge you. I'm just going to end you!"

He watched his uncle's face as he fired the weapon.

# CHAPTER NINETEEN

# Facing the Consequences

Rory called Emily as soon as his cell phone indicated that he once again had service.

"Rory, where have you been? I've been trying to call you for the past hour. I was worried sick." Emily's voice begged him to ease her worries.

"Listen to me, Emily. I have to drive out to my parent's house tonight then I will come back to the hospital. I can't explain right now but I will. Just trust me, okay?" He knew he was asking a lot but he needed to finish what he had started.

"Okay," was all she said.

He hung up and concentrated on the drive out to the ranch. He kept his speed under the limit and his mind on the next steps that he needed to take.

It was nearly ten o'clock when his headlights flashed across the front of his mom and dad's house. They were typically in bed by this time but he figured that his brother, who still lived at home and worked with their dad, might still be awake. He tried to figure out how to deal with him if their paths crossed.

He shut off the engine and sat for a moment watching for any sign of movement inside. His heartbeat echoed so loudly it seemed to reverberate off the car windows. His actions had already been set in an unstoppable motion. At this point, he had only the ability to steer in a certain direction. Neither his father, nor his brother could intervene.

With that in mind, he took in a sharp breath, grabbed the gun and walked quietly to the side door into the mudroom. It would be the quietest entryway and least likely to draw attention. Rodney was in the den sprawled out in the office chair with his feet stretched out before him. He was waiting for his brother. He glanced up.

"Mom seemed off when I came in from the fields this evening," he said. "My gut told me to come in here and check things out. I saw that the .357 was missing and knew you must have figured out where he was." The tone of his voice was simple but the heartache in his spirit was absolute.

Rory looked at his brother for the first time since he had flown into town. The past week had ravaged his innocence and left only shame, anger and grief in its wake. His heart ached for his brother as he realized how many lives had been altered and tainted by the cruel, ugly act of just one man. He shifted his gaze and crossed the room.

"He was up at that cabin we found during our hunting trip," he said simply.

He had already cleaned the gun thoroughly with disinfectant wipes Emily kept in the glove compartment. He grabbed his dad's gun cleaning cloth anyway and wiped it down once more. He wasn't hiding evidence; he was just showing the proper respect for his father's weapon before he returned it to its rightful place. He methodically placed the gun in its designated spot and locked the cabinet again.

"I'm going to the hospital to tell Emily. Then I'm going to turn myself in."

Rodney shot up out of the chair. "What? No! You can't do that. They'll put you away for years. They could even give you the death sentence. That bastard deserved what he got. I can hide him, or I'll take the heat. I'll say that I did it but you can't leave your family again, Rory, I won't let you go down for this. I'm the one who should have done it!"

Rory refused to look at his brother. He focused on a small speck of chipped paint on the wall just behind him. "No, I have to do this. My family needs to know that things have been rectified. I will pay whatever consequences are necessary." He placed both hands on his brother's shoulders.

"I need you to take care of them until I get this worked out, Rodney." His voice was unfaltering and his stare was now direct. It penetrated Rodney's smoky gray gaze, commanding him to make this one vital promise.

Rodney's expression was incredulous but he spoke with resolve in his voice. "I will take care of them, Rory. I swear it."

Rory looked down at his blood-spattered clothes. "I need to borrow some clothes so Emily doesn't see me like this."

Rodney hustled upstairs, gathered a pair of jeans, a t-shirt and a bomber jacket then returned to the mudroom. By then Rory had scrubbed his face, chest and arms with a vicious tenacity. He changed swiftly, bagged up his soiled clothes and handed them to Rodney. "Dispose of those properly. They won't need evidence with my confession."

Rodney swallowed and took the bag. Just before Rory stepped

out, he said, "I will get this worked out."

A surprising air of confidence flowed through his body. A wrong had been righted.

~~~~~~~~~~~~~

Visiting hours were well past over but since he was Callie's father, the nurse let Rory into the ward. Emily was reading by one of small wall lights located beside the bed. The rest of the room lay in soft shadows. She tossed the book aside and rushed to him with a look of exasperation and concern pinching her face.

He kissed her, took her by the hand and led her to the small couch that made a pitiful little bed for her to sleep on. What a terrible nightmare she was going through.

They both sat on the edge of the little pull out. Rory took a few moments to look at Callie's peaceful expression as she slept soundly, oblivious to the events unfolding around her. So precious, so beautiful.

When he turned back toward Emily, he cupped her face in his strong hands and brushed his lips over hers. Emily opened to him. For a heartbeat, Rory let himself forget about the grief and ugliness drowning him and focused only on the love he had for his wife, his rock, his foundation. He savored her familiar taste and comforting warmth.

He began to explore her neck, taking in the scent of her before dragging his lips back to her delicious full mouth again. This would be his last time for an uncertain amount of time. When he pulled back, she searched his face for answers. She knew he was procrastinating and they needed to keep moving forward. Rory inhaled deeply then spoke in a soft, deep voice. With every word, he willed her to really listen and understand.

# The Complexity of a Soldier

"I killed him, Emily. I figured out where he was and I drove up there and I shot him."

Her face fell. "Oh no! Oh my god, Rory! You have to get out of here. You have to leave before anyone finds out!"

Rory shook his head. "No, Emily. I came over here to tell you so you wouldn't find out from someone else. I'm going to turn myself in. I will not change my mind. What's done, is done."

"What? You can't turn yourself in!" She jumped to her feet as her voice escalated.

They both glanced over to see if Callie had been disturbed by her outburst. Once Rory saw that she was still in a deep sleep, he grabbed Emily's hand and pulled her back down. He was desperate to make her see his way of thinking and to help her deal with it before he left for the police station. She shook her head, as she looked down at their linked hands.

"I don't understand. Why did you do this, Rory? They are going to take you away from us. We're going to be without you again."

He felt horrible, inhuman. He was breaking her heart all over again, and this time he wasn't sure she would be able to put on a brave face and survive this last impact. Rory put his crooked finger under her chin and tipped her face up, forcing her to look at him.

"There was no other choice, Emily. I couldn't live another day knowing that creep was walking the same ground as my daughter. Emily needs to recover. The only way she is going to do that is if she knows she will never, ever have to see his face again.

"She needs to understand that people can't just do these types of things and get away with it. She needs to know there are people in this world who would do anything for her. She needs to know that she is worth it or else she will do what every other victim has ever done. She will wonder why her? How did this happen? She will blame herself and it will eat away at her very core." He sighed and shifted on the pull-out.

"That being said, I too have to face my own actions and consequences. I will do it gladly knowing that my daughter will eventually understand what all of this means. She will someday, I have to believe that. This is the only way for any of us to have real closure and move forward. Do you understand?"

"I do understand. I would have done the same thing had I known how. I'm so angry that I feel infested with it but I keep trying to stay positive so that my rage doesn't infect our daughter. We need to be strong for her, to guide her through this. How can we do that now?" The question hung heavy in the air.

"I'm not angry for what you've done. I'm just so concerned for your safety and for our future as a family." She touched his cheek just as his mother had done only hours before. "I do understand, though. Thank you for being the man that you are. I will stand by you through it all no matter what. I'm just so scared."

Rory couldn't believe he was actually going to have to walk away from her again. This time he was stepping into the unknown, territory that seemed to overshadow the horror of his time spent at war. He had been blessed with the gift of being the husband to this wonderful woman and was only sad that he would once again leave her side, not knowing when they would be together again.

He kissed her softly, lingering for an extra few moments, before standing to say goodbye to his sleeping daughter. Lightly kissing the top of Callie's soft brown hair, he said a silent prayer. He hoped she would one day understand why he had done the things he had done. He pulled the collar of his brother's jacket up and pushed his shoulders back. He walked to the door, hesitated, then turned.

"I love you Em!" he said, and quietly pulled the door closed.

# The Complexity of a Soldier

~~~~~~~~~~~~~~

Rory walked into the Baker City police station and asked for the lead investigator on the Callie Nichols case. The only officer on duty in the station stood slowly and shuffled his way around the desk.

"Officer Wayne is at home for the night," he said. "Is there something I can do for you, or is there a message that I can give him? He can get back to you tomorrow."

This had to happen now. Rory wasn't sure he would be able to carry it out the next day. He stood very still and spoke very carefully.

"I'm Callie Nichols' father. I really think you should call Officer Wayne. I have very important information regarding the man that hurt my little girl."

The officer looked at him warily.

"Have a seat." He pointed toward a small waiting room and went to make the call.

Rory walked toward a semi-circle of chairs and sat in a coffee-stained seat. Magazines had been strewn about on two small tables. He listened to the one-sided phone conversation and looked up after the police officer hung up.

"This better be good," the officer said. "Officer Wayne wasn't too pleased at being woken up at almost one in the morning." He started to turn back to his desk then asked, "Do you want some coffee or something?"

Rory's stomach was queasy and felt constricted. He realized he hadn't eaten anything since early that afternoon when Callie's nurse had brought him half of a turkey sandwich, but the thought of food only made the tightness in his gut worsen. He shook his head.

# The Complexity of a Soldier

Fifteen minutes later, Officer Wayne stepped into the station. His head was cocked to the side as if he was trying to recall how he knew Rory. Recognition clicked into place and he raised his eyebrows. "Hey, I know you. You played football with my son Jeremiah Wayne."

Rory remembered Jeremiah. He tried to be polite even though he was anxious to give his confession.

"Yes sir, I remember Jeremiah, how is he doing?"

"He's good. He has two kids now." He paused. "Rory Nichols. You're the father of the little girl that's in the hospital, right? What can I do for you, Rory?"

Rory hesitated, unsure exactly how to proceed. "I want to turn myself in for the murder of Tristian Sutherland."

Officer Wayne blinked once. In an authoritative tone, he said, "Why don't we sit down in the back office. You can elaborate further while you make an official statement."

Rory nodded and trudged forward with the officer close behind. He sat in the only chair in front of Officer Wayne's desk. His back straight, he perched on the edge of the seat, refusing to get comfortable even though the adrenaline he'd been riding was slowly ebbing away. A fatigue unlike any he had ever known before seeped in. He was giving in to the thick cloak of exhaustion and suddenly felt desperate to get this night over with. Then he could close his eyes and escape, if only for a brief time.

"Emily told me that the owner of the Texaco station on the west edge of town had identified a man matching Tristian's description. The man purchased food and water in his store, so there was suspicion that he may have headed into the Elkhorn mountains." Rory waited for Officer Wayne to acknowledge him with a curt nod.

"It took me awhile to connect the dots but a few hours later, I

220

## The Complexity of a Soldier

remembered a small, one room shack my dad, Tristian and I had found on a hunting trip when I was a child. It's about an hour up the Washington Gulch ravine. I somehow knew he would be there, so I went out to my father's ranch, borrowed his .357 magnum, and drove up to the cabin."

His voice was drained of emotion. His words were to the point. "I shot and killed my uncle, Tristian Sutherland. I can give you directions to the cabin so you can locate his body."

The statement was straightforward but it left Officer Wayne reeling. His mouth twitched. He bent over the papers, resumed his chicken-scratch scrawl and noted the last details before dropping his pencil to the desk. After a slight hesitation, he rose up out of his chair. His rigid movements revealed how uncomfortable he was with his duty.

Rory sat patiently as the officer made the robot-like motions demanded by arrest protocol. His voice was devoid of emotion when he spoke. "Rory Nichols, you have the right to remain silent…"

Everything happened in slow motion. Officer Wayne's voice faded out as he recited Rory's Miranda rights.

So much of his life passed before his eyes in those moments… looking into Emily's eyes on their wedding day, holding his newborn daughter for the first time, wrestling with Rodney, the hate reflected in the eyes of the Iraqi man he'd held at gunpoint, J.T. singing. So many glimpses of time all of them rushing in as if tunneled through this last crucial moment. He could see how large his life had been before, how blessed. Now it would all narrow down to a tiny cell.

# CHAPTER TWENTY

# Taking on the System

Rory was arrested in the middle of the night on a Wednesday. His arraignment was scheduled for nine a.m. the following Friday. On a judicial fast-track, he learned that the initial arraignment would be somewhat informal. Its sole purposes were to assign the prosecuting attorney and the judge as well to officially inform the defendant of the charges and his right to counsel. In murder cases, bail could be set at the discretion of the judge if the defendant did not pose any further danger and was unlikely to flee.

Judge Wilmington had been a district attorney in Portland, Oregon for twenty-one years before being appointed judge. He promptly took an open position in Baker City. Years before, his colleagues had talked him into joining a bear-hunting trip. Because he loved the landscape and the small-town feel, he'd left with every intention of retiring there. When the job position came up, it seemed too good to be true. He snatched up the opportunity.

Like all men in his position, he had developed an acute ability to read people only a few minutes after making their acquaintance. Although he tried to stay open and objective, his gut usually indicated where each particular case would head before the trial even began. Over the years, his instinct had proven accurate. He'd learned to rely on and trust his acute powers of observation without question.

He was reviewing the case profile as Rory Nichols entered the room. The man held his head high but didn't appear cocky. He knew he was a military man who had already served two tours of duty in Iraq. And an unspeakable crime had been committed against his four-year-old daughter.

The part of the judge that was a father to two adult daughters, went out to Rory. Still, he remained objective. He firmly believed the system of law that he served would reveal a just and fair outcome. He kept his expression unreadable as Rory's direct gaze caught his own. For a moment the two recognized each other as two respectable men rather than judge and defendant.

The prosecutor walked through the door. His attitude was suddenly the biggest presence in the room. His lack of respect was glaring and the fatigue toward humanity, toward his role in the system, was obtrusive.

"Good morning." The judge refused to let the prosecutor's bad attitude infect him. He was used to attorneys with that sort of demeanor. Although he found it disheartening, he understood it all too well. He had gone through a period during his last five years as district attorney where he'd felt lost, impassioned. He had seized his promotion in hopes that the shift in paradigm would allow him to experience a sort of career rebirth.

He couldn't give up the courtroom. But he definitely wanted to get out of being assigned to cases and having to fight for causes that didn't match his own code of ethics. He was hopeful that changing his perspective within the courtroom would allow him to work within the system in a more neutral fashion. Then he could see both sides for what they truly were.

~~~~~~~~~~~~~~~

Donald Kemper filed into the courtroom carrying a briefcase in one hand and a latte in the other. He was an all business, no nonsense attorney with an immense case load. He was constantly on the go and felt as if he were everyone's lawyer and no one's friend. To say he was overworked and burnt out would have been a serious understatement. He had reached the point where he had long passed feeling resentful. Now he embraced the all-encompassing passive indifference.

He scrunched up his face with disdain as he crossed the room. He hated the way the courtroom smelled. He didn't bother to look at the judge or the defendant until he had placed his briefcase and coffee on the table. When he finally raised his eyes, his face was expressionless and flat. "Good Morning." He forced out a greeting that conveyed his distinct lack of interest.

"Mr. Kemper, have you settled on the official charges that will be filed against Mr. Nichols?" Judge Wilmington asked.

Donald pulled out his paperwork, closed his briefcase and adjusted his glasses. "The state of Oregon is charging Mr. Rory Nichols with murder in the first degree due to evidence showing he had premeditated intent to kill." He spoke in a dull monotone, wanting to move on with the rest of his day.

~~~~~~~~~~~~~~~

The judge nodded and shifted his gaze toward Rory. "Mr.

# The Complexity of a Soldier

Nichols, do you understand the charges?"

*None of it feels real,* Rory thought. Part of him wanted to yell out, *hang on, stop, this isn't right, something isn't right, we need to start over,* but he kept quiet. He didn't know why he was suddenly experiencing an uncomfortable shiftiness, an awkward sensation of being unable to fully grasp the moment. It felt like everything was moving too fast and he was quickly losing his footing. He did however know the answer to the question so he tried to stay focused and gave one sure nod.

"Yes, Your Honor."

"And have you been notified by the arresting officer of your right to an attorney?"

Once again, he gave a single nod. "Yes, Your Honor."

The judge paused. "Well, why isn't he here with you? Have you not found one that you feel is suitable to your case?"

Rory stood with his hands clasped behind his back, unaware he had immediately assumed the military stance common when addressing a superior officer. "No, sir, Your Honor, I will not be seeking counsel. I intend to proceed through the trial representing myself. Pro se."

It was a decision he'd wrestled with since his arrest. He knew he was out of his element in the courtroom up against these two gentlemen but he was determined to fight the good fight on his own wits and integrity.

Donald Kemper snorted with contempt. Judge Wilmington's face revealed only a moment of brief shock before settling back into professional acceptance. Rory wondered if he had ever experienced another case like his. He couldn't possibly be the only person to have refused his right to a court-appointed attorney.

"Mr. Nichols, I will remind you that if you cannot afford an attorney, the state will appoint you one. I highly recommend you graciously accept it for your sake as well as for your loved ones, who probably want to see you receive an adequate and fair trial."

Rory kept his gaze facing forward and his expression stone cold. "I am aware of my rights, sir. I am also aware of how the system operates and frankly feel that though the American justice system was founded on sound principles, it has evolved over time and is now broken.

"Pardon me for saying so, Your Honor, but I feel much more comfortable knowing that my fate rests in my own hands rather than in those of the…" He gave the prosecuting attorney a sideways glance. "Burned out and overworked hands of those that have lost their passion and faith in their own system."

Judge Wilmington was silent as he processed this brave statement.

"I see," he said. The silence in the room was deafening. "Well then Mr. Nichols, how do you plead?"

Rory straightened his spine and threw back his shoulders. "Not guilty, your honor."

He was well aware that the two men knew of his confession. He also knew they would not be expecting him to formally plead guilty with the court. To do so would mean forfeiting his right to a trial by jury and receiving the harsh punishment that went along with his admission.

Pleading not guilty allowed him the opportunity to tell his side of the story to twelve jurors. He hoped to speak to their elemental human nature and demonstrate why he deserved some leniency with the sentence. It would give them the chance to see into his mind and his heart not only as a man and a soldier but as father.

Judge Wilmington wasn't shocked. He merely shifted his gaze to readdressed Mr. Kemper, who now had an irregular and slightly bemused expression. "Does prosecution have anything to offer regarding bail?" Judge Wilmington asked.

"Um...Yes, Your Honor. The malicious nature and obvious intent of the crime show that Mr. Nichols is indeed a danger to society. The state asks that the court deny any request of bail."

"Mr. Nichols?" the judge asked.

"I have no intention of fleeing if released on bail, nor do I have any intentions of committing any other crimes. That said, my family does not have the means to post bail in the amount that I understand is standard for such cases, so it is an inconsequential request." Rory's statement let everyone know he was indeed intelligent and brave enough to carry out this trial on his own.

Judge Wilmington sighed. "Bail will be set at five hundred thousand dollars. We will proceed with the preliminary hearing ten days from now at nine o'clock."

He stood abruptly and retired to his chamber.

~~~~~~~~~~~~

The next day, Emily went to the jail while her parents kept an eye on Callie at her apartment. Callie had perked up significantly within minutes of settling into her own home and already seemed to be gaining strength. She was still unable to walk on her own and using the restroom was a horrific and dreaded experience but she maintained her sweet smile and jovial demeanor.

The social worker assigned to their case had already made arrangements for a pediatric psychologist to begin weekly sessions. That would help Callie and her parents begin healing and give them tools to deal with her persistent nightmares.

As Emily prepared to visit Rory for the first time since the incident, she felt so many conflicting emotions, she wasn't sure which ones to cling to and which to shove aside. The last time she'd seen his face had been when he'd told her he loved her and then walked out of the hospital. He hadn't even been home for twenty-four hours and was already leaving again. She had told him she understood his reasons, and she did but that hadn't stopped her heart from breaking into a million little pieces as her hopes of a reunited family walked out the door with him.

Everything felt surreal as Emily sat on the opposite side of the protective glass. A security guard escorted Rory into the room. He wore the classic bright orange jumpsuit. What should she do? How should she act? She watched him cross the room in a few long legged strides and reach for the phone, never once taking his eyes off hers.

Where did they go from here? She didn't even know what to say to him. So she waited and let him show her how they were to move forward.

~~~~~~~~~~~~

Rory had desperately hoped Emily would visit that day. He was eager to hear her voice and confirm that she was still by his side. He had lain on the tiny cot in the small cement enclosure of his single cell, staring at the ceiling as his mind relentlessly replayed the past week over and over again.

The private telling him of a family emergency. Emily relaying the unforgivable treachery of an uncle. His frail and precious child lying in a much too large and sterile hospital bed, learning of the ugliness of the world at much too young an age. The panicked eyes of his uncle as the gunshot rang out in the night. The look of his wife as he'd told her about his devastating actions.

Pressing his eyelids together, he'd forced the invasive images out of his mind and willed his body to give in to the pressing need to sleep. He had finally drifted off but the jail came alive at dawn when breakfast was served. His body was sore and sluggish but his wife's worried expression had slammed into his consciousness and filled him with dread.

His thoughts had become disjointed. A growing fear had seeped in as he'd wondered if he would lose her heart to this chaotic tragedy. Now she was sitting across from him. He was acutely relieved but also apprehensive. He waited for her speak. It would be their first words since he'd been arrested.

Emily picked up the phone and choked on her greeting. She pursed her lips together then tried again. Her voice wavered. "Hey, babe."

Relief flooded him at the love and devotion in her voice. He wanted nothing more than to reach through the glass and gather her in his arms. He feared allowing his emotions to get the better of him. "How is Callie doing?"

"She tolerated the transfer from the hospital well. I think she just needed to be home. The nightmares have been getting worse." She paused, "When I left, she had mom and dad engrossed with the epic task of naming all her new stuffed animals. There are so many. I think at least half the town sent her gifts. They should be busy with that for a good while."

Her smile was beautiful but it didn't quite reach her eyes. Emotion shifted over her face and he knew something was coming.

"I just have one question Rory." She paused. "Why are you refusing legal counsel?" Her face pinched to a pained expression.

How could he possibly explain his actions? He searched her face. How could he make her understand what he was trying to do, what he needed to do?

"Do you remember that night I talked to you about my time in Iraq?"

# The Complexity of a Soldier

He referred to an evening when, without understanding why, he'd begun opening up to her. He'd told her about the pills and how J.T. had struggled with a short-winded addiction until he'd had a minor breakdown.

"He once told me that he didn't want his actions based solely on what someone in a superior position told him to do. That it was up to us to take responsibility for ourselves rather than waiting for someone else to save us."

Rory caught himself looking at the wall behind Emily staring at flashes of the past. He had looked to her for answers that night, asking her why his friend hadn't been able to follow through with his own realizations.

He glanced around, taking in the stark visiting room. He sighed and trusted that Emily would understand what he was trying to say. He was following through with those same beliefs. His gaze settled on hers.

"I'm just not going to take the pill. I hope you can understand that."

Emily pressed the phone tight to her cheek as if it would bring him closer. "Yes, I understand but it doesn't make it any easier. I'll be at your preliminary hearing,"

The security guard approached. "Time's up."

Neither one glanced his way. Their eyes locked. Volumes translated between them and their hearts were breaking. "I love you, Em. Tell Callie that Daddy loves her."

"I will. I'll see you soon. Love you."

~~~~~~~~~~~

Rory spent the majority of his time reading law books and brushing up on legal terms. He woke every morning, shoveled the surprisingly delicious food into his mouth, then dove into his stack of law books. He was determined to understand as much as possible the process he was about to be subjected to.

By the time his preliminary hearing came he was well aware that even though he was pleading not guilty to maintain his right to a jury trial, he had already confessed. The prosecution had no need to prove his guilt. The hearing would be similar to the arraignment and would basically reiterate everything they had already established.

Rory entered the courtroom feeling a bit more prepared and refocused. Judge Wilmington once again went over Rory's right to counsel and accepted his refusal.

Donald Kemper stated the charges. For the sake of following procedure, he filed his list of evidence with the court.

The entire procedure was over within twenty minutes. The judge said they would select their jury and meet again in exactly sixty days to begin the trial. Rory let out a long exhale. He prayed he would be able to survive the anxiety that would plague him over the next two months.

~~~~~~~~~~~~~

Emily visited Rory at every opportunity and brought him the books he continually requested. He lived for their brief interactions. His eyes skimmed her face and read her subtle cues. She was his link to the outside world and he depended on her to keep him updated on Callie's progress.

"What about the nightmares?" he asked.

The week before, Emily had said Callie's counselor had been teaching her to draw out her fears and scary dreams. At first it had been extremely difficult for her and the night terrors actually seeming to intensify.

Emily was so concerned she suggested they stop the drawing therapy but the counselor insisted it was best to hang in there. By the third week, Callie had a breakthrough. She'd drawn a chaotic black and blue mess of what she called ugly monsters in the dark. With her face contorted in pain and grief much too complicated for such a young girl, she had ripped it to tiny pieces while saying the monsters were going away forever.

Callie had done all those things without any instigation from her or the counselor. Emily was shocked. The next day, again on her own accord, Callie pulled out her crayons and drew her daddy standing inside a big red heart.

"She hasn't had a nightmare since." Emily said. "She's been sleeping through the night. I'm afraid to get my hopes up. I don't know what to make of it."

Every time they spoke of their daughter and her struggles, it left Rory at a loss for words. It was so hard to face his wife every day and know he had failed to protect them.

She looked to him for answers, for support. He felt so inadequate, so lacking. But he had to stay strong and focus on the path he'd started down.

"It's progress, Emily."

"Yeah, I guess you're right. She can walk short distances with her walker now. I didn't even know they made walkers that tiny. It's actually kind of cute. Anyway, the doctor says this way she'll build up her leg muscles again without getting too fatigued."

"Maybe she really can recover from this," he said quietly, more to himself than to her.

Emily looked deep into his doubtful, hurt expression. "Of course she can, Rory, that's exactly what she's doing. I just hope you can, too."

# The Complexity of a Soldier

His gaze snapped up. "What's that supposed to mean?"

"It means that none of this matters if you are going to give in to your obsessive guilt. We are all doing our best to find our way through this mess but you will not be able to join us as long as you are stuck in the mindset that what happened was somehow your fault. What you did in response was extreme, it was murder, but it was also not done in vain. It was an action that will not go wasted or unnoticed by the world as they watch you stand your ground and fight your fight.

"I believe in you and what you are doing and someday so will your daughter. But for now, the only thing you need to concentrate on is learning to let of that guilt. It is useless. It is a distraction. Don't lose yourself to it."

Over the course of the last few years, he had forgotten the spark in his wife's eyes, the well of strength in her spirit when she fought for those she loved. He saw that flame flicker now. It ignited his own inner power, releasing something that had been tearing at his guts for weeks.

His family offered unfailing support and his daughter was fighting her way toward recovery with resilience. So would he.

# CHAPTER TWENTY-ONE

# Taking a Stand

Three days before Rory's first day in court, he was notified that he had a visitor. By that time the guards were well acquainted with Emily as well as Rory's brother and parents, so when they said visitor he was curious about who might be waiting.

The moment he stepped into the room and saw beautiful Abby, his heart warmed. He greeted her at the glass. *Just look at her,* he thought. She looked wonderful. He hadn't seen her since just after J.T. died. It had been eleven months since J.T.'s memorial service. Her hair was shiny and shorter than he'd ever seen it. They picked up the phones. "Abby. I am so glad to see you! You look great!" He meant every word.

Emily had told him that two weeks after she'd returned home, Abby had decided to cut off most of her hair as a sign of mourning. He had heard of cultures that performed the ritual but had never really understood it. For Abby it was a symbol. It separated the past from the future. It was a statement to herself that she would recover and heal in the same slow and steady manner that her hair would grow back.

Rory imagined it must have worked. She looked vibrant and healthy. Only an extremely perceptive person would have caught the tinge of sadness in her eyes but he did. She gave him a gentle smile.

"Thanks, Rory. Wish I could say the same about you," she teased. "Listen, since I have been a paralegal in this town, I have seen Judge Wilmington in action many times. I just want you to know that he is one of the best. He is fair and still has the heart to do what he does."

Rory had surmised as much from the brief interactions he'd had so far with Judge Wilmington. Still, he was grateful to hear confirmation from a good friend who knew her way around the business. Their time was limited, so she pushed on.

"I came here because I have a few things to say. You are one of my best friends and I support you no matter what you have done. Truth be told, I'm proud of what you're doing and so is a large percent of the town."

"I have not yet been blessed with children but I imagine I would be driven to extremes if I had to endure the violation your family has been subjected to. My parents always taught me that the ultimate responsibility is that of a parent. The instinct to protect is so strong it's wrong to deny it. I can't say you did or did not handle it the right way but you did what you believed you had to do."

"Which leads me to something else. I want to speak on the behalf of John Thomas because I know exactly what he would say if he were here."

Rory clenched his jaw. The memory of his best friend was still raw and powerful. In the midst of recent events, he had been thinking less often of him. Hearing his name now brought the old sadness fresh to his mind.

Abby narrowed her gaze. "J.T. would be cheering you on right now. These are exactly the types of situations that ate a hole inside him. He couldn't stand the blatant opposing forces that were incongruent with the morals and values most people espouse."

"We all know what happened to Callie was wrong. Tristian deserved the way he met his end. Most people in the community silently salute your actions. Meanwhile, the legal system forbids you to take such actions into your own hands but often drops the ball further violating the real victims."

"J.T. consistently struggled with misalignments like this. He couldn't reconcile them. He would be proud that you have the courage to face the things that he could not. I'm proud of you, too."

Rory was moved by her words and cleared his throat. "Thank you, Abby. That means so very much to me."

He could never express how much strength she had just bestowed upon him. Her insight would help him get through the rest of the week as he awaited restitution. She gave him one last wistful smile then gathered her purse and blew him a friendly kiss before waving goodbye.

~~~~~~~~~~~~

Monday, July 24th, was a bright and sunny day with not a cloud in the sky. Rory gazed out the windows. He marveled at the beauty as the security guard led him through the hallways toward the court room. Their solid footsteps echoed off the white walls.

He had dressed in his MP uniform. He was freshly shaven with a fresh haircut. When the jury laid eyes on him, the image of a proud American soldier would remind them who he represented, who he'd defended, and where he'd come from. *This is me,* an

# The Complexity of a Soldier

*American. I'm one of you,* was the message clearly conveyed. He would also remind them of the promise he'd made as a parent to his daughter.

Because it was not a federal court, the trial was open to the public. Rory scanned the audience to find his wife, her family, his family, and other familiar faces from his long childhood in the community. There were also reporters and journalists. *Funny, I never really left home,* he thought. For the first time he was proud of his community and where his roots had grown.

Judge Wilmington addressed the jurors with a few rules and instructions. Then he allowed the opening statements to begin. The prosecution was up first. It was obvious from Donald Kemper's smug demeanor that he counted on the trial to be a slam dunk. He stood and rounded the table to face the jurors.

"Today we will begin what should be a short and concise murder trial. Mr. Rory Nichols is being charged with first degree murder by the State of Oregon based on clear evidence and the defendant's official confession."

"This should be straightforward. We ask that the jury keep in mind that murder is punishable by death in the state of Oregon and we intend to seek the full punishment allowable by law. We do not tolerate murder, no matter the cause, in today's civilized society."

He returned to his chair and sat with an air of ambivalent confidence. Rory knew it was his turn. Even though he'd prepared incessantly, he suddenly became jittery. The nerves in his stomach flared and his palms began to sweat. He stood frozen behind the table and looked to the judge. "Your Honor," he said before turning to the jury.

"Ladies and gentlemen, as the prosecution stated, I have indeed confessed to the deliberate murder of Tristian Sutherland. I did kill him intentionally. As far as premeditation, I find the definition by

237

law to be somewhat varied and sketchy. I can honestly say that I had not consciously made the decision to kill the victim until approximately one hour before, at which point I obtained a weapon and sought him out. So there seems to be a very fine line between murder in the first degree and murder in the second. That is a line that you, the jury, will have to define."

Rory paused to gather his thoughts. "Although I am not arguing the charges, I am here to fight for leniency. I will speak frankly about my views and perspectives on what it means to be a man, a father, a soldier and a human being in this country, so that you may have a glimpse into my mind and soul. You might begin to understand how the depths of my convictions concerning this profound turn of events led me to stand before you today."

"In the end, I will graciously accept the sentence you put forth. But be assured that you will hear my side so you can make a solid decision. I thank you for your time."

Rory's knees shook. Grateful he was finished for the time being, he lowered himself into his seat. He hoped the court could not detect his anxiety. He gripped his glass of water and took a slow sip. He willed his limbs to stop quivering as the prosecution began the evidence portion of the trial.

For a moment, Donald looked almost impressed. The moment passed and Rory settled into his hard chair as the prosecution showed exhibit A, a graphic police photo of the victim lying on the floor of the cabin. He described the wound as well as evidence showing there had been a fight or struggle directly before the murder took place, indicating further violence. He followed with exhibit B, the gun identified by the defendant as the weapon.

Kemper described the actions Rory had taken that night to prepare. "Mr. Nichols drove all the way to his parent's house, took the .357 magnum from his father's gun cabinet, drove all the way

# The Complexity of a Soldier

back through town and headed into the Elkhorn Mountains in search of his uncle. He could have gone to the police and notified them where he believed the victim was hiding but he did not do so. Instead he acted on his own accord, and located the cabin.

"The defendant did in fact locate Mr. Sutherland. He then engaged in a violent altercation with the victim before he eventually put a gun to his jaw and pulled the trigger, killing him almost instantly. Not only did the defendant commit the murder he admitted to, he most definitely acted in a premeditated fashion. Although brief, planning and forethought were involved. Therefore murder in the first degree is indeed suitable."

Donald Kemper was clearly pleased with his delivery. He puffed out his chest with his new-found earnestness. His defiant gaze swept over his audience, taking them prisoner with an intelligent and cunning gleem, as he sauntered to his seat.

Rory's confidence slipped further away. He felt as if he'd just stepped into a situation that was much more complex than he could handle.

Judge Wilmington shifted his gaze from Kemper to the jury then to Rory. "Does the defendant have any arguments regarding the evidence just presented to the court?"

*Don't let him get to you,* Rory counseled himself. Just shake it off. He merely shook his head. "No, Your Honor, I do not."

~~~~~~~~~~

The judge lifted his gavel. "This court will adjourn for exactly one hour then return for closing arguments." As he struck the podium with a thud, he thought this had to be the fastest murder trial he'd ever witnessed. Rory was either one of bravest men he knew or one of the stupidest. He felt drawn to the man's plight but

11

couldn't possibly imagine what he could say to the jury to convince them of his right to murder. What could possibly be said to justify his plea for leniency?

It was unsettling to think someone like Rory could have committed such a crime. It was even more unsettling to realize that he and, the judge assumed, many others might have been driven to the crime if put in the same position. He quieted his thoughts, reminding himself that the finely tuned system of law was at least offering Rory the right to a fair trial and he headed toward his chamber.

~~~~~~~~~~

When Emily reentered the courtroom as the hour closed in, her stomach fluttered. They would all soon face a new destiny regardless of their personal hopes and desires. *Please, please, please,* she begged whomever might be listening to her prayers. She wasn't even sure what she was asking for other than safety for her husband and guidance and strength for her family. For the jury to hear his story and understand he'd done what he believed to be right.

She was so proud of the way Rory was conducting himself but she truly feared for his emotional wellbeing. While her nerves where shot, she imagined it must be infinitely worse for him. He sat in a room full of people who were judging his character and his actions. They held his future in the palms of their hands.

She sat directly behind his table, with both of their parents flanking her. They waited patiently for him to reenter the courtroom. She inhaled sharply when she saw his handsome face reappear. Her system settled as his calm, collected vibrations reached her. He was calmer, more grounded than he had been before and it soothed her own worries.

~~~~~~~~~~~~

Rory gave her a quick sideways glance before he sat down. He was grateful for the cloak of serenity that had blanketed him during the recess. He had been allowed to sit in an isolation room and though it might have seemed stifling and claustrophobic to others, it had provided him with a feeling of security and protection as the hour passed.

He had seated himself at the small table in that room. He'd steepled his hands and bowed his head. He focused inward and found a place inside himself that vibrated with peace and acceptance of what was to come. The hour had passed incredibly fast. He had been surprised when the security guard returned to escort him back to the courtroom.

During the closing arguments of a trial, it is standard practice for the defendant to address the court first. Rory sipped his water and waited for the judge to announce that closing arguments could officially begin.

*This is it,* Rory thought. This was his time to tell Callie's story, to let her voice be heard. Rory stood on sturdy legs. This time he rounded the table for a more intimate connection with the jury.

"As I stated before, I did kill Tristian Sutherland. Although you are aware of the details surrounding my case, I want to personally tell you what motivated me to take such drastic actions." He inhaled deeply.

"My young, beautiful, innocent four-year-old daughter was brutally molested by my uncle, Tristian Sutherland. He tried to rape her and in doing so ripped her apart. The doctors had to perform emergency reconstructive surgery to keep her from bleeding to death and to repair the extensive damage he'd caused." He paused to allow the vile nature of the crime to become a vivid and nagging presence in their minds.

"Our daughter has been receiving physical therapy to help her regain her strength and mobility as she tries to make a full recovery. She is making progress. She's amazing. We only hope that her spirit will recover as well. We are hopeful that she will go on to have children one day but in light of such trauma, we are also hopeful that she will be able to function in society without developing horrible fears and psychological conditions. She already suffers from nightmares. I have witnessed her struggle with them. It is disturbing. It leaves myself and her mother helpless." He briefly scanned the jurors to gauge their reaction. They were listening avidly.

"I want my child to grow up in a world where she knows that the people in her community will not tolerate such cruel acts of violence like child rape and molestation. I am well aware that murder is a horrible act of violence. I do not condone it. I am also painfully aware that somewhere along the line, our system has been disempowered.

"Every single day, thousands and thousands of child molesters roam the streets free to live their lives, free to seek out their next innocent victim. I could not live with myself if I continued to move forward with daily life knowing that yet another sick individual would slip through the cracks and walk the same streets as the child he so callously violated."

Rory felt the room become one with him. The audience clung to his heartfelt words and sought to reconcile the struggle within their hearts as the atrocity of his daughter's suffering ripped at their conscience.

"I have spent nearly four years serving as a military police officer in the United States Army. I was finishing up my second tour of duty when I was called home for a family emergency. I want to tell the court right now that I have been proud to serve my country and am proud to be an American. My country has entrusted me to join my fellow soldiers and fight a war on terrorism far across the ocean and away from our loved ones.

"I have seen men die and I have even been forced to kill in the heat of the battle. My best friend could not face the ugliness we have faced and killed himself when he was about to be deployed for a second tour of duty. He couldn't fight for a cause that he no longer believed in or supported."

An image of J.T. flashed into his mind. It filled Rory with strength. He suddenly knew his place in the universe as he fought for his daughter's right to justice.

"I am telling you these things to illustrate that my service to my country has cost me greatly. It has been difficult and challenging, yet I have protected the American people to my fullest ability. Now I must live with the fact that I was protecting millions while at home my family was unprotected and vulnerable to men like Tristian Sutherland. Let me tell you, that guilt weighs heavy on a man." The agony of that weight showed in the tightness of his voice and the tautness of his body as he held his audience captive.

"When I entered the Army, I swore an oath to defend against all enemies both foreign and domestic. I will remind the court that myself and thousands of other American soldiers are fighting a War on Terrorism. I dare to ask. If a child molester isn't a terrorist in the worst form, who is?" He shifted his weight.

"A child molester terrorizes the hearts and minds of innocent children and faces nearly zero consequences in this country. Often the trauma leaves the children broken and sick in their spirit. Unfortunately, without treatment, many will perpetuate that sickness on other children who fall prey to them.

"I ask the court to recognize the heinous and terrible terrorism going on all around us every single day to our precious children. I beg the court to consider sending a message to all of those victims as well as the countless perpetrators, a message that says we will not tolerate this terrorism any longer."

Rory was filled with his righteousness. He was filled with his mission. He was filled with the message he was carrying for every single child victim, including his own.

He took a few steps toward the jury to look deeper into each of their intent faces.

"I understand that I will be punished for my crime. But I want you to understand that the harshness or lack thereof of your sentence will send a message to my child and to thousands of others just like her. What message will you send today?" He felt the jury shift in their seats as the weight of his words hit them.

He pushed on. "I love my country, and when my country called on me to protect them from terrorists, I responded. As far as I am concerned, it will be a sad day when my fellow Americans punish one of their own for protecting his own child to the same degree that they expect him to protect the country."

The court sat silent.

Judge Wilmington watched as Rory crossed the room and took his seat. He shifted behind his podium. "If defense is finished, prosecution may proceed with their closing arguments."

An astounded Donald Kemper looked like he was just as awestruck as the rest of the people within the four walls of that room. He seemed confused, maybe even lost before he gathered his wits and stood to address the court.

"Although even I must admit that Mr. Nichols' words were touching and inspiring, I will remind the court this is still a murder

# The Complexity of a Soldier

trial. A man was killed in cold blood. He did commit a horrible crime, yes. But we must still execute the law as it was intended and punish the person that committed the murder, rectifying the crime that was done to the victim who is not here to plead his case. Rory Nichols admitted to murdering his uncle, and now the jury must find him guilty and sentence him accordingly."

He stopped at that point. Everyone in the courtroom could see his heart wasn't behind his big words.

Judge Wilmington spoke. "The court will recess while the jury excuses themselves and begins their deliberations. When a decision has been reached, notify the bailiff and we will proceed at that time. You have two hours. If a verdict has not been reached by that time, we will return first thing tomorrow morning and pick up where we left off."

He excused the court and returned to his chambers.

Rory exchanged glances with Emily and the rest of his family as he was escorted out. His pulse pounded in his head from the intense emotions that had reverberated within the walls of justice. Somehow he had shared his energy and his drive with everyone there that day. Somehow his intention, his truth had flowed freely and touched every heart. Now they just had to speak their own truth, their own message.

~~~~~~~~~~~~

When the bailiff notified Rory that the jury had reached a verdict only an hour and twenty minutes later, he was not surprised. The straightforward and uncomplicated nature of the case left little to argue. He had felt the group would be able to reach a unanimous decision regarding sentencing fairly quickly. He watched as the jury filed in as well as both legal teams.

# The Complexity of a Soldier

The judge asked, "Has the jury reached a verdict?"

The designated speaker for the jury, a short rotund man, answered, "We have, Your Honor. We find the defendant guilty on the charges of murder in the second degree."

Rory had known a guilty verdict was inevitable but hearing the words still took his breath away. He felt dizzy. The room to spun and tilted for a second before he recovered. He could face a large range of sentences, starting from only ten years and going on up to life or even the death sentence.

He forced slow breaths to fight back the tunnel vision as the jury prepared to deliver the blow.

The designated foreman said in a shaky yet proud voice, "We hereby sentence the defendant to ten years time in the state penitentiary with extensive rehabilitation that will be regularly evaluated by the state."

The courtroom exploded. Judge Wilmington struck his gavel repeating the charges and sentence before excusing a loud and exuberant courtroom.

Rory's relief and elation were overwhelming. The gracious leniency the jury had shown was everything he'd hoped for. Now that he had it, it was nearly too much to comprehend. He risked everything to send a powerful message and they had sent one just as powerful right back. He lowered himself into his chair, placed his forehead into his hands and stared at the table before him trying to grasp the reality of the situation.

"Rory," Emily called.

Her voice was like a caress. He turned to her.

She stood gripping her hands with both sets of their parents by her side. Tears streamed down her face and so many emotions reached out to him he almost couldn't bear it. Heartache, pride, unwavering and undying love clutched at him and he absorbed all

## The Complexity of a Soldier

of it. He would take it with him and hold onto it until he was released.

The security guards walked toward him to take him into custody. He would be transferred from the county jail to the state penitentiary on the outskirts of town. As Rory walked out the back door to the police car that would transfer him, he was shocked. He was greeted by a huge group of supporters who were shouting and cheering as they celebrated his victory.

It was a sight to behold. They were holding signs. They waved their arms in the air. They had smiles on their faces and victory in their hearts as they helped him make a stand. He had never been so proud of the town where he'd been born.

Rory bent his large frame to lower himself into the back of the police car. His emotions were scattered but the crowd's enthusiasm caressed his soul. He couldn't suppress a small smile. *They heard you, Callie,* he thought. They protected you, and gave you justice.

Ten years would feel like forever in the small confines of prison. But the message the jury had sent out to his daughter and to others like her would be heard across the country. He had won.

# EPILOGUE

Four years later, eight-year-old Callie, sat on the ledge of a stone wall circling a flower bed outside the prison. Today was a big day for her family. Since her daddy had been so good while he was in jail, the people in charge, were letting him come home early. It was called probation.

She was so excited. Even though she had visited him every single Saturday to tell him about school and her friends and the new puppy she was trying to talk mommy into buying, she still wanted Daddy to be home. Then she could see him whenever she wanted.

She still remembered the way that mean man had hurt her. She still didn't understand why he'd hurt her. But she did know that her daddy had made it so the mean man would never hurt her again. Her heart felt warm when she thought of that.

She sometimes heard other kids at school talk about her daddy and how he had done a bad thing and that the cops had taken him away. But she knew that sometimes you got into trouble when you did something you thought was right but maybe other people didn't like it.

Her mommy and grandparents told her all the time how much her father loved them all. He couldn't wait to be with her and play with her and take her to school. They also told her that since her dad had stood up for what he believed in, a group of people had helped pass a law that made bad men like the one who'd hurt her spend more time in jail. That way they were less likely to hurt other children. That made her feel safe as well as proud of her daddy.

When she heard her mommy calling, she scooped up the flowers she had picked. Mommy was also very excited about Daddy coming home. In fact, Callie wanted Daddy home for Mommy's sake most of all. Mommy was always good at playing with her and brushing her long shiny hair so it looked like princess Jasmine's hair on Aladdin. Mommy was good at doing all the fun voices at story time. Callie kept telling her she was too big for story time but she secretly looked forward to it.

Even with all the great things Mommy did, she was still waiting, waiting for Daddy to come home, waiting to feel like a whole family again. Sometimes she heard her mommy cry at night. Then she would sneak into her bedroom and snuggle up in bed. Mommy said she'd had a bad dream but Callie knew she was sad and being there would help her mommy feel better until morning.

"Callie, come on, sweetie. I think I see him coming." Emily stood with her feet cemented to the sidewalk staring down the walkway.

Callie leaped off the short ledge and rushed to her side. She was pleased to be wearing her new favorite red dress with the frilly lace. She was happy because it was sunny outside and the birdies were singing their songs.

"Callie girl!" Rory belted out. The emotion in his voice was strong.

## The Complexity of a Soldier

Callie giggled with delight as her daddy walked down the sidewalk. His arms were outstretched and his eyes were filled with love.

"Daddy!" she cheered as she rushed into his arms. He lifted her up and spun her around before taking her and Mommy home.

# The Complexity of a Soldier
## READING GROUP GUIDE

**1)** Why does the author include multiple view points throughout the story rather than stick to Rory's voice? How does this change or mold the emotional and psychological canvas of the events that unfold?

**2)** There is a strong underlying theme that weaves in and out of the characters lives: the quest for individualism and the fight to understand ones own desires and beliefs as opposed to following expectations of authority-whether it be from parents, employers, society, or even a governmental establishment. Each character is faced with challenges that force them to examine this very idea. Explore and discuss the many scenarios that elucidated this concept.

**3)** Rory could have and probably should have accepted professional legal counsel. A case for temporary insanity could have easily been argued given his recent history in battle and the tragic loss of his best friend. Why did the author insist that Rory forego his right to legal representation instead of capitalizing on the argument of post-traumatic stress?

**4)** *Did* Rory act out of psychological disturbance due to post-traumatic stress or was he as stable and consciously deliberate as he portrayed himself to be?

**5)** The author provides historical context via memory flashbacks i.e.- Rory and Emily's courtship and clips of Rory's childhood with his brother, father and mother. What purpose was served by including these memories?

# The Complexity of a Soldier

**6)** In an effort to encourage the court to understand the complexity of his actions from a different perspective, Rory draws a parallel between his duties as a soldier fighting against terrorism and his role as a father fighting to protect his daughter from the trauma of sexual abuse by illustrating the terrorist nature of such a crime. Though his actions are extreme, it is his belief that only extreme actions will bring justice to these insidious acts which are already so pervasive in our current society. Was bringing together two radically different topics – war and sexual abuse – as a means to illustrate a paradigm shift, effective?

**7)** J.T. struggled with deep internal strife concerning his military career, his relationship with Abby, his relationship with his parents and his experience during his deployment in Iraq. He experienced a psychological and emotional evolution as his personal morals and values were challenged. How did witnessing those changes affect Rory and his own decisions?

Made in the USA
Charleston, SC
20 April 2012